1912 WAS GOING TO BE MICKEY RAWLINGS'S YEAR . . .

A small glowing rectangle of color at the far end of the corridor captivated my eyes. The inside of the vertical rectangle was filled with a green so vivid that I could smell fresh-mown grass by sight alone. Almost as luminous was a reddish-brown crescent that cut across its lower left corner. The pure, perfect colors of a baseball field!

About halfway into the tunnel, I passed an intersecting corridor and was startled by a noise—a dull *thunk*—echoing from the passage.

"Hello?" I called out. Listening for an answer, I quietly started walking into the side corridor. I called out again . . . still no response.

About a hundred feet into the passage, a man was slouched on the floor, back to the tunnel wall. He was tilted forward, face down on his left side. I gently grabbed the man's shoulder and brought his face into the light.

But he no longer had one.

WELCOME TO THE BIG LEAGUES, KID . . .

MURDER AT FENWAY PARK

Troy Soos

ZEBRA BOOKS
KENSINGTON PUBLISHING CORP.

ZEBRA BOOKS are published by

Kensington Publishing Corp.
850 Third Avenue
New York, NY 10022

First Kensington Hardcover Printing: April, 1994
First Zebra Paperback Printing: April, 1995

Printed in the United States of America

Chapter One

You've probably never heard of me, but I'm in the Hall of Fame. The Baseball Hall of Fame. *The* Hall of Fame. Well . . . actually I'm in the museum. I was never officially inducted into the shrine like my old teammates Babe Ruth and Cy Young, but I did play big-league baseball and my picture's in Cooperstown to prove it.

I was making my first visit to the quiet lakeside village in upstate New York. It was the last Sunday in July, the day of the annual Hall of Fame ceremonies. As part of the festivities, the Red Sox and the Chicago Cubs were scheduled to play an exhibition game. That's why I was here. As the oldest former member of both clubs, I had been invited to throw out the opening pitch.

About a year and a half ago, some trivia buff went through the record books and found that the oldest ex-major-leaguer was an unheralded utility player named Mickey Rawlings. That's me. Unheralded.

Soon after this momentous discovery, I started getting requests to appear at everything from old-timers games to Little League banquets. I was flattered by the unfamiliar attention, although I didn't quite understand it. As far as I can tell, being the oldest living ex-whatever is not a record of outstanding achievement. There isn't even a question about whether my "record" will be broken—some other codger will inherit my title the minute I kick off.

Anyway, along with the real dignitaries, I sat on a bunting-draped platform in front of the stately Baseball Library. Several thousand folding chairs were neatly arrayed on the sprawling lawn in front of me. They were filled by an eager crowd of baseball pilgrims who came to see the latest additions to the National Pastime's pantheon. The atmosphere *felt* like baseball: the air clean and crisp, but not chilly; the grass vibrant outfield green; the sky a light shade of Dodger blue, set with a glowing golden sun.

The ceremonies began with the baseball commissioner giving a long speech about tradition. As he spoke of the heroes of the past and the popular stars of the present, the sky seemed to grow darker and the sun dimmer. I slipped into a fretful mood, suddenly aware that I was out of place here. Baseball tradition . . . Baseball tradition had skipped over me.

No one remembers seeing me play, no one even recognizes my name—it always has to be followed by the "oldest living player" identification. That description itself seems redundant—does anyone care who the oldest dead player is?

With Hall-of-Famers all around me, I felt conspicuous in the trivial nature of my distinction. I imagined that the crowd noticed it, too, and they seemed to stare at me, silently accusing me of being an imposter. I squirmed in my seat, and twisted slightly to the side, trying in vain to duck out of view. The crowd was right: I didn't belong up here with the game's greatest.

When the commissioner introduced this year's inductees, I realized that I didn't even belong among the fans. I knew almost nothing about the three men whose plaques were being added to the Hall of Fame. They had been stars—excuse me, *super*stars—in the 1970s, during which decade I watched about five games on television and attended none.

While their thank-you speeches and hackneyed anecdotes droned on, I wondered how baseball and I could have grown apart. For most of my life, horsehide and ash were as much a part of me as skin and bone. Now I found myself estranged from baseball, barely recognizing the game I used to know so intimately. The modern game just isn't the one I remember. New teams are playing indoor baseball in domed stadiums, old teams have moved to new cities. The grass is plastic, the light's electric. Hell, the ball isn't even horsehide anymore, and most of the bats are aluminum. . . .

A barrage of sustained applause shook me out of my grousing and marked the conclusion of the enshrinement rites.

With an hour to go before the exhibition game, I slipped off on my own. I first wandered into the Hall of Fame wing of the main building, skeptically wondering what sort of "fleet-of-foot" runners, "heavy-hitting" batsmen, and "iron-armed" pitchers I would find there.

The high-ceilinged gallery consisted of a rectangular hall with alcoves built along two walls. The room contained no furnishings or exhibits other than the bronze plaques that were displayed on the alcove walls, one tablet for each man voted into the Baseball Hall of Fame. The gallery was crowded but quiet: visitors tread softly on the tile floor and spoke in the hushed whispers usually reserved for churches and libraries.

I found myself facing a plaque of Ty Cobb, the first baseball player to be enshrined here. The bronze bas-relief showed a grinning man in a Detroit cap. Many times I had seen Cobb sneer, but I don't think he ever grinned in all his life. The artist who drew him was generous to Cobb in portraying him with such pleasant features—almost as generous as the author who omitted any mention of Ty Cobb's personality in writing the plaque's text.

I moved along, picking out the bronze images of my contemporaries. There was Walter Johnson, the gentle man from Kansas with the simian arms—his smoking fastball brought him more wins than any pitcher in American League history, with over a hundred of them shutouts. And there was Napoleon Lajoie, one of the game's most graceful players and the best second baseman ever.

I continued through the Hall, reading the plaque inscriptions. Some of the more recent ones were far from impressive. Arky Vaughan's: *Homered Twice in 1941 All-Star Game.* Wow. And Ernie Lombardi, who according to the tablet author suffered from *Slowness Afoot.* So much for my "fleet-of-foot" expectations.

I next went into the three-story brick structure that housed the Baseball Museum. I felt this was where I belonged, an artifact from another era.

I was pushed along by the crowd into the Modern Baseball room. Baseball kitsch is more like it. The floor was covered with Astroturf; the green crinkly plastic looked like the stuff used to line Easter-egg baskets and made a crunching noise with each footstep that fell on it. The walls were lined with garish uniforms cased in chrome and glass: the

Seattle Pilots uniform with gold braid and epaulets, the Chicago White Sox short-pants outfit, the Houston Astros uniform with horizontal stripes of Day-Glo yellow and orange. This *wasn't* where I belonged.

As soon as I could, I sidled my way out of the crowded room. The nearest exit led to a staircase that I slowly climbed to the third floor. The crowd was much sparser here, and the exhibits much older. Sturdy oak display cases sat in neat rows on quiet, mottled beige carpeting. Fading photographs and browning prints hung on the walls in dark wood frames.

The first display I encountered was a long wall covered with a century of baseball cards. I'd forgotten how far back those cardboard icons went. Sepia studio portraits from the 1880s showed players frozen in carefully set "action" shots, reaching up to catch baseballs hanging from visible strings.

Cards from the turn of the century were in bold primary colors. Some of them seemed strangely familiar to me, and I felt certain that as a boy I had seen them when they were clean and uncreased, fresh from a package of candy or tobacco.

A decade later, the images were pastel-colored drawings of hatless ball players. Some were so crudely sketched and colored that they looked like comic strip characters. I started to play a game of seeing if I could identify a player by his picture before looking for his name at the bottom of the card. I picked out the faces of Tris Speaker, Smoky Joe Wood, and Jake Stahl; when I checked the bottoms of the cards I noticed their formal names were used—Tristram, Joseph, Jacob.

I was batting about .500 in the identification game when I came to a narrow-faced, wide-eyed player with sandy hair. He looked far too young to be in the big leagues. Drawing a blank on him, I glanced down for the name. *Michael Rawl-*

ings. I looked back at the picture, and startled some bystanders by exclaiming, "Hey! That's me!" The name wasn't quite right—my given name is *Mickey*, not *Michael*—but it was me all right. Did I really ever look that young? Below the name was *Boston (Am. L.)*. I was tempted to call everyone in the room over to see my card. I'm in the Hall of Fame!

I continued to scan the other cards, eager to pick out old teammates and friends. Every couple of minutes I'd glance back to check that my own card hadn't vanished.

Most of the prints in this series showed the players' portraits against a solid red background. One had a dark blue setting: *Harold Chase, New York (Am. L.)* whose rust-red hair required the different backdrop. Another's color scheme made me wince in its similarity to the Houston Astros uniform I had seen downstairs: a head of blazing orange hair was set against a bright yellow background. The face under the hair was even more boyish than the one that appeared on my card. The name read *John Corriden*. John Corriden . . . *Red* Corriden? Of course it was Red—with that hair color who else could it be?

I thought I had forgotten Red Corriden. But he must have lived on in some corner of my brain, because memories that I hoped were buried in 1912 now came roaring to mind.

Chapter Two

The *Yankee Flyer* finally screeched into South Terminal Station at 5:22, three hours and twenty-two minutes after the scheduled start of the Saturday game against Detroit. The train should have brought me to Boston in time for batting practice, but a derailment near Bridgeport voided the timetable.

Because I was so late, a cab seemed more a necessity than an extravagance. I hustled out of the station with a suitcase in one hand and a canvas satchel in the other. I ran up to the first taxi at the cab stand. "Can you take me to Fenway Park?"

The driver stood with one foot on the passenger side running board. His response seemed to come from the black Dublin pipe rooted in his mouth. "Do ye suppose I'm in this business if I can't find Fenway Park, now?" I gave the cabbie a sheepish half smile and threw my bags on the back seat of the dust-spattered Maxwell. While I followed them in, the driver went to the front of the car and turned the starter crank until the engine coughed to life.

As the taxi clattered down Commonwealth Avenue approaching Governors Square, the heavy traffic coming the other way suggested the game had already ended. The cab driver's next question confirmed it. "Now why would ye be heading to the ballpark with the game already over?"

"Well . . . the Red Sox just bought my contract—from Harrisburg. I have to report to them today . . . to play baseball . . . I'm a ball player."

"Are ye now? And what position might ye play?"

A simple enough question, but it threw me for a loss. "Well . . . I play just about everywhere . . . except pitcher. I've caught a few times . . . but I'm not really a catcher. I guess I'll play either outfield or infield someplace."

The cabbie didn't ask any more questions, and I was content to keep my mouth closed. The wheels of the passing carriages and automobiles were churning up dried horse manure into a fine powdery mist that rushed at me through the open cab. The biting spray made talking a distasteful labor and added another layer of filth to the gritty film of soot that had been wafted onto me by the *Flyer* locomotive. Late, dirty, and smelly—what a way to start a new job.

"Well, here ye are me boy. Good luck to ye."

I paid the driver, hopped out of the taxi, and took my first look at Fenway Park.

Last year I had gotten into fifteen games, the full scope of my major-league career so far, with Boston's National League team, the Braves. Home field was the South End Grounds on Walpole Street. It was a cramped, rickety wooden stadium badly in need of renovation or an extensive fire.

Now I gazed in awe at an enormous new ballpark. Fenway Park had opened just a week before as one of the most modern arenas in baseball. With my eyes fixed on the towering structure, I drifted along the sidewalk, my hurry to get there forgotten.

There was a simple majesty to the ballpark's construction. The crisply new red bricks of the high walls; the graceful beckoning arches over the entrances, each with a gray stone inlay at its crest; and crowning it all, a massive white slab atop the left field wall with FENWAY PARK chiseled on it in clean sharp lines. It looked to be a baseball cathedral.

I finally hoisted my bags and strode purposefully to the main entrance. Even the stragglers had left the park by now. The only person visible was a slender, silver-haired attendant who wore his navy blue uniform with a dignified authority.

Respectfully, I called out, "Excuse me! Could you let me in please?"

The attendant walked to the gate at a deliberate pace and politely declined my request. "I'm sorry. I can't let anybody in here."

"But I *have* to get in. I have to see the manager. I'm his new—" Again I wished I could have said "shortstop" or "left fielder," but I could only finish the sentence by spitting out, "—ball player."

The attendant glanced down at my bags and appeared to notice the three weathered bat handles sticking out of my satchel. Looking back up, he scrutinized my face and announced, "You're Mickey Rawlings." The tone of his voice suggested that I couldn't possibly be Mickey Rawlings without his say so.

"Yes! Did they tell you I was coming?"

"No, nobody said they were expecting you. I saw you with the Braves last year. In fact, I saw you steal home—last game of the season, I think it was. That took a lot of nerve."

With a smile, he added, "I like a ball player who'll take chances."

The attendant unlocked the gate and nodded me in. He pointed down a wide corridor and said, "You'll want to see Jake Stahl. He usually stays late after a game. His office is just off the clubhouse." The attendant explained the way to Stahl's office, but in my excitement I didn't quite follow him. Instead of asking for a repeat, though, I said my thanks and headed in the general direction his finger had pointed.

I continued on the curving corridor until the attendant was out of view. I didn't keep count of the hallways I passed, but I had gone by five or six and I figured it was time to try one. I turned into one of the passages that stretched from the field out to the main perimeter I had just traveled.

Stepping into that passage, I instantly forgot that I was in an immense stadium in the middle of a bustling city. I found myself instead entering a very different atmosphere, as I suddenly faced an inviting picture of simple, natural splendor.

A small glowing rectangle of color at the far end of the corridor captivated my eyes. The inside of the vertical rectangle was filled with a green so vivid that I could smell fresh-mown grass by sight alone. Almost as luminous was a reddish-brown crescent that cut across its lower left corner. The pure perfect colors of a baseball field!

The passageway was in quiet shadow. Its cool white-washed walls sucked me gently into the tunnel, drawing me to the growing vision of Baseball Heaven at the end.

Soon this field would be part of me—at least parts of this field would soon be *on* me. I'd be wearing elements of it as badges of honor on my flannels: a streak of bluegrass ground into my chest from a diving attempt to snag a fly ball, cakes of red clay encasing my knees from sliding into second on a stolen base. I already felt myself proudly in uniform, and naturally fell into the distinctive baseball walk, part waddle from the way cleats pull at the feet and part swagger from—just from being a ball player.

I felt that Fenway Park was promising me something: that 1912 was going to be my year.

About halfway into the tunnel, I passed an intersecting corridor and was startled by a noise—a dull *thunk*—echoing from the passage. The jolting sound brought me back to reality and my need to find Jake Stahl.

"Hello?" I called out, figuring that the noise had to be made by someone, and maybe the someone could direct me to Stahl. Listening for an answer, I quietly started walking into the side corridor. Hearing no response, I called out again, louder, "Hello!" Still no answer.

A hundred feet into the passage, in a recessed doorway, a man was slouched on the floor. The light was so dim that I almost tripped on his outstretched legs. I could make out his general form but not his features.

I shouted, "Are you all right?" and rapidly groped the wall near the doorway with my fingertips. I hit the button of a light switch and a bare bulb suddenly flared, lighting our part of the passage.

The man's back was to the tunnel wall, and he was tilted forward, face down on his left side. He wore a blue serge suit that would have been natty had it not been crumpled and stretched by the contorted seating position. I gently grabbed the man's shoulder and brought his face into the light.

But he no longer had one.

I felt my own face blanch and turn cold as the blood

drained from my head, sent plummeting by the horror of what I saw.

I couldn't avert my eyes. I froze where I stood, staring at the pieces of flesh and bone crisscrossed by exposed purple veins, all held together by dark red coagulating blood. A bristly thatch of orange hair stuck out on top of the gruesome mess looking incongruously innocent.

Sudden visceral activity finally caused me to do something. I threw up. Before my external parts could function, a searing torrent of vomit expelled itself. Right on the dead man's chest.

The convulsions in my stomach continued and I doubled over with the pain. At least I was able to turn away enough to avoid further offense to the corpse. Crippled with stomach pain and weak in the legs, I dropped to my knees and crawled across the hallway thinking I was about to faint.

When I reached the far wall, still on hands and knees, I closed my eyes and rested the top of my head against the wall. I inhaled slowly and deeply and tried to compose myself.

Eventually the volcanic activity in my stomach subsided, and I could breathe more easily. I forced my eyes open, and found myself looking down at a baseball bat laying where the floor met the wall. The head of the bat was streaked with fresh blood. Some of it had seeped into the wood, darkening and widening the lines of the grain.

I could clearly see two small pieces of shiny white material embedded in the wood. I spent some minutes puzzling over what they were. It was a relief to have something to occupy my mind, if only briefly. Then I realized they were bone fragments, previously facial features of the man slumped behind me. I slammed my eyes shut and erupted into a vicious bout of the dry heaves.

• • •

Perhaps minutes, perhaps hours, seemingly days elapsed while I remained conscious but literally senseless. My tightly clenched eyelids shut out the hideous sight behind me; the heavy pulsing of my heart left a pounding in my ears that blocked all external sounds; gulping air through only my mouth let no smells past my nose; the only sense of feel that I had was of the spastic constrictions in my belly.

A heavy hand suddenly clutched my shoulder and a loud "Hey!" penetrated the drumbeats in my ears. I was jerked to my feet and roughly turned around.

I faced three very different-looking men. One was the stadium attendant I met earlier. Next to him was a portly man in a gray business suit who kept glancing down at the dead man from the corner of his eye. The hand that had shaken me belonged to a helmeted member of Boston's finest.

The red-faced cop stepped to within inches of my nose, and belligerently demanded, "What the hell's going on here?"

"I don't know," I croaked softly.

"What! Speak up!"

"I don't know. I just found—*him,*" I said, pointing to the body. It was still in the strange sitting position on the floor.

"What are you doing here?"

"Looking for the manager. I'm supposed to report to him. To play ball."

The attendant cleared his throat and quietly said, "This is Mickey Rawlings. He played for the Braves some last year. I let him in about twenty minutes ago and told him how to get to Stahl's office." He frowned at me slightly as he concluded his statement.

The cop glared at the attendant. I think he wanted to get answers directly from me, preferably through a vigorous third degree.

The portly man also looked at the attendant and spoke for the first time. "The kid doesn't follow directions so good, does he?" The deep booming voice sounded like an umpire's; it conflicted sharply with his bankerlike appearance. He turned to me, and with a wry look on his face said, "So you're Rawlings. Welcome to Fenway, kid."

The cop let him speak without interruption or hostile looks, so I assumed the man had a position of authority. He quickly proved me right by barking some commands. He ordered the attendant, "Call Captain Tom O'Malley at the Walpole Street stationhouse. Tell him—uh, tell him what we have here. And I want him to handle it personally. Bring him to my office when he gets here." He directed the policeman: "You stay here until O'Malley shows up and tells you what to do." To me he said, "Come along with me," and firmly pushed my elbow to get me started. I followed him through a course of passages without trying to keep track of the turns.

We arrived at a door that had ROBERT F. TYLER painted on it in gold letters. My companion unlocked the door, and we stepped into an office that was large in size, but seemed cramped from all the ornate dark wood furniture that filled it. He moved as if the office was his, so I took it that my escort was the advertised Robert F. Tyler. I watched as he closed the door behind us and silently walked over to a sideboard. Tyler wasn't as soft as he first appeared. There was a power to his movements that indicated an athletic past. He did have a prominent belly, but that was a sign of prosperity that no self-respecting executive would be without.

Tyler filled a shot glass with amber liquid from a decanter and gulped it down. Emitting a satisfied sigh, he picked up another glass, filled it to the brim, and brought it to where I was still standing just inside the door. "Drink this. It will do you good."

I took the glass, tentatively took a sip, and shuddered at the taste.

"All of it. Drink it right down."

I tilted my head back and obeyed. My first attempt at drinking liquor, when I was about twelve, had made me sick. This second attempt had the same result. I did make it to a cuspidor though, and I did feel somewhat rejuvenated by the liquid fire that poured in and out of me.

Meanwhile, Tyler moved behind his desk and into a high-backed leather chair. When I looked as if I'd safely finished with the spittoon, he told me to have a seat. I sank into an armchair on the other side of his broad desk.

I had the feeling we weren't alone. I looked around and noticed three pairs of eyes staring at me—the dead glassy eyes of one moose and two deer whose heads were mounted on the walls.

Tyler took a neatly folded white handkerchief from his pocket, wiped his forehead, and finally introduced himself, "I'm Robert Tyler. I'm one of the owners of the Red Sox. Officially, I'm the treasurer." He didn't extend his hand, and I didn't offer mine. I suppose meeting over a corpse allows for dropping some of the social graces.

My new boss went on, "I handle most of the business activities of the ball club. Ticket sales, player contracts, travel arrangements." He thought for a moment, then suggested,

"Why don't we take care of some business now, and try to forget about that situation out there until the police get here. I have your contract somewhere . . . Yes, here it is. You need to sign at the X." He slid the paper to me, pulled a gold fountain pen from a desk drawer, and slid that to me, too. He didn't say how much I'd be paid, but I saw on the contract that it would be $1,400 a year—more than a hundred dollars a month!

While I quickly signed, Tyler continued, "Everybody knows what a terrific outfield we have, but we can use some shoring up in the infield right now. Injuries. A week into the season, and we already got injuries. Jake saw you with the Braves last year, said you looked pretty good, figured you could help us.

"We could use another pitcher, too. And maybe somebody to give Jake some time off at first—he's not getting any younger. We'll get whoever we need. I don't plan to come up short at the end of the year because of bad luck at the start."

I pushed the signed contract back to him.

He settled deeper in his chair, and muttered mostly to himself, "New ballpark . . . best outfield in baseball . . . Honey Fitz is crazy about us . . . we should be all set." Tyler was no longer looking at me; his thoughts were obviously elsewhere. I wondered what a "Honey Fitz" was.

Three delicate raps joggled the door, and the attendant stuck his head in. Before he could speak, an overweight policeman wearing captain's insignia elbowed past him into the room.

The officer and Tyler exchanged nods of recognition and curt greetings.

"Bob."

"Tom."

The captain turned to face me and asked, "Is this the suspect?"

Suspect? Me? I was too astonished at the question to say anything.

Tyler answered, "This is Mickey Rawlings. He just joined the club today. He found the body."

O'Malley grunted in response and squinted hard at me, trying to make his eyes look penetrating. "Was he dead when you found him?" he demanded.

"Yes," I answered. "I think so . . . I'm sure he was. I didn't really check him. I mean, he was so . . . He must have been dead. I yelled at him but he didn't answer. He was dead."

"Do you know who he was?"

"No. Who was he?"

"I'm asking the questions!" the captain bellowed angrily. "Did you see anyone?"

My first impulse was to answer that I hadn't. But after a moment's thought, I wasn't so sure. Once I set eyes on the dead man's face, I was oblivious to all else. Perhaps there was someone there, and I just hadn't noticed. I answered, "I don't think so."

O'Malley rolled his eyes. "Did you hear anything?"

"No—well, yes. I mean I heard a noise—like something fell, but that was before I went in the hallway."

"Like something fell," the officer repeated. "Did you hear footsteps? Somebody running away? Anything else?"

"No, I don't think so."

"Didn't see anything. Didn't hear anything. That's a lot of help."

I shrugged in apology.

Tyler spoke up again. "Do you need Rawlings for anything else?"

"Not right now," O'Malley answered, but as a final note he warned me, "Don't leave town."

Tyler overruled him. "He has to leave town. We start a road trip tomorrow." O'Malley scowled, but silently capitulated. Ignoring the captain, Tyler swiveled toward me. "You've had a helluva day, and we're leaving for New York in the morning." He scribbled on some stationery. "Take this to the Copley Plaza Hotel. Get yourself a good night's sleep and make sure you're at South Station by ten sharp." He held out the note, and with a token attempt at a smile said, "See you in the morning."

I stepped around the glowering O'Malley and took the paper without returning the smile. Mumbling, "Thank you," I picked up my bags and stepped out of the office.

The attendant was waiting outside the office door. Without exchanging a word, he escorted me all the way to the stadium exit.

Chapter Three

The whitecaps of Mystic Seaport sparkled through the window to my left; less than twenty-four hours ago, I'd admired them through a window to the right. Since Boston and New York both prohibited Sunday baseball, today was used for travel, with the entire Red Sox team on the train heading to Grand Central Station.

Tyler's generosity in putting me up at Boston's newest hotel had been wasted. Last night was a sleepless one—every time I closed my eyes, I was jolted awake by the full-color image of a viciously battered face. Exhausted from yesterday's catastrophes and drowsy from lack of sleep, I dozed off after boarding the train and napped until the sunlight skimming off the water penetrated my eyelids.

Before leaving the hotel this morning, I had stopped at the newsstand for a paper. The lobby had been surprisingly tranquil—I'd expected to encounter newsboys shrieking lurid headlines, "Murder at Fenway Park! Red Sox Rookie Stumbles on Stiff! Read all about it!"

I now scanned Page One of the *Boston American* and saw that the crime didn't make the front-page news. Most of the articles were still about the *Titanic,* although it had been two weeks since it sank. The death toll was up to fifteen hundred, but I was unaffected by the enormity of that tragedy. I was concerned with just one death, one victim who had lain shattered before my own eyes.

I turned the pages, puzzled to find no mention of the crime. Eventually, a small item headed GRISLY DISCOVERY caught my eye. But the story turned out to be about a robbery victim who had been found beaten to death in Dorchester. There was nothing about the body at Fenway Park.

I felt a need to know something about the man I'd found. I wasn't looking for a particular piece of information, just something that would humanize him: his name, where he lived, his work. Anything would do. If I could associate him with some other aspect of his identity, then maybe when he entered my thoughts—and I was sure he would on many nights to come—I could envision him in some way other than as that shockingly mutilated face.

Until I could picture him differently, I would just have to try to avoid thinking about him at all.

With some effort, I gradually prodded my thoughts away from the dead man.

And there were indeed more agreeable musings available to occupy me. For despite the disturbing start to my association with the Red Sox, I had every reason to look forward to what was ahead. Particularly to our immediate destinations: my first appearances in New York and Philadelphia as a major-league baseball player.

• • •

I grew up in Raritan, New Jersey. It was perfect for seeing major-league baseball, even though the state itself didn't have a single team. In a journey of less than two hours I could reach the home grounds of any one of five big league clubs: the Giants in upper Manhattan, the Highlanders—or *Yankees* as some papers called them—in the Bronx, the Brooklyn Dodgers, and the Phillies and Athletics in Philadelphia.

I was raised by my aunt and uncle. Uncle Matt ran a general store in town and taught me baseball. And he gave those tasks about equal priority. My earliest memories are of playing catch with him in the backyard.

My uncle took me to major-league games whenever he could, usually to the Athletics' Columbia Park, where I could cheer for my favorite player: Rube Waddell, a hard-throwing eccentric pitcher who spent his off-time wrestling alligators and chasing fire engines.

As I was growing up, I worked hard to polish the baseball skills I had and learn the ones I didn't have. I rarely attended school, finding it useful only for rounding up enough other boys to play a full-scale ball game. I tried to get into every baseball game that the boys would organize, though I dreaded the choosing-up-sides ritual. Not once was I the first boy picked. I was smaller than most of the other kids, and despite all my practice, there was always one boy who could throw harder than I could, another who could run faster, and many more who could hit the ball farther. But I was usually the best fielder and best place hitter, so I was never the last picked either.

When I was fourteen, my aunt died after a brief illness. Uncle Matt didn't feel like playing catch or doing anything else anymore. With my aunt gone, my uncle totally withdrawn, and school holding no interest for me, I was on my own.

I always knew that my career would be in baseball. I also knew that I would never be a star. But I figured I could have a pretty good career as a journeyman ball player and then go on to coaching and maybe managing.

The first teams that paid me to play were factory teams. Many companies would give jobs to men or boys who could play on the firms' baseball teams. I worked and played for a variety of industries across the Northeast, including a snuff factory in New Jersey and a shipyard in Connecticut. I once took a job with a cotton mill in Rhode Island, but quit after just three days. Most of my coworkers in the mill were children, as young as ten. They labored sixty hours a week for forty cents a day, breathing air that was foggy with lint. I was getting twelve dollars a week to play baseball. My conscience couldn't reconcile itself with the unfairness, so I left. I knew my departure didn't help those kids any, but I liked to think that it hurt their employer by weakening the company team.

During those semipro years, I sharpened my playing skills, learned to get along with different kinds of people, and picked up the rudiments of a dozen industrial trades. My only book-learning came from what I read while killing time in railroad depots: dime novels, *The Police Gazette,* and *The Sporting News.*

I made it to the minors a year ago, and played most of the season with Providence until the Braves bought my contract. To my delight, old hurler Cy Young was on the team, playing his last season after more than twenty years and five hundred victories. The highlight of my stint with the Braves was that someday I could tell my grandchildren that I had been a teammate of Cy Young.

I had always assumed that once I made it to the majors, I would stay there. It didn't occur to me that I could head down the system as well as up, and I was devastated when the Braves released me after the season. At age nineteen, I thought my career was over.

But now the Red Sox were giving me another shot at the big leagues, and I intended to make the most of it.

• • •

A sharp cough snapped my mind to attention. I looked up to see the stadium attendant I met yesterday standing next to my seat. He wore a navy suit almost identical to his uniform, with a red polka dot bow tie protruding from a high tight collar. I was startled to see him on the train—surely the Highlanders and Athletics had ushers for their own ballparks.

"I don't believe I ever introduced myself," he said, extending his hand. "My name is Jimmy Macullar." I took his grip. "Mind if I sit down?" I shook my head, and he gently settled into the seat next to me.

In a low voice Macullar said, "I was feeling badly about yesterday." The bumping train caused his words to rattle softly through his teeth. "It's a terrible thing that happened. You must have been very shaken up." He looked at me sympathetically as I murmured agreement. Considering my embarrassing physical reaction to the situation, I thought him gracious in understating my condition as "shaken up."

"One way or another, I've been in baseball more than forty years," he said. "I don't go back quite as far as Abner Doubleday, but I've seen just about everything in the game since then. I want you to know that I've never been as excited about any team as I am about the 1912 Red Sox. Even before the season started, it seemed like everything was coming together for us. We already had the players, and now the new owners have taken care of everything else.

"Stop me if you like, but I thought you might want to know something about the ball club." I didn't stop him, so he went on. "A new group of owners bought the team last year. Some of them had been players, some managers—all of them have a solid baseball background. They know the game on every level.

"You met Bob Tyler. He's the treasurer and general manager—handles all the day-to-day business decisions. I'm his assistant and sometimes I help out at the gate or do odd jobs. Mr. Tyler used to work for Ban Johnson—"

"Really?" I interrupted. I couldn't picture Tyler working for anyone but himself—although if anyone could order Tyler around, it would be the American League president. "What did he do?"

"Mr. Tyler was the league secretary for six years. He knows more about league affairs than anyone but Ban Johnson himself.

"Jake Stahl is quite a man, too," Macullar said. "I think you'll like him. He owns about ten percent of the club. Player, manager, and owner all at the same time. It's a lot of responsibility, but he handles it well.

"Anyway, what I wanted to say is that we have the ideal owners for a baseball club. They know the game from the playing field to the league president's office. The first thing they did was move us out of the Huntington Avenue Grounds, and put up Fenway Park. Beautiful ballpark isn't it?"

I shook my head up and down in unrestrained agreement.

"Opening Day at Fenway was a grand time—the game was postponed three days by rain, but that just made it more exciting when we did get it in. Mayor Fitzgerald and his Royal Rooters were there in force. They kept singing "Tessie" over and over—that was our fight song in ought-three when we won the first World Series.

"Anyway, we beat the Highlanders 7–6 in extra innings opening day. I took it as a good sign for the season. It seems like the whole city is excited by the team. Of course, with Honey Fitz our biggest fan, everyone is eager to get behind us." I deduced that Honey Fitz was the mayor of Boston.

"Well, I've talked too much," Macullar concluded. "Mr. Tyler asked me to bring you to his car, but I wanted to take a few minutes to let you know that this is a very special team, and you have a lot to look forward to." He smiled confidently. "We're going to the World Series."

Macullar rose to his feet. I stood up and followed him through the train, wondering why he had made such an effort to talk up the team's ownership.

We both entered Bob Tyler's private car. Tyler was seated in a plush chair, his hands folded on the large gold head of a walking stick that stood between his knees. He glared at Macullar, silently asking, "What the hell took you so long?" Verbally he told him, "That will be all for now, Jimmy." Macullar quickly ducked out of the car.

In addition to the cane, Tyler had an aggie-sized diamond stickpin in his tie and a hefty gold watch chain draped across the vest of his striped brown suit. Buff spats covered his ankles. He reminded me of some of the factory owners who used to hire me to play: petty autocrats who thought they could impress the world by sporting the sort of trappings I now saw before me. Usually, the most adorned and pompous men ran the shabbiest factories.

I was in my one good traveling suit, which was still grimy from yesterday.

Tyler pointed me into a seat, and adopted a grave tone. "Mickey, Captain O'Malley's investigation isn't going very well. In fact, he seems to think you're the leading suspect."

"But I didn't have anything to do with it! All I did was find the guy!"

"Well, if it's any consolation, I believe you." With a grimace, he added, "I never heard of a killer who pukes on a man he's just murdered. I'm not the police though—it's their opinion that counts. And you *were* found at the scene of the crime." Tyler allowed me to squirm uncomfortably. I stared at his face, and noticed with some surprise that he was younger than I thought at first; he probably wasn't out of his forties. His brown hair was thick, without a hint of gray. From his dress and bearing, he wanted to appear older—to bolster his autocratic manner, I figured. He finally went on, "However, I'm not without influence. The team does have a certain status in the city of Boston, and we can probably protect you somewhat from any hasty accusations by the police."

"But why would I need protection? I didn't do anything wrong."

"You're a major-league baseball player. You're in the public eye now. If he wants to, a cop or a reporter could get a lot of attention for himself just by accusing you. That kind of publicity tends to stick, though, and that's bad for all of us. The point is that a ball club can do a lot to protect its players." Tyler glanced up at the ceiling for a moment. Then he said in a confidential voice, "I'll let you in on something:

every couple of years, Ty Cobb gets in one of his rages and assaults somebody. Then Frank Navin has to calm down the cops and try to keep it out of the papers. You remember when the Tigers played the Pirates in the World Series?"

I nodded. It had been just two or three years ago.

"Cobb had to travel outside the Ohio border every time they went from Detroit to Pittsburgh. You know why?"

I shook my head.

"Because he knifed some hotel worker in Cleveland, and there was a warrant out for his arrest. Navin took care of it in the off-season. He's a good owner. He takes care of his players' problems. If the Tigers can keep it quiet when a famous player like Cobb really commits a crime, we should be able to protect a nobo—a, uh, lesser-known player who was just in the wrong place at the wrong time. You're going to have to do *your* part, though." I started to ask what that was, but he talked over my question, already answering, "You don't say anything to anybody about anything that happened."

"But what about the police? What if they want to ask me more questions?"

"Of course we want to cooperate with the police—just like we expect them to cooperate with us. If Captain O'Malley has any questions for you, you should answer them—just make sure I'm there, too."

"You mentioned the papers. I saw today's paper and there wasn't anything about it."

"Well . . . Boston's a big city. People turn up dead all the time."

"At *Fenway Park?*"

Tyler looked annoyed. "We wouldn't want Fenway to be mentioned, would we? Look. Nobody even knows who the man was. I don't know if this occurred to you, but he may not have been some innocent victim. What if he was killed in self-defense? What if he was a hoodlum who had it coming? Look. This is what it comes down to: you don't need trouble, the team don't need trouble. The cops will do their investigating, but they'll have to do it quietly. If O'Malley wants to talk to you, that's fine—I'll just come along and make sure your interests are protected. Other than that, you don't say a word to anybody. Understood?"

I didn't feel like I understood, but I nodded that I did.

With a forced smile Tyler said, "Good. Let's get this behind us, and concentrate on baseball. Jake's probably going to start you in tomorrow's game." He clapped his cane on the floor to signal an end to the conversation. "Send Jimmy in on your way out."

I did as he asked and returned to my seat. I wasn't able to get my thoughts on baseball, though, so I fruitlessly mulled over Tyler's words. This business with the police and the papers and the ball club was beyond my experience. I could make no sense of the situation.

But I could tell that this didn't look like it was going to be my season.

Chapter Four

My new teammates milled about home plate, coordinating their moves so that each time I tried to step to the batter's box I was blocked out. This came as no surprise; preventing rookies from taking a turn at batting practice is a standard part of the hazing ritual new ball players have to endure. For form's sake, I maintained a pretense of expecting a chance to hit, but I really didn't mind when other players elbowed in front of me and stepped to the plate. I was engrossed in scanning the Hilltop Park stands. This was the first time I'd been in a stadium as a player where I used to come as a spectator.

The grandstand behind third base was filling up with fans: office clerks taking an afternoon off to attend a nonexistent aunt's funeral, and courting couples who sat high in the stands to enjoy the view of the Jersey Palisades across the Hudson River.

Outside the right field foul line lay the open bleacher seats, bare pine boards occupied mostly by kids who couldn't afford better vantage points. Less than ten years ago,

I was one of those eager faces dreaming of actually being *on* this field some day.

Box seats between home plate and the dugouts held middle-aged men in business suits and derbies who looked as if they could afford the best. I had never been able to get a ticket for one of those seats, and gloated that today I would be sitting in an even better location: the dugout bench.

Everywhere, the ballpark was alive with sounds that had been dormant all winter and now burst out with the coming of April. From a hundred directions came the sociable buzz of friendly arguments—about off-season trades, which teams would make it to the World Series, which players were over the hill and which were promising rookies. Over the chatter, vendors barked *Peanuts!* and *Beer!* and fans shouted their orders for same. From the field came the sharpest sounds: loud cracks of wood on leather as hitters teed off on soft tosses from the batting practice pitcher; and hard pops of leather on leather, as baseballs were thrown into mitts eager to snap them up.

Ten minutes to game time, Jake Stahl called us in to the dugout. Contrary to what Bob Tyler predicted, Stahl had decided not to start me. He said he'd let me get adjusted to the team before putting me in the lineup. I wondered if he was also letting me recover from the episode in Fenway Park, but he said nothing about it.

I sat by myself at the end of the dugout bench. I knew the first rule for rookies: they should be seen and not heard. I also knew the second rule: they shouldn't be seen either. To my teammates I had as little stature as a batboy. It would take a while for me to be accepted by them. Usually the way it worked was that a rookie would be paired with a veteran player on road trips. After the veteran showed the youngster around and gave his approval, the other players would start to think of him as part of the team, too. My roommate was to be Clyde Fletcher, another utility player, but only his luggage made it to our hotel room last night so we had yet to meet.

The game got under way with Harry Hooper leading off for us against Hippo Vaughn. The Highlander pitcher looked as huge as his name implied, but I thought he was more imposing in appearance than he was in performance (of course it's always easy to think that from a safe spot in the dugout or the bleachers). Hooper had no trouble with him, lining a single back through the box on the second pitch.

While the next batters took their turns, I fixed my attention on Hal Chase at first base. I was oddly comforted by his presence there. Not because it was Chase—famed equally for his fielding prowess and his unsavory character—but because he was a player I had watched as a boy in this very ballpark. When I was a kid, sitting in the bleachers and fantasizing about playing in the big leagues, I always envisioned in my daydreams playing against the very players who were on the field in the very ballparks where I watched them. Those players had been leaving the game, though, and huge new stadiums were replacing the homey ones I used to know. So it was with a feeling of comfortable familiarity that I sat in old Hilltop Park, reassured to see Hal Chase manning first base for the Highlanders.

Six and a half innings went by with the Sox hitters methodically driving singles and doubles off of Vaughn and circling the bases for seven runs. Our pitcher, Bucky O'Brien, just as methodically mowed down the New York batters, holding them scoreless with only two hits. Already some fans were crossing the corner of the outfield to get to the exit gate in the right field fence. It seemed odd to see people walking through fair territory while a game was in progress, but it was one of the quaint facts of life at Hilltop Park.

"Rawlings! You come here to sleep or play ball?"

I looked up at the angry voice. "Huh?"

Stahl was standing in front of me, clutching his mitt in one hand and pointing toward the infield with the other. "I said you're playing second. Get out there! We're not paying you to sit on your ass."

I snatched my glove and stumbled out of the dugout, running to second base. Jake followed close on my heels to take his position at first. O'Brien threw his last warm-up pitch, and the Highlander leadoff man stepped into the batter's box. I was now officially in my first Red Sox game. Stahl must have figured that with a 7–0 score it was safe to put me in.

I was a tight bundle of nerves anyway. To settle down, I went over the fundamentals: if it's a grounder to me, I throw to Stahl at first . . . a bunt toward first, I cover the bag . . . a hit to right field, I move out for the cutoff throw . . . a drive to left, I cover second.

None of these situations developed, as O'Brien struck out the first two batters and the third flied out to center. I jauntily trotted off the field, having accomplished nothing but feeling satisfied at having done nothing wrong.

I didn't get a turn at bat in the top of the eighth, as our side went down in order. In the bottom half, my first fielding chance came as Hal Chase himself hit an easy one-hopper to me. I played it cleanly, and felt my confidence grow.

I was due up fourth in the final frame, so I wasn't sure if I'd get to bat at all. Tris Speaker then led off the inning with his second double of the game and my chances improved. Speaker moved to third base on a fielder's choice, and I moved to the on-deck circle. I swung two bats together to loosen up. They weren't my usual bats, but new ones that I bought in a sporting goods store earlier in the day. The short stubby pieces of wood had roughly the same heft as the homemade bats I'd left in my hotel room.

Stahl struck out looking, and I approached the batter's box slowly. As nervous as I first was in the field, I was more so coming to the plate. At second base there was always a chance that I wouldn't be involved in a play, but in the batter's box there was no place to hide. It would be just Hippo and me.

I took my place in the box, kicking my right spike into the dirt. When facing a pitcher he hasn't seen before, a hitter will usually take the first pitch looking. But I didn't like to let good ones go by, so I would choose one spot and one type of pitch, and if it was served there, I'd take a rip at it. I now tried to pick a location for the first pitch, but absolutely nothing came to mind. While I frantically tried to think of the pitch I wanted to look for, I unconsciously kept kicking with my shoe.

"Hey, busher! Dig it a little deeper! You're gonna git buried in it!" Hippo got my full attention with that yell. I called time and backed out of the box. Glancing sideways at him, I could see that Hippo did not look happy—no surprise since he'd taken a beating from the Red Sox hitters. Okay, so I have to expect one at my head. No pitcher likes to have a batter dig in on him, and none would let a rookie get away with it. Just what I need: something more to think about. Okay, if it's a fastball knee-high down the middle, I'm swinging. If it's at my head I'm ducking. But Speaker's on third; if Vaughn throws a wild pitch, he'll score, so maybe he won't try throwing at me. But if he hits me, the ball's dead and Speaker can't advance, so he will throw at me, but he'll make sure not to miss me. Hmmm . . . Only one thing is for certain: it is impossible to think and hit at the same time.

I took my stance in the box. In less than a second, I gracelessly dropped to the ground as Hippo tried to keep his word. He *was* mad—the ball was thrown *behind* my head. That's where you throw it if you really want to hurt somebody; the batter's instinct is to duck back into the path of the ball. But the ball missed me, and the catcher missed the ball, so Speaker trotted home with another run. Vaughn apparently didn't care if he lost 7–0 or 8–0.

Okay, this isn't working out badly. We have another run, and my pants are still dry. Considering the scare I got, I should get an RBI for that run.

The next pitch from Hippo was right where I wanted it. I pulled the trigger, but a little too early. The ball cued off the end of the bat and rolled up the dirt path from home plate to the pitcher's mound. Vaughn threw me out before I was halfway to first base. A pretty good at bat: I got some wood on the ball, and earned that moral RBI for Speaker scoring.

The clubhouse was boisterous after the easy victory over New York. The players kidded each other, snapped a few towels—and sawed my new bats in half while I was in the shower.

When I discovered the useless pieces of lumber they left me, I loudly let loose with most of the cuss words I knew—a considerable repertoire after all my years around ball players. My teammates laughed at my reaction to their little prank. Welcome to the Red Sox, kid. What they didn't know was that I was really relieved. One more aspect of the hazing was over, and I could safely bring in my good bats.

A stocky player with a small towel around his waist and an enormous wad of tobacco in his cheek shuffled up to me.

Lush patches of wiry black hair sprouted on parts of his body where I didn't even know hair could grow. "I'm Clyde Fletcher," he said, spraying a shower of tobacco juice in saying the "tch" of his last name. "We're gonna be roomies. I got plans for tonight, so if Jake comes by for bed check, tell him I went out for cigars. Got it?"

"Yeah, sure."

"Goo' boy." Fletcher belched out a dribble of brown juice, turned around to reveal a broad back that was nearly as hairy as his belly, and returned to his locker.

I remembered reading once that Rube Waddell had a clause put into the contract of his roommate that prohibited him from eating crackers in bed—Waddell said the noise kept him awake nights. I had a feeling I would soon be wishing for a roommate whose most annoying habit was munching crackers.

• • •

I was back at the Union Hotel by half past six. I walked up three flights of stairs to my room, intending to lie down for an hour and then go out for a late supper. But my bed was already occupied.

Neatly laid on top of the cover was Mabel, my favorite bat. She was lengthwise, with the knob toward the foot of the bed and the barrel denting the pillow—right where my head would be.

I turned to look on either side of the door. No one there.

Who put the bat on my bed? And how did he get in? I quickly examined the door lock: it was intact, no sign of force. And I'd needed the key to open it. I swept across the room to the one window—it was unbroken, securely locked, and sealed up with thick beige paint.

I checked the rest of the room. The two sagging iron-rail beds were still made up. Fletcher's bags were at the foot of his, the same as they were last night. A pitcher of water and my shaving tools were in place on the washstand. I sifted through my luggage and the dresser drawer where I'd stashed my clothes; nothing was taken or moved. Everything looked in order.

Staring at Mabel, I sat down on the room's only other piece of furniture, a pinching straight-back chair with legs of unequal length.

This was no prank by playful teammates. Nor was it an attempt at burglary or vandalism. This was a message. The context of the message was obvious: it had to do with the man I'd found at Fenway Park. But what was the content—what exactly was I being told?

Was it a warning, telling me to keep quiet about my find or I'd end up the same way? Or was it a notice, the calling card of some perverse killer? Had the dead man at Fenway also found a bat in his bed? I read all sorts of ominous scenarios into the sight of one round piece of wood.

I'd made Mabel when I worked in a furniture factory. Instead of the usual ash, I selected a choice block of hickory, turned it down on a lathe, and sanded it smooth. As the bat took shape, I named it for movie star Mabel Normand, and "it" became a "her." I spent long hours honing her with a hambone to keep her from chipping, and rubbing sweet oil into her to protect the wood. Now, as I worried over the message she bore, I couldn't even bring myself to touch her. What I had so lovingly created repelled me.

Not until Jake Stahl knocked and announced himself at

the door could I move her; I grabbed her delicately at each end and stashed her under the bed.

When I let him in, Stahl took a glance around the room, and wearily asked, "Fletcher out getting cigars?" I nodded, but doubted if I seemed convincing.

"Uh-huh," he grunted. Stahl wore a tired expression and a blue herringbone suit that looked a size too small. "Don't worry about it, kid. You did okay today. Tomorrow you're starting at second. When we get to Philadelphia, you'll fill in at shortstop. Get some sleep."

He turned to go out the door, and added, "Oh . . . don't bother to wait up for Fletcher." When Stahl left, I thought his was a job I didn't envy. He was expected to bat .300, field his position at first base, run the team in the day, and baby-sit it at night.

With my bed now free, I undressed and tried to take Stahl's advice.

Once I was under the covers, it occurred to me that whoever left the message might return, perhaps to clarify its meaning. I tried to sleep lightly, keeping one eye open to spot any intruder. I found that it can't be done. All I accomplished was tire my eyes by trying to close only one at a time. I was soon asleep.

I awoke with a ringing in my ears. Was that the alarm clock? No, it's still dark out. Wait a minute, are my eyes open? I chafed my right eyeball by sticking a fingertip in it. Yes, my eyelids are open. So, it's still night. Why am I awake?

Hchoowook. Shptoo. *Ping!*

That was the noise. I sat up.

"You up, kid?"

"Mmm . . . yeah."

Hchoowook. Shptoo. *Ping!* Fletcher hit the spittoon with

another gob of tobacco juice. "Well, you oughta go to sleep," he said. "We got a game tomorrow." With that helpful advice, Fletcher spit out his wad and plopped into bed.

• • •

The next day, I did get a turn at batting practice, probably because nobody else wanted one. It was a chilly sunless spring afternoon and there were bees in the bats. Unless the ball was hit with the sweet part of the bat, it stung like hell to make contact.

Since I was starting the game this time, I paid attention to the field instead of the bleachers and the fans. And to get my mind off the message that was left in my room, I tried to concentrate on the proper use of a baseball bat. After taking my practice hits, I checked out the ground near home plate. I wanted to see how far a bunt would travel, and in what direction. Some groundskeepers graded the foul lines so that balls would tend to roll either fair or foul, depending on their own team's bunting skills. The ground here looked level, but it was packed hard. To keep the ball from skipping too fast and far, I'd have to deaden a bunt by holding the bat loosely.

I headed back to the dugout where most of the Sox sat huddled in their red plaid warm-up jackets. Without a jacket of my own, it struck me how drab the Red Sox uniform was in comparison with the bright coats. The entire outfit was flat gray with faint blue pinstripes, even the bill of the cap; the only extra decoration anywhere was BOSTON spelled out on the front of the jersey in navy block letters. The Red Sox's new ownership may have done a great job building Fenway Park, but Bob Tyler and his partners would have done well to snazz up the team uniforms some, too.

Only two other players lacked the colorful overcoats: pitcher Charlie Strickler and catcher Billy Neal, an aging battery that just joined the team. Continuing his effort to bolster the injured Red Sox roster, Tyler bought the duo from Frank Navin for $5,000 cash. It gave me some degree, if only a day's worth, of seniority on the team.

Holding the lineup cards in one hand and a battered brown megaphone in the other, the plate umpire faced the crowd behind home plate and announced the starting lineups. He must have given the names of both nines, but all that caught my ear was *Rawlings, Second Base.* I savored the sound as it echoed through the stadium.

The Highlanders were throwing Jack Warhop at us. Smoky Joe Wood, the only Sox player who looked as young as I, was pitching against him.

Harry Hooper again led off the game, this time by popping out to third. Duffy Lewis and Tris Speaker went down easily, too, and I trotted to second base as the Sox took the field.

I quickly discovered why Joe Wood was called "Smoky": he threw the ball so fast that the only thing visible was the smoke that seemed to trail behind it. I used to think this an exaggeration by the sportswriters, but the blur of the speeding ball really made it look like it had a tail of steam. Smoky Joe had his best stuff this day; he shut down the Highlander batters in the first inning, striking out the side.

The game was still scoreless when I led off the top of the third. I chose my spot for the first pitch: curveball, belt-high on the outside corner. That's where Warhop put it, and I took a cut. The ball broke sharper than I expected, and I topped it a bit, hitting a hard grounder between third and short. I tried to leg it out to first, as the shortstop went in the hole to field the ball. I should have been out by a step or two, but the play didn't click somehow. As usual, Hal Chase had been playing a deep first base, and he didn't get to the bag in time for the throw. The ball skipped off Chase's glove and flew into the stands. I went on to second base as the umpire retrieved the ball from the fan who caught the overthrow.

That play felt funny. The timing was off, and it shouldn't have been. I looked to first base, and saw Chase smirking as he moved back into position. Was he playing his games again? Although Chase was unquestionably the best fielding first baseman in the game, he was known for slacking off at times. Rumors had it that he was friendly with gamblers and would sometimes throw games for his pals. But I don't think anyone ever actually caught him at it. Perhaps the stories circulated only because there are always rumors about odd people—and Chase was certainly that. Who but a screwball would throw lefty and bat righty?

While I speculated about Chase, Warhop picked me off second. It is impossible to think and run at the same time.

The innings passed quickly with neither team scoring.

Whenever the Sox batted, I kept my eyes on Hal Chase, looking for any funny business. If he was trying to throw the game, he'd have to blow some more plays.

In the fourth, Duffy Lewis grounded to third and again Chase didn't make it to the bag in time. He did look to be hustling, but again the rhythm of the play was wrong.

My next at bat came in the sixth. With a 2–2 count, Warhop served up a low lazy curve. I slid my right hand up the barrel of the bat and rapped down at the ball with a short stroke. The ball shot off the wood, down onto the hard earth. It hit a foot in front of home plate and bounced up to the height of a pop fly. By the time it came down, I had crossed first base safely. Hal Chase glared at me with pale gray eyes and greeted me with scorn, "*Nobody* hits Baltimore chops no more." That's okay—so what if I'm old-fashioned? I'm on first base with a single. But there I stayed, as the hitters who followed me went down on outs.

The game remained scoreless into the top of the ninth inning. And that's when I figured out how Hal Chase did it.

Jake Stahl hit a grounder to third to open our half of the inning, and I kept my eyes on Chase from the moment the bat made contact. While the ball skipped to the third baseman, Chase stayed anchored well off the first base bag. Then just before the ball was fielded, he broke for the base. When the third baseman's throw arrived, Chase was hustling as hard as he could to take the throw at first—but his initial delay ensured that he wouldn't be in time to catch the ball cleanly. The son of a bitch. He was really throwing the game.

Yesterday, with the sight of a dead man still fresh in my eyes, I would have thought that murder was the most heinous of crimes. But now I'd seen Hal Chase try to throw a baseball game. It was an offense that seemed worse than murder—a crime less gruesome, but a sacrilege more sinister.

Chapter Five

Before the first game in Shibe Park, I worried that I would be intimidated by playing against the Athletics. Not only were they my old boyhood favorites, but just off their second straight World Series win, they would likely be Boston's toughest competition for the American League pennant.

Once the first game began, however, my awe for the Athletics faded away. Maybe because it wasn't the same field where I had watched them as a boy.

My nonchalance lasted only until the next day, when we faced Gettysburg Eddie Plank. Plank had been pitching for the A's since I was nine years old. He was one of those hurlers I batted against time and again in countless daydreams. Somehow the prospect of trying to hit him in real life didn't seem as promising as it did in my fantasies of years ago.

My first at bat against Plank turned out to be an embarrassingly futile effort. I felt physically weak, with no strength in my legs or power in my arms. I swatted at three pitches and struck out without even a foul tip.

In my second try against him, I was just angry enough

with myself that it offset the nervousness. The net effect was that I felt strong and sharp. On his second pitch, I tagged a line drive single up the middle, just inches over Plank's head. At first base, I cheered to myself: I can hit Eddie Plank! Yes, I belong in the big leagues.

I ended up one for four, but that one felt like plenty. Plank won the game, giving Philadelphia a split of the first two games of the series.

After the game, the locker room was the usual babel of talking, groaning, cussing, and spitting. Still generally ignored by teammates, I changed quietly, barely paying attention to the intermittent comments that buzzed around me.

"He got himself killed."

That caught my attention. I wasn't sure who said it, or what preceded it. I lifted my head and tilted it this way and that, angling my ears to try to extract additional information from the fragmented words and phrases that darted about the room.

"Look at these goddam corns—my feet are killin' me."

"Anybody seen my towel?"

Hchoowook. Shptoo. *Splat!*

So far nothing useful. Come on, somebody ask *who* got himself killed.

"I gotta get myself some new spikes."

"Okay, who took my towel?"

"Who's pitchin' tomorrow?"

"Found him under a railroad bridge."

There! That was a strange sentence for a baseball clubhouse.

I began to successfully filter out the extraneous conversations, and pick up only those comments that didn't fit in with typical locker room chatter. In no particular order, I was able to gather that a baseball player had been killed, the fellow's name sounded like "Carrigan," he played third base for Detroit, his body was found under a railroad bridge in Boston, it was discovered after the Tigers' last series there, and he had died as the result of a mugging. Since Detroit had preceded us in Shibe Park, I figured that's how this news started to get around.

I was hoping for information about the dead man I stumbled upon in Fenway Park, and was disappointed. The locker room conversation obviously referred to someone else. I remembered the newspaper story I read about the body that was found in Dorchester, and this fit what I heard in the clubhouse.

Instead of going straight to the hotel after leaving Shibe Park, I took an aimless walk through the streets of North Philadelphia. My thoughts were confused and largely incoherent, but they eventually agreed on one frightening conclusion: a deadly trend was developing.

Although my find at Fenway Park was a horrible one, it was the horror of one gruesome sight, one shocking experience. Now, even more chilling, was the possibility that it wasn't an isolated incident. Two violent deaths—was it two and counting?—had occurred within a short time of each other. And both were connected with Fenway Park. One victim—maybe a fan—was found *in* the stadium, and the other had just played there. Could the splendid new ballpark be jinxed?

The walk didn't help me sort things out any, so I grabbed a cheese steak sandwich at a street vendor and went back to the hotel room.

Laying on my bed, staring at the ceiling, I realized that I wasn't going to clear anything up just by thinking. If I wanted to find out what happened, I would have to talk to people, ask what I wanted to know. But talking could get me in trouble.

Tyler had made it clear that I'd better keep my mouth shut about the dead man at Fenway Park. Of course I knew that his main concern wasn't my protection as he claimed—he probably wanted to avoid bad publicity more than anything else. Whatever the real reason for his orders, Bob Tyler seemed a man who would not tolerate having them disobeyed.

And then there's the police. If they failed to find the real killer, the cops might decide to clear up the case by convicting the handiest suspect. Having been found at the crime scene, Captain O'Malley already had me pegged for that role. Asking questions would only draw additional attention to myself.

I wasn't entirely sure which would be worse: facing Tyler's wrath or O'Malley's handcuffs.

Wait a minute . . . I *can* ask questions about the Detroit player—it was only the body at Fenway that Tyler had told me to keep quiet about. If Tyler gives me hell for asking about the dead Tiger, I'll swear I did as I was told, and pretend it never occurred to me that the deaths were connected.

I was still awake when Clyde Fletcher came into our room, much earlier than usual, grumbling about the insufficient nightlife in Philadelphia.

Hchoowook. Shptoo. *Ping!*

I looked at him as he sat on his bed. His head seemed to list to one side to balance the massive chaw of tobacco that puffed out his cheek. It gave a tilt to the one huge bushy eyebrow that spanned across both his eyes as it tried to stretch from ear to ear.

Although he seemed unpromising as a source of information on anything but vices, I decided to try to talk with Fletcher. If there was no response, at least I wouldn't be losing out on much.

Trying hard to sound as if I just wanted to pass the time, I asked him, "You know a player named Carrigan?"

"Bill Carrigan?"

I shook my head at the name of the Red Sox catcher. "No, this guy is with Detroit. Or he was, anyway. Some guys in the clubhouse were saying he got himself in a scrap."

Fletcher looked puzzled, then seemed to remember him. "Oh. *Corriden.* Yeah, Red Corriden. He was in the last series in Boston. Too bad about him. Just a kid. Musta been about your age." Hchoowook. Shptoo. *Ping!*

"You know what happened to him?" I prodded.

"Nah. Just what I heard the boys saying. I guess he was out where he shouldn'ta been. Somebody beat him up and took his roll. Happens sometimes. Shame though."

"Third baseman, wasn't he?"

"Yeah, I think so, but he hadn't played much. Oh yeah, I think I saw him with the Browns a couple years ago. I think maybe he did play third." Hchoowook. Shptoo. *Ping!*

Fletcher ended the brief conversation by killing the light and saying, "Well, might as well get some sleep. Nothing else to do in this goddam town."

Chapter Six

After thoroughly washing my hands to avoid leaving even the faintest smudges, I struggled to attach a new stiff collar to a brilliant white shirt. I almost cut off the blood supply to my head in the process, but I succeeded in getting the collar on, as well as a crimson silk necktie. I was wearing a good part of my first Red Sox paycheck, and looked almost dapper. Even more so when I peeled off the shreds of tissue paper that were stuck to my face. I had only four hairs worth shaving, but I managed to inflict five cuts attempting to remove them.

Everything I put on was new: from my socks and the garters that held them up to the blue-striped seersucker suit that had cost me $40. There was something about wearing new clothes that made me feel a new man; it gave me hope of getting off to a fresh start. I topped off the outfit by placing a straw boater over my slicked-back hair, and looking in the mirror, decided never mind "almost," I *did* look dapper.

This was the first week of May, back in Boston after the Philadelphia series.

I had started the final game against the Athletics, but

since the locker room talk about the murdered Detroit player, and with the silent mystery of the dead man at Fenway Park continually occupying my thoughts, I found myself unable to focus on baseball. After one throwing error and two fielding errors in the first three innings, Jake Stahl demoted me to the bench.

The only positive thing that happened before leaving Philadelphia was that another Red Sox player finally spoke to me, making me feel a little more like part of the team. Bucky O'Brien, a native Bostonian, suggested a rooming house in Back Bay that he said was clean and cheap. Seeing that his evaluation of the place was accurate, I moved into the house when we returned. It turned out to be owned by Bucky's aunt.

Since our first full day back in Boston was a Sunday, I was free to find an amusement that would divert my mind from thoughts of murder.

I didn't share the usual ball player passions for liquor, tobacco, or gambling, but I did have one weakness, and I was going to Scollay Square to indulge it.

The late-afternoon sun was still warm when I stepped out of the rooming house. I walked slowly to prevent working up any sweat that might spoil my clean crisp appearance. I strolled casually toward my destination, taking in the sights along Beacon Street.

Turning into Tremont Row, I spotted the building I was seeking. As I approached it, I glanced about to see if there was anyone around who might recognize me. I did not want to be seen going into this place.

My heart raced, and with a deep breath I stepped inside the door.

My excitement waned considerably when I got a look at

the chunky, graying woman who greeted me. Though disappointed, I decided to carry through with my plans anyway, and walked up to her.

"One please," I said, sliding a dime through the ticket window.

She handed me a paper stub back, and said with a smile, "Go right in."

I removed my hat, and found an empty seat in the darkened theater. A Mack Sennett comedy flickered on the screen in front of me.

About five years before, I had started going to the moving pictures. As a gypsy ball player, I was always finding myself with time to kill in unfamiliar towns. Almost every burg, no matter how tiny or remote, had a tavern, a church, and a nickelodeon. Since I wasn't good at drinking, and figured I wasn't bad enough to need churches, I took to the flickers. They were supposed to be bad for the hitting eye, though, so to avoid getting in trouble with my managers, I kept my vice a secret.

It was through my interest in moving pictures that I had met Miss Peggy Shaw. She was actually *Mrs.* Peggy Shaw, but I preferred not to be a stickler about that.

During a Saturday rainout last year, I had come to this theater for the first time to see the Mary Pickford picture that was advertised. At the ticket booth was a shapely young lady with light honey hair and sparkling green eyes. She looked like a Gibson Girl who just stepped out of the pages of *Collier's.* I was instantly smitten.

As the movies began that day, the visual delight from the ticket window sat down at the piano. She played beautifully, choosing music that complimented each scene perfectly, and performing as if she were in a concert hall instead of a nickelodeon. Mary Pickford got barely a glance from me as I kept my eyes in the direction of the piano, eager for every glimpse of the musician that the flickering illumination from the movie screen provided.

I went back to the movie house almost every day the Braves were at home, and soon found out that the daytime ticket-taker and nighttime piano player was named Peggy Shaw. It wasn't long before we started seeing each other outside of the theater.

Although we'd had no communication since last fall, I simply assumed that she would still be working here. It was my eagerness to see her again that had made me so particular about my appearance. And it was seeing someone else in her place at the ticket window that had sent my hopes plummeting. Feelings of guilt crept upon me as I sat and fretted in the theater. Could she have believed it when I said I'd write? I thought it was just a standard expression that people used to make goodbyes seem less final. Now I wished I *had* written.

I was only vaguely aware of the Keystone Kops capering on the screen in front of me, as I reviewed last autumn's scenes of Peggy Shaw and Mickey Rawlings.

Although she looked about my age, Peggy had five years on me, and had once been married. At twenty-one she'd married a newspaper writer. Less than a year after the wedding, she became a widow when her husband was struck down with yellow fever while reporting on construction of the Panama Canal. She'd been widowed almost three years when I met her.

I wasn't comfortable enough with the subject of her late husband to ask about him, but now and then Peggy would reveal bits of information about their brief life together. I gathered that her husband was the sort of reporter Teddy Roosevelt would call a muckraker. I also had the impression that he discussed his work with her a great deal, and that she had a deep interest in it. She once mentioned working for passage of child labor laws. I told her of my experience in the cotton mill, and she seemed impressed that I had quit the mill in protest.

Peggy also told me she had once dreamed of being a concert pianist. As a girl, she practiced for hours every day. Then, like me, she realized that she didn't have the natural skills to be great. She stayed with music, though, giving lessons and playing at theaters. Just as I was determined to be the best utility baseball player, she intended to be the best nickelodeon piano player. This similarity between us seemed to cement our friendship, and raised in me hopes of becoming more than friends.

Now it seemed I would never have a chance to find out.

I should have written.

Chapter Seven

I showed up two hours early for practice Monday morning. Except for that interrupted view through the runway corridor, it was my first real look at the Fenway Park playing field.

It was the damnedest baseball field I had ever seen. There was a *hill* in left field! About twenty-five feet in front of the left field fence, the ground began an upward slope, rising to a height of ten feet where it made contact with the wall. The rest of the park was strange, too. It seemed as if it had been squeezed in several directions to fit into the shape of the building lot. The outfield fence went from shallow to deep to shallow as it wound its way from the left field corner around to right, with a number of interesting nooks and corners that would make playing the outfield far too much of an adventure for me.

I was surprised that my roomie also arrived early to get in some extra fielding practice. As my counterpart in the outfield, Clyde Fletcher filled in for Speaker, Hooper, or Lewis if they needed relief. He hadn't played so much as a single inning this year, but here he was, eager to shag some flies. I had dismissed him before as a dissipated sloth, but he obviously took professional pride in his play, and I grudgingly discovered that I was developing some respect for him.

Since there were no other players around, Fletcher and I traded off. He hit me practice grounders, then I hit fungoes out to him in left field. He looked pretty comical stumbling up the hill trying to go back for fly balls, but I had to admire his determination. He said if he never got into a game all year, he was going to conquer that hill. I suggested that if he got rid of his enormous wad of tobacco, he'd be a lot lighter and could run up the slope faster. He suggested I do something to myself that I unfortunately had never yet experienced doing to anyone else. I decided Clyde Fletcher and I might get along after all.

Soon other players joined us on the field, and fans trickled into the stands. I picked out the Red Sox stars as they warmed up—the ones who played with ease and grace, the natural ball players Clyde Fletcher and Mickey Rawlings would never be. We could fill in for the stars when they were hurt, but we'd never have their fame and stature.

Centerfielder Tris Speaker was the team's leader and second only to Ty Cobb as the best all-around player in the American League; he was exchanging long throws with Duffy Lewis and Harry Hooper in the outfield. Jake Stahl, coming to the end of the line as a player but still batting .300, was hitting pepper to the infielders. Baby-faced fireballer Smoky Joe Wood threw light pitches to Bill Carrigan along the right field foul line. Next to him, throwing more seriously, was today's starting pitcher, Bucky O'Brien.

This team could win it all. Jimmy Macullar could be right: the Red Sox could be on the way to the World Series. If the current roster survived the season. A fan, an opposing player . . . could a Red Sox player be next? Would the first year of this magnificent, peculiar ballpark be ruined by more tragedies? I wanted to yell out to the players who were warming up so leisurely. To scream a warning at them. And, just as strongly, I wanted to keep utterly quiet—to forget all I knew and all I feared.

I didn't yell. But I knew I wouldn't keep my thoughts to myself much longer.

When the ball game against the visiting New York Highlanders got underway, Clyde Fletcher and I were both relegated to the pines. As the Red Sox regulars took the field, the two of us sat together at one end of the nearly deserted dugout. Hal Chase led off for the Highlanders, and I remembered our last game in New York. I nudged Fletcher with my elbow and asked him, "Hey, Fletch, do you believe the stories about Chase?"

"What stories?"

"That he throws ball games."

Fletcher looked down the length of the bench, and seemed satisfied that we were out of earshot. Veterans don't like to be seen talking to rookies. Hchoowook. Shptoo. Schplat. "Well, I don't *know* that he throws games, but I'm *sure* of it."

"What do you mean?"

"I don't think nobody ever caught him at it, and I never heard him admit it, so I can't say that I *know* it. But from what I do know about the son of a bitch, and what I hear from other guys who know him, I'm sure of it."

I suppressed an impulse to tell Fletcher that *I* had caught Chase blowing plays. "Why does he do it? Money?"

"I dunno . . . maybe money. Mostly I think it's a game with him. He likes the idea of pulling something over on somebody." Fletcher grimaced. "It's not just ball games, either. He took me in a card game once."

"Cheated?"

"Oh yeah. I didn't realize it till after the game, but no doubt about it. I watch for that in poker, but this was a goddam bridge game. Me, Addie Joss, Billy Neal, and Hal Chase. Chase took all of us, got away with a bundle. He seemed too sure of himself during the game, grinning like it was some kind of joke. His goddam joke cost me two months' salary. But—nothing I could do about it."

"Jeez."

Hchoowook. Shptoo. Schplat. "Yeah."

One thing about his story surprised me. Joss had been one of the best pitchers in baseball until he got sick and died the year before. I couldn't imagine Fletcher palling around with a star player. "You knew Addie Joss?" I said.

"Not real good, but yeah, I knew him. I was with him in Cleveland."

"He could have been a *great* pitcher."

"He *was* a great pitcher. He just died too young. Barely thirty years old."

I suddenly wondered how old I'd get to be.

With the Highlanders side retired and the Sox fielders coming into the dugout, our talk ended.

Fletcher and I remained on the bench throughout the game, and thus avoided contributing to our 3–1 loss. The fans were vocally disappointed, not only at losing, but for hometown favorite Bucky O'Brien who was charged with the defeat.

After the game, O'Brien stopped by his aunt's rooming house for dinner. I welcomed what I thought was an opportunity to get to know him better, but he was in a surly mood after the loss to New York and didn't say much at first.

His aunt, a short, round, chatty woman who seemed to think of herself as a mother to her boarders, explained that her stuffed cabbage was the only thing that could console Bucky after a loss. Whenever he was pitching in Boston, she would prepare it for supper. If he won, he'd go out to celebrate with the other players, leaving plenty of extra food for her boarders; if he lost, he would visit her and gorge himself with cabbage.

After filling himself this evening, Bucky revived a bit and became more talkative. The two of us went into the parlor after dinner, and after settling ourselves in overstuffed chairs, he started to review every pitching mistake he made in the game. I liked the fact that he only criticized his own performance; he didn't complain about scoring opportunities missed by the Red Sox hitters, or lack of hustle by the fielders, or poor pitch selection by Bill Carrigan behind the plate.

Bucky had arrived in the big leagues late. His aunt told me that his thirtieth birthday was day after tomorrow, and I knew he was in only his second major-league season. He seemed determined to do everything in his power to stay in the majors for whatever good years he might have left. Too many seasons in the minors—grueling travel, cheap hotels, bad food, worse companions—had taken a toll on him. Bucky's short brown hair was neatly groomed and a stylish blue suit draped his muscular frame, but he had sunken eyes and an overall grizzled look that would be his forever.

After he had gotten the self-criticisms out of his system and relaxed a little, I decided to broach the subject of the dead Tiger player. "Say, Bucky, I heard one of the Detroit players got killed during the last series here."

"Yeah, Red Corriden. I struck him out three times in the last game. Couldn't touch my spitter." Bucky was still thinking like a pitcher.

I tried to move off of Corriden's batting ability. "Clyde Fletcher was telling me he thought Corriden used to play with the Browns."

"Sure did. Don't you remember what he did in the batting race a couple years ago?"

"The batting race?"

"Yeah. Where you been? The Browns tried to give the title to Nap Lajoie. Remember?"

"Ohhh, okay. I thought his name sounded familiar. That's where I heard of him."

"Yeah, it's a damn shame. Now the kid's just going to be remembered for being a sap."

"I read about what happened, but it seemed awful mixed up. I still don't think I know what all went on. It was over a car, wasn't it?"

"Not just a *car,* it was a *Chalmers 30.* I don't make enough in two years to buy an automobile like that. I don't know if it was really about the car though, or because Ty Cobb's such a mean son of a bitch that everybody hates him."

"I remember Cobb and Lajoie went just about all of 1910 neck and neck for the batting title—and whoever won the title would get the car as a prize. Right?"

"Yup. Then it came down to the last day of the season. Cobb was ahead by a few points, so he didn't play—didn't want to risk going hitless and blowing his lead. Son of a bitch is as gutless as he is mean. Anyway, the Tigers let him sit out.

"Lajoie and Cleveland were ending the year with a doubleheader against the Browns in St. Louis. I just finished another year in the minors—with Des Moines in the Three-I league. Jack O'Connor was managing the Browns and I heard he wanted to buy my contract. It was my first nibble from the majors, so I followed everything that went on with the Browns pretty close.

"When Lajoie came into St. Louis, he needed to get a hit just about every at bat to beat Cobb. And he did it. Got eight or nine hits, and he should've had the batting title and the car."

"But the hits were gimmes, weren't they?"

"Yup. The Browns third baseman was playing him back on the outfield grass. So Lajoie just kept dropping free bunts down third."

"And the third baseman was Red—"

"Red Corriden, yeah. Wasn't really his fault though. Turned out he was told to play back for Lajoie. He was a rookie, so he did what O'Connor told him."

"The Browns fired O'Connor, didn't they?"

"Yeah. Him and Harry Howell. Howell was coaching or scouting or something for St. Louis. Don't remember how he was mixed up with it. But Ban Johnson kicked O'Connor and Howell both out of baseball. Huh! Ban banned 'em. Get it? Ban *banned* 'em."

"Yeah. That's a good one."

"First I thought, there goes my shot at the majors with O'Connor being out. Then the Sox bought my contract, so it worked out even better." Bucky belched vigorously and stood up saying, "I gotta get me something for my stomach. My aunt's a great cook, but this goddam cabbage keeps repeating on me."

He left me alone in the room to think over the pathetic aftermath of the batting race scandal. Ty Cobb was finally awarded the hitting title by the American League—but he was exposed as someone so despised by his fellow players that they would go to incredible lengths to cost him personal gain and glory. Jack O'Connor and Harry Howell were banned from baseball. And Red Corriden, who was publicly painted as a sap, would now never have a chance to live down that reputation.

Chapter Eight

In one way, it was a relief to remember where I'd heard of Red Corriden before. The nagging feeling that I knew his name from somewhere, but couldn't place it, was finally gone. On the other hand, it left me overly free to concentrate on the more upsetting mystery of the body I had found at Fenway Park.

At least with Red Corriden's case, his identity was known and there had been some mentions of his death in the newspapers. But I still had heard nothing at all of the murdered man in the Red Sox's new ballpark. Sometimes I'd start to wonder if I imagined the event in some intensely gruesome nightmare. Then that savagely shattered face would come flashing into mind, and I would again taste the acrid nausea and know that the awful experience at Fenway had really happened.

The total shroud of silence that enveloped the incident was its most disconcerting aspect. No one discussed or even acknowledged the man's existence much less his death. There was nothing in the papers, no locker room gossip, no more meetings with Bob Tyler, no additional questioning by the police.

My curiosity was becoming overpowering, and I knew I would end up violating Tyler's warnings about talking. I would have thought that it should be the easiest thing in the world to just keep my mouth shut—one assignment that wouldn't strain the limits of my abilities. But it was becoming increasingly difficult. Questions pounded at the inside of my mouth struggling to be let out, my ears ached to hear answers. Who was the dead man? Has the killer been found? Am *I* still the leading suspect?

And more perplexing: what was the relation of the dead man to Red Corriden? Was the connection Fenway Park? Would there be more killings? Was *I* next on the list—is that what the bat on my bed meant? Who put it there?

In everything I did while awake, and every night when I tried to sleep, the nagging fears and questions tugged and grabbed at my thoughts and dreams.

These worries no longer affected my play on the ball field, but that was no consolation. I had no chance to play, because Jake Stahl still had me benched.

After the move he made in Tuesday's contest, I started to wonder if Stahl had given up on me. We were down three runs in the bottom of the ninth, when our third baseman Larry Gardner doubled. He hurt himself sliding into second, and looked like he'd have to come out of the game. I stretched my legs, assuming I would pinch run for him. I almost fell down when Stahl sent in Clyde Fletcher instead. Sure, I'd started to take a liking to Fletch, and didn't begrudge him a chance for some playing time, but how the hell could Stahl put in a guy who's fat and slow instead of me? Fletcher didn't get beyond second base (he'd have been thrown out had he tried to steal third), and Charlie Strickler took the loss for the Sox.

Feeling stymied in my desire to learn what had really happened in the tunnels of Fenway Park, and worried about a baseball future that was looking increasingly bleak, I decided to try the one thing I was sure would help: a moving picture show.

Less meticulous this time about my appearance, I again headed to the Comique Theatre in Scollay Square. I didn't know what movies were playing, and it didn't matter. I intended to be fully caught up by whatever stories appeared on the screen.

Half a block from the theater, I slowed and looked behind me. Anybody from the Sox around?

I wasn't sure, but I thought somebody ducked into a doorway. A man, but an unidentifiable one—he'd lowered his head so his cap blocked his face.

I backed behind the protective bulk of a cigar store Indian and waited, watching. Nobody came out. What the hell, it could have been my imagination—the square *was* pretty crowded.

I scooted out from behind the wood statue. I quickly walked to the Comique as if I was going to pass by, then took a sharp turn inside.

When I entered the theater, I suddenly wished that I had paid more attention to my attire. At the ticket booth were the same hair and eyes that had appeared so regularly in this past winter's dreams. I was at first indecisive, torn between my eagerness to be near her and the need I felt to go home and put on a cleaner collar. I saw that she spotted me, too, so the choice was made for me, and I slowly approached her.

I drank in the sight of her, working my eyes from the ticket counter upward. Peggy's blouse was sparkling white, with a ruffled front and sleeves puffed at the shoulders. Around her throat, setting off her fair skin, was a black ribbon choker with a small silver and black cameo on the front. Her honey-blond hair was piled into a high wide bun. Long wisps of it had come loose at her temples and waved down, framing her slender face. A fine spray of freckles, not much darker than her hair, dotted the bridge of her nose.

Peggy's eyes, green and sparkling, had a smiling look of glad recognition, but her voice was controlled and chilly as she said, "Hello, Mr. Rawlings. It's good to see you again." Those were the words she used, but what I heard in the tone was "You didn't write like you promised."

I decided not to return her use of formality. "Hello, Peggy. It's nice to see you, too."

Her voice was just slightly warmer when, after a pause, she said, "I think you'll like today's pictures." With an amused smile she added, "No Mary Pickford, though, I'm afraid."

I could think of nothing else to say, but was saved from embarrassment by a flock of matrons lined up behind me. They pressed me into the theater, where I selected a seat near the center. I ended up spending more than four hours in it.

I paid no attention to the pictures. Instead, I wondered to myself if I was mistaken about what Peggy and I had last year. Was it a romance—or the prelude to a romance? Or by reviewing its highlights over and over, had I magnified it in my thoughts beyond what it had actually been?

Then, as the movie program was repeated for the evening audience, the piano began to tinkle gracefully. Like the first time I saw her there, my gaze remained fixed on the nape of Peggy Shaw's neck.

After the last strip of celluloid had been run for the night, the house lights came up and the rest of the audience trickled out. I remained immobile in my chair while Peggy closed the cover over the piano keys and put her sheet music away.

She smiled at me when she turned around and saw me waiting for her. I felt from her smile that she knew I would still be there.

I extricated myself from the seat and, ignoring the dull cramps in my legs, walked over to her. She looked more inviting now, her initial coldness gone—or at least not visible.

I asked, "Uh . . . Would you care to go for a walk . . . If you have the time . . . Tonight?" To my ears, I sounded stilted, and I felt flushed and shaky.

Peggy smiled and nodded. "I'd like that."

She had a few things to take care of in the theater office, then we were off toward the Boston Common. She seemed excited, and I flattered myself by assuming that it was because of seeing me again. I wondered what dreams she'd had last winter.

"I came to the theater Sunday. I thought you would be there," I began, then added in a quieter tone, "I was kind of disappointed when you weren't."

"This past Sunday?"

"Uh-huh."

"I was in New York for the weekend. Didn't Helen tell you?"

"Uh . . . no. Well, I didn't think to ask. When I didn't see you there, I guess I just figured you weren't at the theater anymore."

Peggy smiled. "I went to Manhattan to march in the suffrage parade."

It was seldom that I knew anything of the various social movements, and eager to show that I knew something of this one, I piped up with a quip I had once come across, "Suffragette: One who has ceased to be a lady and not yet become a gentleman." Peggy's eyes made it immediately clear that I had said something wrong. My body fluids seemed to vaporize under her fiery glare, and I lamely tried to diminish the damage, mumbling, "I read that someplace."

After letting me stew in her silent reprimand for a few moments, Peggy continued about the big march in New York City, "It was wonderful. Women from all over the country joined together to march down Fifth Avenue. *Fifteen thousand.* And John Dewey led a men's contingent. And the crowd *cheered* us this year. The *New York Times* said half a million people watched the parade. It was a great feeling. Invigorating. It felt like being part of history."

As she talked about the march, I realized that her excitement wasn't about being with me. She was still bubbling over with residual enthusiasm from the weekend.

"We actually had our own cavalry! Fifty women led the parade on horseback. Inez Milholland was one of them. She looked so fresh and lovely on her white horse, and she seemed to charm everybody. A lot of people seem to think that suffragettes aren't feminine. I suppose Inez is our best answer to that argument."

There was a sudden gap in Peggy's report of the march. I think I just missed a cue to say something.

Then she picked up with her story again and was regaling me with more details of the parade.

I wanted to talk to her about everything that happened to

me since I arrived in Boston. She was so enthusiastic about her weekend in New York, though, that I couldn't bring myself to be that selfish. I squelched the desire to spill out everything that was troubling me, and instead relaxed and tried to share her excitement. After I succeeded in putting my own urges on hold, I easily found it satisfying enough just to look at her as she spoke.

We walked for almost an hour, slowly and circuitously, before reaching her town house on Beacon Hill.

I left Peggy at her door. Although I hadn't unburdened myself to her, I felt almost as relieved as if I had. Just being with her again was a comfort that made any situation bearable.

I slept peacefully that night, my dreams refreshingly free of any visions of mangled faces or bloodied baseball bats.

• • •

The next afternoon, Jake Stahl gave me the happy news that Larry Gardner's ankle was severely sprained. I bit my inner lip to keep from grinning as he told me I would be starting at third base until he recovered.

I played all of Wednesday's game against the White Sox with no errors. I also got two singles to bring my season average over .250.

Before Thursday's game, the clubhouse talk was about Ty Cobb. As I was changing out of my street clothes, Clyde Fletcher yelled at me, "Hey, kid! Yuh hear? Cobb went into the stands at Hilltop. Beat up some crank who was giving him the business." I was grateful to Fletcher for bringing me into the exchange. It was his way of letting the other players know I was okay.

I quickly took advantage of the opening to give my opinion, "Great! It's about time somebody stood up for himself." All ball players have been subjected to vicious verbal abuse—and sometimes projectiles—from spectators at one time or other, and it was thrilling to hear that one of the rowdies got his comeuppance. My teammates voiced a variety of loud, unreserved agreements.

When I read the rest of the story in the paper that night, the thrill turned to disgust. The man Cobb went after was a cripple. As Cobb pummeled the heckler, other fans tried to pull him off, screaming at Cobb that he was punching a man with no hands to defend himself. Cobb yelled back, "I don't care if he has no feet!"

The Georgia Peach defended his action to reporters, claiming he had been grievously provoked by the fan. Cobb was quoted as saying, "When a spectator calls me half-colored I think it is about time to fight."

Unfortunately for Cobb, Ban Johnson was in a field box at the game and witnessed the episode. The league president announced that Ty Cobb was suspended indefinitely.

On Friday, the locker room was still buzzing about the Ty Cobb incident. The Tigers were now saying they wouldn't play unless Cobb's suspension was lifted. The furor about Ty Cobb assaulting a crippled fan became overshadowed by arguments over his teammates' threatened strike. Everyone from politicians to labor leaders to the press had strong opinions either condemning or encouraging the Detroit ball players.

I stepped out of the clubhouse shower to hear Fletcher ask Charlie Strickler, "Whadda yuh think, Strick? Your old pals really gonna sit out a game?"

Strickler shrugged and snapped, "How the hell should I

know? I don't give a damn what they do." A former star on the downhill side of his career can be as ornery as a cantankerous old dog.

Bucky O'Brien tried our other ex-Tiger. "Billy! How 'bout you? What do *you* say? Tigers gonna strike?"

Billy Neal answered without hesitation. "Not a chance. Ain't one guy on that team who'll give Cobb the time of day. They sure as hell ain't gonna lose their jobs for him."

On Saturday afternoon, Neal was proved wrong. With Ban Johnson still not giving in to the Tigers' demands that Cobb be reinstated, the team carried out its threat. The Tigers went on strike, refusing to play Philadelphia.

The Tiger management was prepared: to avoid paying a fine to the league for failing to field a team, nine local amateurs were recruited to represent Detroit. In the farce that followed, the Athletics hitters fattened up their batting averages, teeing off for twenty-four runs against the sham "Tigers."

An outraged Ban Johnson canceled the Tigers next game.

To me, the world seemed to have gone slightly crazy. *Baseball players on strike?* In support of *Ty Cobb?*

I played poorly in our Saturday game at Fenway, my head filled with a perplexing jumble of bewilderments. The baseball world was the one that had always made sense to me. I understood the game and every nuance of its strategies. And, until now, I knew what ball players thought and felt. Even under suspicion of murder, I had been able to find a small haven of stability on the baseball field. But with Balldom now beginning to resemble Oz, I could find no respite anywhere.

The Sox were scheduled to leave for a western road trip on Sunday. This would mean two weeks without seeing

Peggy, a separation I didn't look forward to right now. Even if no romance would bloom, I still felt a need for her friendship.

After the game, I decided that I had to talk to Peggy and tell her all that had happened.

I rushed to the theater, and ran up to Peggy at the ticket booth. "I really need to talk to you tonight. I have to leave for a road trip in the morning. Can I come back here after the show is over?"

Peggy looked taken aback, but she nodded and said, "Yes, certainly."

"Okay, great. I'll be back later." With that, I bolted from the theater.

I returned two hours later, after eating a fast supper and packing my bags. A chilly drizzle had begun outside, so instead of leaving the theater for a walk, we stayed inside, sitting next to each other in two front-row chairs.

I kept my eyes fixed straight ahead, staring blankly at the stark white screen in front of me. By not looking at Peggy, I was less self-conscious, and the words poured out of me in an uninterrupted torrent.

I quickly recounted the off-season I had spent playing winter ball and pickup games. To help excuse my failure to write, I tried to make my activities since last fall sound especially hectic.

With a deep breath, I proceeded to detail my arrival at Fenway Park, the horrid experience of finding the body, the questioning by the police captain, Bob Tyler's warning not to talk, and the nearly unremitted distress and confusion I felt ever since I came across the murdered man. I told her, too, of the death of Red Corriden, and my suspicion that the killings might be related, possibly part of a series.

Finally, I turned my head to look into Peggy's eyes, and confessed, "I don't know what to make of all this. I just know I feel terrible. I feel I have to find out what happened—or what's happening. But the police think I'm a suspect, so if I start asking questions they may think I'm trying to cover myself somehow."

Peggy looked thoughtful, not at all shocked, as she absorbed all I said. She seemed to take my strange tale in stride, and I admired—and envied—her composure. After minutes of silence, she spoke slowly and calmly, "Well, first off, I don't *think* you're in any real trouble. If the police considered you a suspect, I doubt they'd leave you alone. They would have questioned you again by now."

"Maybe Tyler has the police holding off. He told me the day after it happened that *he* didn't believe I had anything to do with it. And he did seem to have a lot of influence over the cops who were at the park."

"Do you think Mr. Tyler meant it about believing you, or was he just trying to sound supportive?"

I was ashamed, but I filled in a detail I had previously omitted. "Well, I, uh, I got sick when I found the body. Tyler said a murderer wouldn't throw up"—I decided I didn't have to be completely detailed and skipped the fact that I vomited on the corpse—"at the scene of the crime."

I quickly looked at Peggy to see how she would react. There was no sign of amusement on her face. She said, "Oh. Well, he probably does believe you're innocent then."

She fell silent and her brow furrowed a little—and I couldn't help noticing that her frown looked very endearing. After some more minutes, she said, "I suppose you're going to have to find out what happened somehow. But I don't know how. Can I think about it, and we'll talk when you get back?"

"Yes, sure. I didn't really know what I thought you could do. But just telling you about it helps."

I walked Peggy home through a light steady rain, neither of us saying much. She kissed me on the cheek when we got to her door, and I went home feeling much better that at least someone else was sharing my worries.

But I hadn't told Peggy everything. I didn't tell her about the bat left on my pillow. I didn't tell her that being considered a suspect wasn't my only worry.

Chapter Nine

The weather cleared by early Sunday morning. It looked as if it would be a beautiful day for a picnic or a walk through the Arnold Arboretum. I wished that I could spend the day with Peggy in one of those deliciously genteel pursuits. Instead I was on my way to South Station to join my extremely nongenteel teammates for our long western road trip. And I was on my way to finding out what happened to the murdered man at Fenway Park.

I'd decided that I would have to take some initiative and find out what occurred that first day I entered the Red Sox ballpark. I was going to start asking some questions. But what questions? And who would have answers?

Should I look into the Fenway murder by itself or should I start with Red Corriden's death and try to find the connection to the other man. Were their deaths necessarily connected?

It could have been coincidence. Corriden was a likely enough mugging candidate: a young fellow in what was probably an unfamiliar city. He easily could have wandered into a rough part of town and stood out as an inviting robbery target. As for the dead man at Fenway Park, he was in a stadium that had just been filled with thousands of people including drunks, gamblers, and pickpockets. In the hectic congestion that followed the game, almost anything could have happened. He could have been pulled aside to be robbed, or maybe he met someone for a fight. After all, as much as I distrusted him, Bob Tyler was truthful about one thing: Boston is a big city with its share of violent crimes.

Robert F. Tyler . . . I'd thought about his warnings to me, and concluded they were mostly scare tactics. It was obvious that he was lying when he pretended to be so concerned with protecting me, and I'd started to think—and hope—that maybe he wasn't honest with me when he claimed I was Captain O'Malley's leading suspect.

Then there's Jimmy Macullar. I didn't have a clear read on him, but he seemed a decent enough man. The only strike against him was that he worked for Bob Tyler. Macullar could be my best bet for answering questions. He might not know much, but I had a feeling he was aware of a lot more than Tyler would want him to know.

I decided I would talk with Jimmy Macullar on this road trip and see what I could find out. And then—I wasn't sure.

• • •

The train ride from Boston to Cleveland was a grueling one. I never could sleep in a sleeper car—especially not in the criminally uncomfortable upper berths to which rookies and utility players are assigned. This Pullman was even worse than usual. The heavy curtains of my berth trapped in the odors of all its previous occupants, few of them sufficiently bathed. And a recent occupant apparently tried to mask the smell with a cheap stogie, only adding to the vile stench.

I felt drowsy and sluggish when we arrived at League Park late Monday morning. This was the day when the game scheduled between the Tigers and the Athletics in Philadelphia would not be played. Since Detroit was the next city on our road trip, we didn't know if we would have any games to play when we got there. When would the Tigers be playing baseball again?

We lost an unmemorable game to Cleveland, with both teams preoccupied with the more interesting contest of Ban Johnson versus the Detroit Tigers.

That evening, the *Cleveland Plain Dealer* reported the resolution of the Tigers strike. Between Johnson's typically heavy hand, and uncharacteristic cooperation by Ty Cobb, the Detroit players were convinced to call off their walkout. Johnson threatened the Tigers with banishment from baseball if they didn't return to the field. Cobb thanked them for their support, and urged his teammates to play again. Johnson then announced that Cobb's suspension would run ten days more. This was great news for the Red Sox: our series against Detroit was on, and the Tigers would be without the services of Ty Cobb.

With the Tigers situation settled, I paid more attention to our second game against the Naps. Larry Gardner's ankle was getting better, but not well enough yet to play. I was still filling in for him at third base. In the fourth inning, I suddenly had the eerie feeling that I was in Red Corriden's shoes when Nap Lajoie dropped a bunt down the third base line. He had it beaten out easily, but I threw anyway, well over Jake Stahl's head, giving Lajoie an extra base as the ball landed in about the twentieth row of seats. Stahl let loose with some loud cussing, making up fascinating combinations I had never heard before. He left me in for the rest of the game, though—he had no choice, with Gardner as lame as he was.

In the final game, each time Nap Lajoie came up to bat I again had the feeling I was standing in the spikes of a dead man. Somehow I felt connected to Red Corriden though I never even met him. The unnerving sensation made my legs go soft and quivery, and reminded me that my primary mission on this trip was to talk to Jimmy Macullar.

We left Cleveland by boat, my first experience with that evil means of transportation. The choppy waters of Lake Erie left my insides so shaken that I longed for the relative comfort of a Pullman car.

In Detroit, we went on to a three-game sweep over the Cobb-less Tigers. After the series, the trip half over, I told myself that I really should talk to Macullar soon.

I tried to prod myself into action again after we took two out of three from the White Sox in Comiskey Park. Only a few days of the road swing remained.

These western cities must have had plenty of attractions in the nightlife department. Clyde Fletcher didn't make it back to our hotel room once in the first three cities. He did show up at the ballparks, but not looking very well. In the West, he didn't even get to recuperate from Saturday night outings, since Sunday baseball was legal here.

I wanted to ask Fletcher if he knew anything about Jimmy Macullar. I thought it might be a little easier to approach Macullar if I had a better feel of what the man was like. I knew that if my roommate could manage to find activities to occupy his nights in Cleveland, I would never see him at our hotel in a wild town like St. Louis.

Before the final game with the White Sox, while the rest of our team was taking batting practice, I approached Fletcher as he sat on the dugout bench looking bleary-eyed. "How's it going, Fletch?"

Hchoowook. Shptoo. Schplat.

I tried to sound casual. "Say, you know that fellow Jimmy Macullar at all?"

"Who?"

"Jimmy Macullar. He seems to be with Mr. Tyler a lot. I think he's his assistant or something."

"Mister Tyler?" Fletcher smiled and spat again. Then he grumbled, "Hell, Bob Tyler ain't nobody. Used to be a flunky for Ban Johnson, that's all. That's how he got where he is now."

My attention was distracted by shouts from the dugout runway. The echoes of the words made them tough to decipher, but they were definitely angry ones. They grew louder as they neared the dugout, and clearer. One voice was Jake Stahl's, threatening, "It's gonna cost yuh fifty if yuh don't get your ass out there *now.*"

"What the hell should I practice *for?* I been here a month and all I do is sit the goddam bench. I don't gotta practice *sitting!"* This voice was a gruff one; I wasn't sure whose.

"I'll decide when you play. *I* never wanted you anyway."

"Well you *got* me, so you goddam well better *play* me."

"You don't tell me what I better do. I'm sure as hell not benching Carrigan just to make you happy. Now get out there!"

Billy Neal sullenly plodded out of the runway, his face a picture of angry frustration. He slowly climbed the dugout steps and walked out to the batting cage. He was doing as Stahl told him, but flaunted his unhappiness with each step.

I felt sorry for Neal; I could sympathize with wanting to play but being blocked by better players. It was a situation that was very familiar to me.

I nudged Fletcher, and nodded out to the field. It didn't seem a good idea to let Stahl see us sitting down. We were on the infield grass before Stahl came out of the dugout.

I got back to asking Fletcher, "What about Jimmy Macullar?"

"Hmm? Oh, yeah. I guess now Tyler's got a flunky of his own. Don't really know him, though. Why?"

"I don't know . . . no reason . . . guess I was just wondering. He always seems to be around, but I wasn't sure what he does."

"Probably just a charity case. Heard he used to be a ball player once. Hmmph—musta been about a hundred years ago. Got washed up, so now he hangs around doin' errands and whatever. Hope I never got to kiss the ass of somebody like Tyler to get by." Hchoowook. Shptoo. Schplat.

Fletcher hadn't told me much, but what little there was didn't encourage me. If Macullar's livelihood depended on the good graces of Bob Tyler, he might not want to tell me anything that Tyler could object to. But I'd see when we got to St. Louis.

The series against the Browns turned out to be another easy one for us as we swept them without one close game. I had a pretty successful road trip, playing every inning of every game. I knew my performance wasn't good enough for me to keep the position when Gardner's ankle got better, though. I'd need to boost my batting average by a good fifty points to have a shot at his starting job.

The trip wasn't quite over yet. Before getting back to

Fenway Park, we had a two-day train ride ahead of us. Only two more days to talk to Jimmy Macullar.

• • •

Lurching my way down the aisle of a sparsely occupied club car, as our train passed through Pennsylvania farmland, I spotted Jimmy Macullar alone in a window seat staring quietly out through the pane. This was it: my best chance so far, and possibly the last one I would have before reaching Boston.

I approached his seat without him noticing me. He seemed absorbed in either his thoughts or the passing cornfields.

"Mr. Macullar?" I had to repeat his name once more before he heard me.

"Oh. Hello, Mickey."

"Is anyone sitting here?"

"No. Would you like to?" He sounded vague and distracted.

"Uh, thanks." I sat down next to him and he smiled at me vacantly.

I tried to start off the conversation with a safe subject. "I heard you used to be a pretty good baseball player," I said. Fletcher had mentioned nothing of Macullar's skill level, so that was my own embellishment. I figured it couldn't hurt.

Macullar seemed flattered. "Oh, I don't know if I was *good.* But I wasn't bad." His voice faded as he added, "My, that was a long time ago." Then he turned his gaze back to the window.

I tried to bring him to what I was hoping would be a conversation. "You were in the majors?"

He turned to me again. "Hmm? The majors? Oh, yes. I played six seasons in the big leagues." He added with a smile, "That was just after there was a major league to play in." He paused, and then somewhat more animatedly asked, "You know who the first team was I played for?"

I shook my head no.

"Syracuse. *Syracuse* had a big-league club. Eighteen hundred and seventy-nine that was." Macullar's head now faced forward, tilted slightly up, his eyes focusing on sights that were history by the time I was born. The array of wrinkles that fanned out from his eyelids seemed to perk up at the view. He talked on, steadily and softly. "The Syracuse Stars. One year in the National League and that was it. A one-year franchise, and now it's forgotten. . . .

"It was different back then. All this fuss now about statistics, RBIs. There was no such thing as an RBI when I was playing. And stolen bases—nobody kept track of them.

"The game was played different, too. Take pitching. I remember this: when I was with the Stars, the pitcher's hand had to go below his belt—they weren't even allowed to throw sidearm. It all had to be down underhand . . . I saw one pitcher get around that, though—he had his pants cut extra long so his belt was up across his chest. He looked like a clown, but he beat the rule—seems there's always somebody who thinks he's better than any rules or laws."

Macullar paused, and I prodded him along in his reverie, "What position did you play?"

"Oh, we used to play wherever they needed us pretty much. Usually a team only had one extra player. Mostly I played shortstop, and a fair amount of outfield."

"Where did you go after Syracuse?"

"Nowhere for a while. I was out of the big leagues 'eighty

and 'eighty-one. Longest years of my life. I thought I'd never get picked up again. Seemed like my life would be over if I didn't get back in the big leagues. I played semipro those two years. It was still baseball, and I did love to play the game, but it's just not the same after you've had a taste of the major leagues. Then I got lucky. They started the American Association, and I got signed by Cincinnati. I was a big-league baseball player again. Five more years. Two with Cincinnati and three with Baltimore."

I felt guilty about interrupting his memories—especially since I enjoyed hearing them—but I had to bring him around to the present eventually, so after a sufficient silence I asked, "How did you come to be working for the Red Sox?"

The expression on Macullar's face became grimmer as he responded, "Well, playing baseball doesn't leave you with a lot of useful skills when your career is over. From the first time I picked up a ball and bat, all I ever wanted to do was play baseball. Then when they started paying ball players, that's what I wanted my career to be. It didn't much matter what would happen afterward, so I never gave any thought to it—didn't plan for anything else." Macullar sighed. "But, I had my time in the big leagues and I was satisfied. I felt like I got to live a dream playing baseball with the greatest players in the game.

"I was born in Boston, so I moved back there after Baltimore let me go. I picked up work with semipro teams wherever I could. Each year, I got older and it got harder to find a spot as a player. Then when Boston started an American League team, I took a job as a gate attendant. That's when we were still at the Huntington Avenue Grounds. I've been with the club ever since. And now I work for Mr. Tyler." With his last sentence, Macullar grimaced slightly.

Okay, time for the big question: "You remember when I first came to Fenway?"

Macullar nodded, but didn't face me.

"Well, I was wondering what happened. The police never asked me any more questions. And I haven't seen anything at all in the papers or anything. Did they find out who the dead man was? Did they catch who did it?"

Macullar sat silently, still staring straight ahead. Eventually he answered, slowly and carefully, "As far as I am aware, the case has not yet been solved." Then he looked at me and asked, "Have you spoken to anyone else about this?"

I didn't want to mention Peggy, so I came up with an answer that was partly true. "No, you're the first man I've talked to about it." I quickly went on, "It's just that Mr. Tyler told me I was a suspect. I was getting worried . . . I'd just like to know what's going on."

Macullar looked thoughtful and then said matter-of-factly, "You don't have anything to worry about. Not from the police."

"I don't?"

"No."

We both sat in silence for a while, neither looking at the other. Then he spoke up again, "That—what happened at Fenway Park—it never happened."

"Huh?"

"Well . . . You are not going to discuss this with anyone else. *Anyone.* Right?"

"Okay."

"Well . . . you have to understand that the Red Sox's financial situation is not very strong. Mr. Tyler and his partners are not millionaires. And they put a lot of money into the new ballpark. If attendance isn't good, they could be out of business—"

"But the stands are *filled*. We're in *first place*."

Macullar held a hand up and shook his head at my interruption. "Yes. Everything is going our way right now. People are coming to the games . . . Mayor Fitzgerald and the Royal Rooters have adopted us . . . we should be on our way to the World Series. But what do you think would happen if there was publicity about a fan being killed at a game? There'd be a scandal . . . people would think it wasn't safe to come to the ballpark . . . attendance would drop . . . the city would be embarrassed. . . ."

I couldn't help interrupting again. "But it *did* happen."

Patiently, Macullar answered, "No, not officially. Officially, nothing happened at Fenway Park." Then, with a low, flat voice, he said, "The body was moved. To another part of town. Dorchester. It was found there. So . . . officially, nobody was killed at Fenway Park."

"The body was *moved?*"

Macullar turned his head to look back out the window. His response was barely audible. "I moved him. The police officer and I moved him. We put him under a railroad bridge. Mr. Tyler said to. He said it couldn't matter to the dead man where his body was found—it wouldn't bring him back to life. But if people knew it was at Fenway Park, that *would* matter, and it wouldn't be good for anyone."

I was speechless.

Then I made the connection, and gasped out, "The dead man was Red Corriden!"

Macullar shook his head, "We didn't *know* that at the time. Nobody knew it was a ball player. We all assumed some fan got into a fight or got robbed . . . there are some rough sporting types who come to the games—and after nine innings of beer, they can be trouble. We didn't know who it was until after he was found in Dorchester."

"Jeez. That was Red Corriden." I felt queasy thinking of what his face looked like when I found him.

I had expected that learning something about the nameless man I discovered would make me feel better somehow. It didn't. Attaching an identity to him made it worse. Hell, he was a ball player. A rookie baseball player. It could have been me. I suddenly felt a tingly spasm shoot through my legs.

Neither Jimmy Macullar nor I said another word. After I recovered enough from the shock to get to my feet, I walked off to another car to sit alone. And suddenly wondered, what did he mean, *Not from the police?*

Chapter Ten

The day after the Red Sox returned from the West, I went to see Peggy to report on my talk with Jimmy Macullar. She was again out of town, but had left a note for me at the theater. Helen handed it to me saying, "Peggy's down on the Cape. Her aunt took sick, so she went right down to take care of her. Wonderful girl that Peggy is."

"Mmm," I agreed.

"Make a mighty fine wife for some lucky fellah."

"Uh. Did she say when she'll be back?"

"No . . . I suppose it depends on when her aunt gets better. Why don't you read the note? Maybe she says there."

There was no additional information in the note. Peggy did include her aunt's address in Hyannis, however. Was that supposed to be some kind of hint?

Unable to tell Peggy what I'd found out about Red Corriden, I was left to pursue my own thoughts on the matter. They were muddled conjectures, and I couldn't assess what was realistic and what was farfetched. I felt I needed to bounce my ideas off somebody if only to hear them spoken and see them take shape. By myself, I couldn't get a grasp on the ramifications of Macullar's information.

His revelation had one surprising effect on me. For six weeks, I'd been trying to forget the sight of the facial remnants I had seen in Fenway Park. But once I knew whose face it was, I had an inexplicable impulse to revisit the tunnel under the park. To look at the place where Corriden had been killed, and bring the vision back before me. Perhaps there was something I had seen or heard that hadn't registered before. As much as I dreaded reliving the experience, I decided to check out the scene of Red Corriden's death.

But I'd have to be careful. I didn't want anyone to see me wandering under the ballpark. Certainly not Tyler. Nor his minions—Macullar, the stadium cop, whoever else might be in his command . . . Besides, it was like paying respects at a gravesite, the sort of thing that should be done alone.

After a game against the White Sox, I claimed a sore shoulder and had the team trainer give me a rubdown while my teammates showered and changed. Then a long shower of my own, shivering in the cold water that was left me, and when I'd finished the clubhouse was empty. There would still be stragglers and cleaning people in the park, so I dressed in my street clothes and ducked into the equipment room to bide some more time. I sat amid the bats and balls and bases for about an hour, until I figured everyone would be gone.

To get my bearings, I first headed out to the main hallway that circled the park. Dusk had come, and few minutes of daylight remained. I quickly strode the hallway, my shoe leather clacking on the concrete floor. I stopped briefly at the entrance of each passageway and glanced at each view of the field. I remembered my first sight of the Fenway field, how the clay arc of the infield cut across the bottom left of the outfield grass, and looked for the same picture.

I finally spotted it—dimly, but the layout was right.

I walked into the passage, toward the field. Last time, the tunnel invited me in and drew me gently; now it repelled me. The walls squeezed together, and I had to force myself to keep stepping forward against their suffocating grip.

A turn to the right, into the hallway where I'd found Corriden. It was almost completely black, and I preferred leaving it that way. Not until I thought I was close to the actual murder scene did I try to find a light. I felt a doorway—was this the one? And a light button; I punched it in.

The bright yellow glare showed nothing but empty hallway. No body, no crusty patches of blood, no bat. Of course they would have all been removed. I wondered what happened to the bat . . . Tyler had it burned, probably. In the dressing room stove maybe? The Red Sox could have been warmed by the heat of a murder weapon.

A closer look revealed one trace of what had happened here. A patch of wall adjacent to the doorway had an extra coat of whitewash. It was thicker and brighter than the rest of the paint on the wall. I squatted down, and could barely make out faint dark splotches under the white. I had no doubt they were splatters of Red Corriden's blood.

I stood, and looked back up the hallway, trying to remember exactly what I'd seen and heard the last time I was here. Then I closed my eyes and let memory take over. It was all in my mind, more durable than movie film. I replayed the entire episode, stopping at different points to study particular frames, rewinding to look at earlier scenes.

When I was first approaching the field that April day, I'd heard a noise—the *thunk.* What caused the sound? The bat being tossed down by the killer? Then the killer must have evaporated—he couldn't have walked away without me hearing his footsteps clomping in the corridor. It wasn't the bat.

I focused on the way Corriden had been slumped: legs stretched out, bent over at the waist, head down on the floor. The head. That was it.

Corriden is standing, perhaps facing his attacker, when the beating starts. He staggers back to the wall, is hit again, and slides down. He's sitting now on the floor, head and back balanced against the wall. His face is an easy target for the bat and the attack continues. Finally, the killer stops, his rage spent or his cruelty satisfied. He drops the bat and leaves. But is Corriden dead? No, there's some life still in him, life that flickered out about the time I entered Fenway Park. Then a last gasp of breath or first spasm of death upsets his balance. He slumps down to his left, his head bouncing on the concrete floor. *Thunk!*

That could be how it happened. I opened my eyes, and again scanned the wall for any signs that would indicate otherwise.

The whitewashed patch of wall suddenly went black. An explosion roared at me through the runway and a delicate shower sprinkled my head. I ran my hands through my hair; it was dry. Then I felt wetness on my palms and biting pain. It was shards of glass that rained on me.

I didn't grasp what had occurred. The order threw me: black, boom, shower. But that's how it happened . . . Somebody shot out the light!

I hit the floor, ignoring the broken glass that crunched on impact, and rolled to the wall opposite the doorway. I laid face down in just about the spot where I'd found the bloodied bat.

The thunderous gunshot had filled the tunnel—I couldn't tell how far back it had originated, how close the shooter was. I remained motionless, listening. No sound of approaching footsteps, no more explosions.

My planning skills could use some work. Staying late after the game ensured that fewer people would be around to see me, but it also left me isolated. If somebody was keeping an eye on me, I had put myself in easy view. And now no crowd remained to hear any gunshots. No one to come to my aid.

My instinct was to crawl further into the tunnel, away from the shooter. I raised my body off the floor to make less noise on the broken glass. With my weight resting on knuckles and toes, I awkwardly began to crawl forward.

After fifteen feet of walking like a crab, I stopped. My instinct was wrong again: I should head to the open, not further into the winding depths. I wasn't sure where these passages led; going deeper could just get me into a corner. With the gunman following behind. And the sound of a shot kept muffled within the tunnel walls.

I had been in a passage facing the field when I'd made a right turn into this one. So the next left should take me out to the field. That's it. The shooter would expect me to head directly away from him. Maybe by doing the opposite, I could fool him and get away in the dark.

I veered off to the left-side wall and scampered ahead on my knees, still keeping low. I dragged the fingertips of my left hand along the wall, feeling for a corner.

About twenty more feet, and my hand lost contact with the wall. I almost keeled over from the loss of balance.

Crawling around the corner, I breathed with relief. I was out of the line of fire.

I plunged forward—and rammed my head into a door. The wooden bang sounded even louder than the earlier explosion. Idiot! This was no escape. And I'd just signaled the gunman where I was.

No reason for silence now. I stood and felt my way back out of the doorway. From behind me, I heard the soft grate of a footstep on broken glass.

I quickly continued in the tunnel until I felt the next gap in the wall. This time, I kept my hand out and walked straight to feel the width of the gap. It was wider than a doorway. I turned into it, a hard left. I walked steadily forward, my hands out in front like a bug's antennae. Ten steps with no obstructions, then I felt a gentle draft on my face.

I came out into the park along the right field foul line. Into fresh air that I inhaled deeply. Onto soft grass that quietly cushioned my footsteps.

I trotted toward center field, feeling safe in the open. Nobody's going to fire a gun out here—somebody in the neighborhood would hear the shot and call the police.

A growling rumble came from the tunnel I'd exited. I hit the ground and hugged the turf to my chest. Grass blades stabbed the open cuts in my palms.

I was wrong again. Bullets travel: the shooter could stay in the tunnel and fire out to the field—where his idiot target was standing in open view.

At least this bullet wasn't close—I didn't hear it hit anything. Or maybe it was—what sound does a bullet make when it strikes turf? It might *schplat* as softly as a shot of Clyde Fletcher's tobacco juice.

I lifted my head. There was light from a handful of stars

and a quarter moon. It didn't shine strongly, but I was sure I could be seen. Fortunately, wispy clouds rolled across the moon and cast wavering shadows on everything below. Even laying motionless, I would be a moving target, harder to hit.

I remained near the middle of the park, resisting a temptation to get out of view. I might feel more protected along the sidelines or the outfield wall, but I could end up putting myself in closer reach of the gunman there. With my elbows, I dragged myself behind second base, to a spot more nearly centered in the field. If he came after me here, I could run away from him no matter from which direction he came.

I lay on my stomach for some time, then propped myself up on my elbows and looked around the perimeter of the park. No one approached me, there were no more shots. Finally, I seemed to have made the right choice.

The night air was getting cooler. I estimated that I'd been on the field for an hour. But it could have been three hours—or ten minutes. Everything was distorted. Everything.

Fenway Park wasn't even a baseball field now. A ballpark was a place of warmth and sunshine, where even in the chill of early April the summer game could be played before thousands of cheering fans.

This stadium was haunted. The passing clouds filled the seats with mute darting ghosts. The grass felt dank, the air clammy. I wanted to sleep and dream—to see sunlit bleachers filled with straw hats and white shirtsleeves, to hear kids rooting, even hecklers taunting.

It occurred to me that I could be stuck here all night. Assuming the shooter was gone, could I find my way to an exit? Would the gate be open if I did? The answers were "Maybe," and "Unlikely." And the assumption about the gunman might not be a wise one. I would spend the night here.

I wasn't going to sleep in the middle of the field, though. The dugout bench was a possibility. No, stay away from the sidelines—too accessible to the gunman. I looked around, and made my choice: I'd go into the stands and join the ghost crowd. And I saw my exit route: the hill in left field.

I curled into a crouch position, then bolted for the left field wall. No shots followed my sprint. I hit the incline fast, and scooted up to the peak. With a leap and a stretch, I grabbed the top of the fence and swung my body over into the first row of seats.

If the gunman was watching, he would have seen me. But he also would have shot, and he didn't, so he must be gone. I took added precautions anyway. Keeping low, I crawled away from the spot where I'd gone over the wall. When I reached the middle of the center field bleachers, I stretched out between two rows of seats.

Averting my eyes from the eerie shadows of Fenway Park, I stared up at the stars and moon and clouds. I lay with my hands over my head, palms up to bathe them in the night air. It must have looked like I was on the wrong end of a celestial stickup.

I watched the stars glitter white and yellow, some steady, some blinking on and others fading out. Clouds washed over the face of the moon in dark blue streaks.

Eventually, like a piece of film stuck before a hot bulb, the scene before me glowed red, melting into oblivion. Then the stars were gone, banished by the sun, and the sky was blue.

When the sun was at about nine o'clock, I staggered my way through the stands and out to the main gate. Jimmy

Macullar was there, stocking the concession stand with scorecards and pencils.

He looked surprised to see. "You're here early," he said.

"Uh, shoulder's still bad. I want to ice it down before practice."

"Ice is no good. *Dr. Pritchard's Snake Oil,* that's the thing. Mix it with some liniment and rub it in good. Then throw. Lots of throwing. You've got to work out a sore shoulder."

"Thanks, Jimmy. I'll try that." I walked off in the direction of the clubhouse. Now I'd be stuck in the ballpark until game time.

I went to the dressing room and cleaned the cuts and scratches on my hands. Then I stripped off my clothes and napped on the rubbing table until batting practice.

Chapter Eleven

We were a confident team going into June.

The Red Sox had possession of first place with a five game lead over the third-place Athletics. Washington was in second place, only three games behind us, but this was mostly due to an April hot streak; the Senators could be counted on to do their traditional nosedive soon, and we didn't give them much concern.

I think June is my favorite month for baseball. It's late enough in the season so that the players are warmed up and their reflexes sharp, but early enough so that the accumulating aches and pains haven't yet taken their toll.

It's the time of year when one can best appreciate the beautiful balance of the game. The warming weather has the pitchers' arms loose, and gives them a more sensitive feel of the ball. But the batters have their hitting eyes honed, so the pitcher-batter matchup remains even. The legs of the base runners are limber, and they get quick jumps in their sprints to steal bases. But the catchers have developed snappier releases, so the catcher-runner duel also stays close. The critical matchups are ideally balanced this time of year, with all of the combatants at the peak of their powers, and every skirmish of mind and body a close and exciting contest.

I had time to dwell on such thoughts of the game. Too much time.

My nocturnal adventure in Fenway Park had left me in a state of mental paralysis. Trying to find out what had happened to Red Corriden accomplished nothing but put me in the path of a bullet.

Who did the shooting?

Did the Fenway tunnels have some deranged inhabitant who killed those he considered trespassers? Maybe that's why Corriden was killed. And why I became a target when I went to the same place where Corriden had been.

Or was I followed? Were the shots intended to kill me, or were they just a warning? *Just?* It was a hell of an effective warning. It stopped me—temporarily—from pursuing Corriden's death any further.

When I tried to take action, I ran into trouble. But I had a feeling that doing nothing could be worse. A moving target has a better chance than a sitting one.

• • •

The first week of Peggy's absence, I concentrated on baseball. By now I was on friendly terms with enough teammates that I could find players willing to pitch me extra batting practice or hit me ground balls to sharpen my fielding.

Clyde Fletcher kept coming early to Fenway, too, in his continuing effort to conquer the left field hill. This had become a prime entertainment attraction for the team. The Red Sox players would stand along the left field foul line yelling encouragement and suggestions at Fletcher as he scrambled up the hill to catch the fungoes I hit out to him.

Even the team's biggest star got into the act. Tris Speaker spoke to me for the first time as I was hitting fly balls to Fletcher. With a deep rumbling voice, he said, "Let me hit him a few, kid." He reached for the fungo bat, and I handed it over with pride. The way I chose to look at it, this meant Tris Speaker was substituting for *me*.

Fletcher did get better, although he never made it up the hill as fast as I had. Most of the time now, he could run back to the fence without falling on his face. But all his hard work seemed to be for nothing; Duffy Lewis still played every inning for the Red Sox in left field during the games.

By our second week back in Boston, with Peggy still on Cape Cod, I started to read the newspapers. Any page without box scores on it was unfamiliar territory to me, but I decided to explore the news sections and find out what was going on in the world—not due to any sudden interest in international affairs, but because I thought it would give me more to talk about with Peggy.

Since the presidential nominating conventions were coming up, it seemed a good time to start following the campaigns. I read about the opening of the Republican convention in Chicago, expecting it would be straightforward and easy to understand. I assumed that President Taft would automatically be nominated to head the Republican ticket again. But then Teddy Roosevelt's followers got mad at Taft's nomination by what they called "conservatives" and went off to form a "Progressive Party." Great—just when I start to follow politics, they complicate it by forming a third party. Well, at least it's supposed to go smoothly with the Democrats; according to the papers, Champ Clark is an easy winner for their nomination. Not that it mattered—I wouldn't be old enough to vote yet.

Eventually, I exhausted the available pool of ordinary topics with which I tried to occupy my thoughts, and returned reluctantly to the murder of Red Corriden.

In the weeks since my talk with Jimmy Macullar, I had reviewed our conversation a hundred times. After each rehash, I was a little more troubled than the time before. By now, my perspective was quite different from what it was immediately after speaking with him. It led me to a difficult and uncomfortable decision. I was eager to talk it all out with Peggy and was frustrated by her absence. What should have been an obvious thought finally dawned on me, and I put the address she gave me to use.

It seemed a good idea to redeem myself for the winter's omissions by writing to her. Damn, I hate to put anything in writing. If I had shown up at school more often, I might be more comfortable writing letters. But I hadn't and I wasn't.

At Mrs. O'Brien's, I sat down at the small writing desk in my room to endure the strange and perplexing experience of trying to compose a letter.

Dear Peggy—No, that's no good. Sounds too familiar.

Dear Miss Sh—Oops, it should be "Mrs."

Dear Mrs. Shaw—Nope. That doesn't sound right—too formal.

Well, if I were talking to her, I would call her "Peggy," so that's what it'll be here. Okay, now that that's decided, what do I say?

After two hours of intense labor, endless uncertainty, and a floorful of crumpled sheets of paper, I finally put together a letter that sounded pretty good:

Dear Peggy,

I am sorry your aunt is sick. I hoped to see you when I got back. Cleveland, Detroit, Chicago, and St. Louis were good. I played okay. I hope your aunt will be fine. How are you?

Sincerely,
Mickey Rawlings

Deciding on the closing caused me more distress. I again didn't want anything to sound either too formal or too familiar. I was tempted just to sign my name without any closing, but she might have thought that I didn't know how to write a proper letter. Well, when she gets back I'll just have to see if she's pleased, disappointed, or insulted.

• • •

She was pleased. Very pleased. And I discovered that, after all the time and agony I had put into its composition, the content didn't matter a bit. Merely that I had thought to write was enough. I'll have to keep this in mind for the future—maybe I can cut the time in half on the next letter if I don't have to worry about what goes in it.

It wasn't until the third week of June that Peggy returned to Boston. We would overlap in the city for less than two days, then I was off on the Red Sox's next road trip.

As soon as she got back, she invited me to dinner. I had never been inside Peggy's home before. It seemed excitingly improper to be alone with a woman in her house . . . at night . . . with no one else there . . . just the two of us.

Peggy's parlor and dining room—the only rooms I got to see—were immaculately kept and tastefully furnished. Not that I was entirely sure what "tastefully" meant, but it looked the way I assumed "tastefully" would be: elegant but functional, not the intimidating don't-touch-anything sort of decor. The parlor was dominated by a glossy black piano. A wood-trimmed blue couch and matching chairs with white throw pillows were artfully placed about the room, not cluttering it, but appearing to be exactly where one could ever want to sit. The walls of the room were lined with overflowing bookcases whose contents were slightly torn and scuffed from use. A tall Victrola spewed the scratchy voice of an Irish tenor into the room.

Through dinner, Peggy and I chatted pointlessly about her aunt, the weather on the Cape, the weather in Cleveland, Detroit, Chicago, and St. Louis, the Red Sox's prospects for taking the pennant, my misfortune in Larry Gardner's ankle healing . . . the conversation seemed consciously kept on a tedious track. I helped keep it in that rut, though I wasn't sure if it was sweet talk we were avoiding, or if it was murder that wasn't a fit topic for dinner conversation.

After eating, we retired to the parlor and Peggy brought in a tray of coffee and gingersnaps. The polite trivial chatter was left behind in the dining room, and we picked up with the more important subject we last discussed almost a month ago.

Peggy took off on an odd tack. "I looked through some old detective books of David's. I brought them with me to the Cape. If Aunt Phyllis hadn't gotten sick, I wouldn't have had as much chance to read. So it was lucky in a way that I had to stay with her. Well, not *lucky*—because she *was* sick. But she's fine now. *Fortuitous*—that's what it was. There, that doesn't sound as callous.

"So anyway, I went through Sherlock Holmes, and Edgar

Allan Poe's Dupin stories—but I don't think they'll help. And Jacques Futrelle. He's a wonderful writer. *Was* a wonderful writer. Did you know he died on the *Titanic?*"

I shook my head no, and wondered who Jacques Futrelle was. I also wondered what the point was of reading through her husband's detective books. This is no way to go about solving a murder. And I know—I've read the *Police Gazette* for years, and I don't remember one case where a crime was solved by somebody reading books.

Peggy started to go off again, but I held up my hand. "Time out. Uh, maybe I should tell you what I found out first. It turns out things weren't really what they seemed."

"Yes! Tell me!"

Readily breaking the promise of secrecy I had given him, I filled her in on my conversation with Jimmy Macullar, leaving out the reminiscences of his playing days. And leaving out his *"Not from the police"* comment.

Peggy paid rapt attention. When I concluded, she gave a yell of relief, "Oh, that's wonderful! You're not in any trouble then!"

"Well, that's what I thought at first."

"You *are* in the clear, right?"

"I suppose I am. But I was thinking . . . there isn't any mystery anymore about the body. It was Red Corriden. And I'm not really a suspect . . . so it has nothing to do with me anymore. Right?"

Peggy looked puzzled, but nodded.

"Well, then it occurred to me: with Corriden's body moved, how can his murder be solved? I mean, the police will be looking for somebody who killed him in Dorchester. But that's not what happened. So how are they going to solve it?"

"But didn't Mr. Macullar say a policeman helped him move the body? So won't the police *really* be looking for a killer at Fenway Park?"

"No. I thought about that. The officers who were at the ballpark weren't detectives. I think the one was just a stadium cop. The other man—the captain—he seemed to be a crony of Bob Tyler. They both did whatever Tyler said. I *don't* think they'd have told the police department what they did.

"So anyway . . . there's no good reason for this, I guess . . . Maybe it's because he was a ball player—or because I'm the one who found him, I don't know. But nobody else is trying to get him any justice. So this is something I'm just going to *have* to do: I am going to have to find out who killed Red Corriden."

I wasn't going to say anything to Peggy about being at risk myself, certainly not about getting shot at. She'd have just worried. I didn't like being dishonest with her, but it seemed better than scaring her. And if she thinks that my reason for wanting to solve Corriden's murder is more noble than self-preservation, so be it.

I expected that Peggy would respond with a very reasonable argument against taking on such a preposterous task. Instead, her eyes sparkled with excitement, and she offered, "Can I help?"

"You *want* to?"

"Yes."

"Well, sure, I'd like that. But . . . There's just one thing: I don't know how to go about solving a murder."

"That's all right. Whatever we can do will be better than doing nothing."

"Okay . . . so, what do we do?"

"I'm not sure either."

We both sat in silence, with no idea of how to implement our good intentions. Finally Peggy suggested, "Maybe the first thing we should do is come up with a sensible plan for investigating the case." Up to now, I had only a vague notion about finding out what happened to Red Corriden. When Peggy said "investigating the case" it suddenly struck me that this was going to be serious.

We agreed that we would each try to develop a plan while I was on the road. When I returned, we would then put together one strategy and see if we could find out who killed Red Corriden.

I felt that Peggy and I had become partners of a sort tonight, and I found it difficult to break away from her.

At eleven o'clock I rose to leave, and she walked me to the door. As we stood together to say good night, Peggy softly closed her eyes, and tilted her head back slightly. Oh my, this was not going to be just a quick peck on the cheek.

Chapter Twelve

It took about a week, and we were halfway through the road trip, but I finally came up with a plan to solve the Red Corriden case. Well, not a plan, but a couple of steps toward developing a plan.

First I wondered whether I should call Corriden's death a "killing" or a "murder." I figured if Corriden was a random victim, who died at the hand of a robber or a madman, then it was a "killing"; if he was killed by someone who specifically wanted *Corriden* dead, then it was "murder."

In the first case, if Corriden was just in the wrong place at the wrong time, anyone could have killed him. I had no idea how to pursue that avenue, so I decided to concentrate on the second possibility.

It seemed that the best way to start the investigation was to find out as much as possible about Corriden himself. Maybe uncovering something in his past—or in his personality—would reveal a reason why someone would want him dead. This then was my immediate mission: to gather every bit of information that I could about Red Corriden.

First I tallied what I already knew about him, and was

discouraged to realize that it totaled only three facts: he briefly played third base for the St. Louis Browns in 1910, his only renown came from being mixed up in the batting race scandal that year, and he began this season with the Tigers.

For the sake of finding out about Red Corriden's past, I wished that we were on a Western road trip. There should be more information about Corriden in the cities where he played. I could talk to his former teammates, see where he lived, and . . . well, do whatever else one did in pursuing an investigation.

In the Eastern cities, meantime, I would try to approach some of my teammates, and maybe some of the opposing players, too, and ask if they knew anything about Corriden.

We were two games into a four-game series with the Athletics by the time I decided on my plan of action. Since we had already finished the New York series, the opportunity to question Highlander players about Corriden was gone. Although I tried to make use of the remaining two days in Philadelphia, I completely struck out in trying to learn more about Corriden. At least the investigation provided me a chance to strike out—Jake Stahl hadn't given me a single at bat in more than a week.

I first talked again to Clyde Fletcher. He knew nothing more than what little he had first told me.

Then on to questioning the Philadelphia players. I managed to speak to half a dozen of the Athletics players before the series ended. To a man, each said he didn't know any Red Corriden. It bothered me to discover that not one of them even remembered Corriden as the ball player who had been killed. It seemed he was already forgotten just two months after his death.

I hoped to have better luck in Washington, my first visit

ever to the capital. We came into Washington on Saturday night, giving me all of Sunday to explore the city and see the sights.

In the morning, I made the rounds of the White House and the Capitol building. I toured absentmindedly, giving only token attention to the standard attractions. After stopping for a sandwich at a lunch counter, I worked my way over to the Washington Monument. A few years before, when Gabby Street was with the Senators, he'd achieved instant fame by catching a baseball dropped from the top of the monument. Craning my neck to look up the structure, I couldn't believe he did it—or that he'd be crazy enough to try it. Inside, I climbed the steps to the top, and looking down at the miniature people below, I believed it even less. Hell, the damn fool could have been killed. Killed . . .

What little hold the national monuments had on me vanished completely as my thoughts went back to Red Corriden's death.

I picked out two more Boston players for questioning: Charlie Strickler and Billy Neal. It was still tricky for me to grill my teammates, since my rookie status would last the entire season and with it the unspoken injunction to mind my own business. Strickler and Neal were both veterans, but I had a slim margin of seniority over them as a Red Sox player, and so found them less intimidating. I picked Strickler as the one I would speak to first. I'd seen him pitch a few times when I was a boy, and that seemed to make him more approachable.

Monday afternoon, Charlie Strickler was given a spot start to open the series for us against Washington right-hander Long Tom Hughes. The Senators were still hanging right behind us in the league standings.

Strickler struggled his way to a 2–1 win, relying on the only weapon he had left in his arsenal: irritation. Between each pitch, Charlie would rub the ball, tug his cap, kick the rubber, hitch his pants, and shake off Bill Carrigan's signs until they were repeated. Having thus nagged the hitter into a fit of impatience, Charlie would finally serve up the pitch: never a fastball, usually a combination of change-up and slow curve, always a tantalizing powder puff. More often than not, the batter would pull the trigger too soon, dribbling an easy grounder or tipping a pop-up.

After the game, I gave myself a chance to talk to Strickler. He was taking his time in the locker room, so I dawdled, too, timing my dressing to ensure that I'd be ready to leave the park with him.

Watching Strickler dress, I found myself wondering if his slow pitching tactic was by clever design, or if he was in fact putting all he had on his pitches and did the stalling to catch his breath. He had a roll around his middle that caused him difficulty when he bent over to tie his shoes. He was no longer in shape for baseball—probably not even for gardening—and though he won this day, he couldn't win many more.

The final product of Strickler's dressing was a man who would never be taken for a ball player. Under a misshapen suit that barely restrained his bulges, he wore a soft-collar shirt with no tie. His hair was so short that the graying stubble blended into the bald spot that capped his head, and his face had a droopy look of general resignation to it.

When Strickler started to leave the clubhouse, I joined him on the way out and told him, "Say, Charlie, I saw you pitch against Addie Joss once when you were with Philadelphia."

"Oh. Did I win?"

"Uh, no. You pitched real well, though."

"Mm. Thanks for bringing it up."

"Well, there weren't many who could beat Joss."

"Yeah, he was tough. Shame about him getting sick like that. The good they die young."

"Yeah, that's what they say. Red Corriden, too, I guess."

"Red Corriden, too, what?"

"Dying young."

"Oh. Too bad. Who was he?"

"Uh, he was with you on the Tigers. This year . . . Third baseman . . . Got killed in Boston."

None of this seemed to register with Strickler. "Don't remember . . . Red Corriden, huh? Must have been a rookie . . ."

"Yeah, he was."

"Oh. I wouldn't notice a rookie."

"Yeah, well, good talking to you, Charlie." We were out on the street and each took off our own way. I knew I'd lose my baseball skills, too, someday, but I hoped I could hang on to my faculties longer than Strickler.

During warm-ups before the final game in Washington, Strickler and Billy Neal were tossing a ball on the sidelines. Professionally, Neal was similar to me—or what my career would be like after I had his ten years of experience. He was a journeyman ball player, never a star, who bounced around from team to team. Neal had one advantage over me though: catchers were always getting hurt, so Neal was always in demand to fill in for injured starters. It seemed every time I saw his name in the box score, it was listed for a different club. Since joining the Sox, he had gotten into only a handful of games, taking Stahl's place at first.

When Strickler yelled, "That's 'nuff," and started walking to the dugout, I put myself in Neal's path. I said, "I'm not loose yet. Feel like throwin' a few more?"

"Yeah, okay."

We started exchanging throws. I moved toward him a few steps, wanting to stay within talking distance. "Arm's a little sore. Just short ones, 'kay?"

Neal shrugged his indifference to the range of our tosses.

"How you like playing first?" I began.

"Haven't got to play much. But it's okay. Rather catch, but Carrigan seems to have a lock on the job."

"Yeah, he's real solid. Plays no matter how bad he's hurt. You do much catching with Detroit?"

"Enough to keep me happy. They gave me a chance at Detroit—not like that bastard Stahl."

"Uh, yeah . . . Oh—wasn't Red Corriden with Detroit?"

"Who?"

"Corriden. Red Corriden. Third base."

"Oh yeah. Rookie, wasn't he?"

"Think so. Did you know him?"

"Nah. Not really. He was just around a couple weeks. Heard he got himself killed."

"Yeah, I heard that. Why the hell would anyone want to kill a guy like Corriden?"

"Damned if I know. Thought he got robbed or something. Why? What's the big deal with Corriden?"

"Nothin', I guess. Just wondering what happened to the poor guy."

"Don't know. Damn shame though. Seemed like a good enough kid." Neal held on to my last throw and called a halt to the warm-up and interrogation. "Let's get in. Almost game time."

I jogged up to Neal and we walked back to the dugout together. One more question occurred to me. "You remember who he roomed with, Billy?"

"Who? Corriden?"

"Yeah."

"Mm . . . Oh, sure. Charlie Strickler. He was always complaining how the kid drove him nuts."

"Really? How so?"

"Damned if I know. But them two sure didn't get along. What are you asking me for anyway? Strickler's sitting right there. Ask him if you're so interested."

"Oh, I'm not! I was just wondering is all."

"Uh-huh."

So Charlie Strickler lied to me. There's no way he could have forgotten Red Corriden after just a couple of months.

I felt betrayed—though not as much by Strickler as by the investigating process. It was difficult enough for me to figure out who I should approach for information and what questions to ask. If I wasn't going to get honest answers, this could be really tough.

Chapter Thirteen

I decided to hold back on telling Peggy about the progress I made. First I'd let her tell me if she had gotten anywhere—I expected she hadn't. Then I'd impress her with my success in discovering a possible suspect: Charlie Strickler, Red Corriden's roommate at the time of his death, who now denied even having heard of him.

We were again seated in her parlor, with coffee and chocolate cake on the table in front of us. I was comfortable and at ease. It no longer felt tantalizing, but instead homey and familiar to be in her house.

Peggy was trying to explain her approach to the case: "At first I got wrapped up with the notion that it was like a detective story—you know, somebody's killed in a secluded mansion, the place is full of weekend houseguests, and they're all suspects, and a detective figures it out, and he gathers them all together in the library to reveal the murderer. But of course real life isn't like that."

"No, that sure doesn't sound like what happened to Red Corriden."

"Then I just tried to think of it the way a detective would.

The situation is different—no mansion and houseguests, and all that—but the way a detective approaches a murder case would be the same. Motive, means, and opportunity. That's what they look for."

"Motive, means, and opportunity?"

"Yes. To find a killer, you have to look for motive, means, and opportunity."

"Okay . . . I understand motive. That's the *reason* he was killed. That makes sense. But what about those other things?"

"Well, the means would be how it was done. So if he was shot, the killer would have to have a gun. Opportunity would be—well, *opportunity*. The killer had to have a chance to kill him. So if he was shot on a day when your suspect was in a different city, then he didn't have opportunity, so he can't be the killer."

"But Corriden wasn't shot."

"No, but we can apply those same *principles* to this case."

"Oh. I see. Well, we know the means. He was beat on the head with a baseball bat." Peggy grimaced; that's all right, it's better than what I did when I saw the body. "So the means would be a baseball bat."

"Right. Now: opportunity. It had to be someone who was there."

"Wouldn't it *always* have to be someone who was there?"

"No, not always. You can give somebody slow-acting poison and be miles away when it takes effect."

"Time out. I'm getting confused. Can we leave out guns and slow-acting poison? I think I'd be able to understand this better if we stuck to what happened to *Corriden.*"

"Oh, of course. You're right."

"Anyway, what was it about opportunity?"

"Well, it had to be somebody who was there. I went to the library and checked a newspaper for April twenty-seventh. It said there were a little over twenty-two thousand people at the game—"

"Oh great. *That* sure narrows it down. Twenty-two thousand. And how about the vendors, and the people who work in the ballpark? The players? The *umpires?* That brings it to what? Twenty-five thousand suspects?"

I must have sounded frustrated and hopeless. Peggy tried to be patient with me, but there was a hint of exasperation in her voice. "No. It doesn't mean twenty-five thousand suspects. I didn't check the paper to see how many suspects there were. I wanted to see if anything unusual was reported about the game."

"Oh . . . *Was* there anything unusual?"

"No, not as far as I could tell. I thought perhaps there was a fight in the stands that could have carried over after the game, something like that. But there wasn't anything."

Peggy was dragging me along on this unfathomable tour of her detective logic. Trying to follow it and failing, I became skeptical about this whole detecting process. "I still don't get it. How exactly do we find *one* killer out of *twenty-two thousand* people who were there?"

"Well, not everybody who was at the game is a suspect, of course. Motive, means, and opportunity all have to go together. It had to be somebody at the ballpark who had a reason to kill Mr. Corriden and could use a baseball bat to do it."

"But even putting it all together, it still seems like it could be practically anybody."

"No . . . How many people in the park that day even *knew*

Red Corriden? And how many of them could have killed him with a baseball bat?"

"Oh, I see. They'd have to be strong. It wasn't a woman, or a child—"

"That's right! They wouldn't have had the *means.* And opportunity: how many people would know their way through the corridors under the stands? Fenway Park is a new stadium. Most people have trouble just finding their seats. I think the key, though, is the motive."

"Do you have any ideas who would have had a motive?"

Peggy shook her head. "No, not yet. I tried to think of the usual motives. Money is probably the most common. Does anyone benefit financially from Mr. Corriden's death? Husbands and wives tend to kill each other a lot, too. Let's see . . . revenge, jealously, I don't know what else. I gave a lot of thought to the motive possibilities. So I thought it would be helpful to find out about Mr. Corriden's background, and then see if that could give us a clue to the reason he was killed. I started to find out a few things." Peggy looked about the room, then walked over to a bookcase and took a notebook from a shelf. "Here it is. Let's see what I have . . ."

She sat back down, and referring to her notes, proceeded to astonish me. "Okay. He was born in Indiana. Twenty-four years old this year. Not married. Average size. Five foot seven, hundred and thirty-five pounds. Right-handed.

"Let's see . . . Began his career with Keokuk in the Central Association. Nineteen-eight. The next year, too. Nineteen-ten, the St. Louis Browns bought his contract. They sent him to play in Omaha, then brought him up to the Browns at the end of the year. Then what happened . . . Ah! The Browns acquired Jimmy Austin to play third base for them last year, so they released Corriden. He spent the year with Kansas City in the American Association. The Detroit Tigers bought him from Kansas City at the beginning of this year. They paid fifteen thousand dollars for him—that seems awfully expensive for a baseball player. . . ." Peggy concluded with a satisfied look, "Well, that's all I have."

I hesitated a moment, then couldn't help asking, "Where's *Keokuk?*"

She answered with a giggle, "It's in Iowa."

I was incredulous. "How did you find all that out?"

"Just a couple of telephone calls. I started with the Detroit Tigers office. Then the Browns. Then I called the *Sporting News* in St. Louis. That was it."

"The *telephone!* I can't believe I didn't think of that. I was going to wait until we traveled West again to see what I could find out. Jeez . . ." Maybe I really wasn't cut out for this investigating business. This venture was starting to seem overwhelming. I tried to shake the confusion out of my head—to no avail. I thought coffee might help me think straight, and picked up the cup in front of me. The coffee was cold, but I gulped it down anyway. It didn't help either.

The door knocker unexpectedly sounded out four evenly spaced taps. Peggy bolted up, exclaiming, "Oh! He's early. I wanted to tell you first—" She swept to the door and pulled it open to admit a man I had never met.

"Who the hell is he?" almost blurted from my lips, but I swallowed it, mumbling only a garbled "whmph," which went unnoticed.

Although handsomely dressed, the man didn't look like much. A bookkeeper. No, an assistant bookkeeper. More like the errand boy of an assistant bookkeeper. In every aspect of his appearance, he was thin and wiry. From his spindly arms and legs to his tightly pursed lips to the sparse strands of receding brown hair plastered across his skull—even to the dainty steel-rimmed spectacles perched on his bony nose. If he were a baseball player he'd be penciled last in the batting order, after the pitcher. And when he was sent up to the plate, he'd be told, "Crouch real low and try to draw a walk." I didn't like him.

"Mickey, this is Karl Landfors. He's a—was a friend of David's. They worked together in New York. Karl, this is Mickey Rawlings." "Mickey" suddenly sounded like a kid's name.

Landfors distastefully stuck his hand out and I tried to shake it. Our flesh made barest contact as he quickly slithered his fingers out of my grasp. I imparted a brusque, "Hi. Mick Rawlings."

"Yes, so I gathered."

"Coffee?" Peggy asked Landfors.

"Yes, please. If it's no trouble." He used a different voice—almost lifelike—when he addressed Peggy.

She tried hard to sound cheerful and light, as if she were throwing an afternoon tea party. She babbled about something or other while she filled the third coffee cup that was on the tray. Another indication that I might not make much of a detective: I had noticed the extra cup earlier, and assumed it was a spare in case I broke one.

Peggy settled back on the couch, and Landfors slipped past me to take the spot next to her—where I had been seated minutes before. I had a choice of pulling him off the couch or sitting by myself in a chair. I reluctantly took a chair.

"I thought Karl would be able to help with the murder case," Peggy said, in a tone that sounded as if she were still trying to maintain a tea party mood. "He does a lot of investigative reporting."

"You told a *stranger* about it?"

"He's not a stranger—I've known him for years. He and David used to write for the same newspaper. He's very reliable and I trust him completely."

"You're a reporter?" I asked him.

"Yes."

"So you're planning to write about this. For a newspaper."

"No. I promised Peggy that this would all be off the record. I only agreed to help as a favor to her." He smiled slightly. "I don't do routine crime-reporting anyway."

I turned to Peggy. "What exactly did you tell this guy?"

"Of course if you don't want my assistance," Landfors continued, "I don't intend to force it on you. But Peggy certainly seems to think you can use it." Do I have to ask him to take his glasses off, or can I just go ahead and punch him?

Peggy answered calmly, "I told him about the murder, and about Mr. Tyler having the body moved, and that the police might think you're a suspect—everything you told me. I think this whole thing has to be resolved. Once and for all, to get it behind you. And Karl could be a lot of help."

I was furious that she would tell somebody about the murder, and about me, without first asking me. "Really? How is *he* going to help?"

"I have contacts, and I know how to dig up information." Landfors ended every statement with a wispy sniff. I wished he'd either blow his nose or shut up.

Peggy continued to champion Landfors. "And Karl knows what will hold up in court. We can't just guess at who the killer is. There has to be evidence, evidence to—"

"Evidence," Landfors took over, "to obtain an arrest warrant, then an indictment, and finally to convince a jury." I didn't like him finishing her sentence. And I wasn't sure what an indictment was.

"I already did some checking on your Robert Tyler." Landfors addressed me in a slow, distinct way, as if he were explaining something to a rather dull schoolboy. "Did you know that he used to work for Ban Johnson—president of the American League?"

Barely holding my tongue and fists in check, I answered, "I *know* who Ban Johnson is. And yes, I know Bob Tyler worked for him." This is supposed to be helpful?

Landfors went on unperturbed. "In fact, Tyler pretty much ran the New York office. Do you know how he raised the money to buy his share of the Red Sox?"

My silence told him the answer was no.

"It seems the New York American League team has a player who intentionally loses games—a Harold Chase."

"Hal Chase."

"Yes, whatever. As I was saying, Chase loses games for gamblers who place bets on the opposing team. Do you know who Arnold Rothstein is?"

"No." Get on with it already.

"He's a gambler. One of New York's more notorious. He pays Chase more money to lose games than the Highlanders pay him to win."

"Everybody knows Chase throws games. What does this have to do with Bob Tyler?"

"What it has to do with Tyler is that a baseball player who is known to be dishonest is still allowed to play major-league baseball."

"Yeah?"

"Charges have been brought against Chase a number of times—not in a court of law, but to the league office. Two of Chase's managers, Norman Elberfeld—"

"*Kid* Elberfeld."

"—and George Stallings, have both filed complaints about Chase. The curious thing is that nothing was done to Chase, but both of those managers were fired." Landfors paused, relishing my puzzlement before coming to the point. "It turns out that Arnold Rothstein paid a certain highly placed person in the American League office to ensure that Hal Chase could continue to play baseball."

"Bob Tyler?"

"*Very* good. And that's where Tyler got the money to buy into the Red Sox."

Jeez. "How do I know this is true? How did *you* get this information?"

"Getting information is my business. Of course I don't really follow *baseball*, so I talked to Fred Lieb, one of our sportswriters. He filled me in on some of the details." Landfors smirked with satisfaction. His revelations about Bob Tyler impressed me. *He* didn't, the revelations did.

Peggy then threw a curve at me. "I had an idea. It may sound a little bizarre, but what if it wasn't really Red Corriden? The body, I mean."

"*Sure* it was," I said, feeling on firm ground. "That's the only thing that *is* solved. Jimmy Macullar said he and the cop moved the body to Dorchester. Remember? It *was* Corriden."

"What I mean is, what if the body at *Fenway Park* wasn't Mr. Corriden?"

"How? I don't understand."

"You said his face was completely battered. Then how was the body identified? What if Mr. Corriden wanted people to *think* he was dead, so he gives the *real* murder victim his identity and disappears. That could even make Mr. Corriden the murderer. He could have killed the man, and put some papers or something with his identification on it in the man's pocket. See?"

"Is that from some detective story?"

"No, it isn't."

Landfors piped up, "It would make a good one though." He was trying to flatter her. "I think that's a theory that should be explored." This from a guy who calls Kid Elberfeld "Norman."

I felt *I* was the one with the most useful expertise here, and asserted myself. "Keep in mind that we're talking about baseball players here. Corriden, Tyler—okay, he's not a player, but still . . . And Hal Chase, and Jimmy Macullar was a player. I think I'm in the best position to investigate the case. It needs somebody who's in the game. Baseball's my profession, and—"

"Profession!" Landfors mocked. "You don't really consider baseball a *profession,* do you?"

I lost patience with him. "What the hell do *you* do that makes you such a big deal?"

"I don't waste my life playing a silly game." A silly game?

"Didn't you ever play ball?" I asked.

Landfors looked taken aback. "Well . . . A little. When I was young. I don't think playing games is much of an occupation for a *man* though."

"You were the one they always picked last, weren't you?"

"What?"

"When they chose up sides for a game. You always got picked last, didn't you?"

"I did not."

"Betcha did."

"Mickey! Karl! *Please.* You both sound like little boys."

I got up to leave. "I think I better go. I have things to do. *Real* nice meeting you, Landers."

"Land*fors.*"

"Mickey! Please!" Peggy sounded frantic. Her little party was not ending on a happy note. I stalked out the door, impervious to her pleas to come back.

I sauntered down the steps and out onto the street at a carefully casual pace intended to show that I was thoroughly indifferent to what Peggy and her friend thought of me.

Chapter Fourteen

Until I saw Peggy and Karl Landfors in the same room, I hadn't realized how ridiculous my romantic intentions toward her were. I must have been crazy to have had hopes for Peggy and me as sweethearts.

I never before asked myself the simple question: *Why* would Peggy be interested in me? True, I was a fairly good-looking guy, and being a major-league baseball player gave me some kind of celebrity. But those qualities were probably low on Peggy's list of requirements for a beau. No, a college boy was the type for her. Unhandsome as he was, and lacking as he was in personality, Karl Landfors was more her type than I. There were looks that passed between them that showed me they thought the same way. And if they thought the same way, maybe they felt the same way—and maybe about each other.

Peggy and Landfors had me pretty disoriented, not only personally, but about the investigation. Peggy actually seemed to think of it as just some kind of parlor game—although maybe I was somewhat to blame for her attitude, since I hadn't told her how serious it had become.

And the talk about evidence and the courts left me uncertain about my approach. I figured you just find the killer, tell the cops who did it, and then leave the judges or the lawyers or the police to work out the details. That's it. Case solved. Peggy and Landfors seemed to think there's more to it than that.

Landfors did get my interest up with his information about Bob Tyler, though. If Tyler was involved with gamblers, that could put a new slant on things . . . somehow . . . I suppose. If Landfors was right, that is. How did I know he had accurate information? He might have made the story up out of whole cloth just to impress Peggy. The conniving little . . .

I didn't know how I was going to go about solving Red Corriden's murder now. The only thing I was sure of was that I wouldn't be working on it with Peggy anymore, and certainly not with Landfors. But somehow I'd figure out how to proceed, and when I solved it on my own, I'd make sure Landfors knew about it.

I finally put Peggy and her irksome friend out of my thoughts, and turned my attention to the upcoming Independence Day doubleheader.

July Fourth was the fifth straight day of a blistering Boston heat wave. It was the scalding, still kind of heat that makes you move around in the vain hope of getting out of its way. The exertion then leaves you instantly exhausted from the effort, and hotter than you were before. So you try moving again . . . and you're singed some more.

The first game of the holiday doubleheader turned out to be a runaway, and Smoky Joe Wood breezed—he was the only breeze this day—to an easy 6–0 win. The New York batters looked so spiritless and inept, that *I* could have pitched a victory against them.

During the break between games, while the infield dirt was dragged and fresh lime was applied to the foul lines, our territory was invaded by the enemy. Hal Chase walked across to the Boston side of the field as if claiming it for his own. He stayed away from the players, though. It was the box seats next to the dugout that attracted him. Or, rather, their colorful occupants did.

A front-row box in this location would usually be occupied by VIPs in somber-colored suits. Tickets for these seats took not only money but front office connections. The four men who greeted Chase were no politicians or industrialists, though. They would have been more at home at a racetrack. They wore loud checked suits and caps cocked at arrogant angles. They must have been hilarious wits, judging from the incessant, raucous howling that came from the box.

Chase greeted them all loudly, then focused his attention on the least noisy of the four. The man was in a lime green suit with the vest buttons unfastened. A lemon yellow cap covered all his hair and drooped over his left eye. A black cigar not much smaller than a baseball bat stuck out from under a light-brown Teddy Roosevelt mustache.

Chase clearly reveled in his notoriety. I couldn't believe he would flaunt his friendship with gamblers in front of an entire stadium. I was relieved when the teams were called in to the dugouts and he left our side of the field. The air seemed to smell better with his departure. The gamblers remained, but they didn't offend me by themselves—a ball player fraternizing with them was what I couldn't stand.

The second game continued where the first left off. Bucky O'Brien was now the beneficiary of the Highlanders' lackluster play and the Red Sox's scoring barrage. After three innings, we already led 7–0. The commanding lead and the hellish heat prompted Jake Stahl to give the bench-warmers some playing time.

I took over at shortstop, Billy Neal finally went in for Carrigan behind the plate, and to the delight of all the Sox players, Clyde Fletcher trotted out to substitute for Duffy Lewis in left field.

I was eager to see how Fletch would handle the wall. But O'Brien was on a roll, striking out a string of Highlander hitters, so neither Fletcher nor I had a fielding chance in our first two innings.

In the bottom of the fifth, with the bases loaded, Fletcher came up to bat against Jack Warhop. Down the left field line of the ballpark, next to the scoreboard above the fence, was a huge billboard that read:

MUMM'S
EXTRA RYE
WHISKEY

Taking a hopeful rip at Warhop's first pitch, Fletcher tagged a screamer right up the line. It was still rising when it struck the word RYE—just inside fair territory—for a grand slam home run. It was Fletcher's first hit of the season, but he trotted around the bases as nonchalantly as if he hit a homer every day.

I ran from the on-deck circle and joined the scoring runners in greeting Fletcher on his triumphant arrival at the plate. I teased him that the whiskey sign was just his kind of target.

I then took my place in the batter's box knowing full well that I was going up as a target for Warhop's wrath. Sure enough, his first throw—he didn't even pretend it was a pitch—came straight for my head and I hit the dirt to avoid it.

Then he threw again and caught me by surprise, almost nailing me in the neck. One duster is expected, but two is out of line. My teammates moved to the front of the Sox dugout, yelling curses and threats at Warhop. Undeterred by their yells, his third pitch plunked me in the ribs. With tempers already shortened by the heat, the Red Sox stormed the field, Jake Stahl leading the charge. Both benches emptied, and fights broke out all over the field.

I noticed that Clyde Fletcher ran directly toward Hal Chase, dodging more reachable opponents to get to him. I figured Fletch was going to administer a payback for Chase cheating him at cards. Chase spotted him, and ran to face him head on. Maybe heat waves affected my vision, because the two of them looked like that scene from the movies—the one where lovers lope across a meadow in slow motion to meet in the middle and embrace.

I grappled with the Highlander catcher. We wrestled a while to no decision, he impeded by his catching gear, I in pain from my bruised side, and both of us wilted from the sun and the exertion.

Like most baseball fights, the scuffles subsided after lots of pushing and shoving and few good punches. Umpire Silk O'Loughlin then tossed Stahl and Warhop out of the game. Warhop looked relieved to be leaving the field.

I trotted to first base with an affected limp, trying to look as if I was in too much pain to run well.

Since Warhop's replacement was brought into the game

after a ruckus on the field, I figured it would take him awhile to get settled. So on his first pitch I swiped second base in a clean steal. Some of the New York players, Hal Chase especially, started yelling at me for trying to show them up. Everybody knows you don't rub your opponents' noses in it by stealing bases when you're up by a bushel of runs. Well, that's just too bad if they don't like it; you don't throw at a guy three straight pitches, either.

I hadn't exacted enough of a revenge yet, so on the next pitch I stole third base. I slid safely under the third baseman's tag, then felt fresh pains as he jumped on top of me and started punching. Again both benches emptied. This time it took longer to restore order, with the Highlander third baseman the only player banished by O'Loughlin.

Before leaving the field and dugout, Stahl had appointed Bill Carrigan acting manager—then continued to call the shots from the dugout runway out of sight of O'Loughlin. Since O'Brien had gone the five innings he needed to get credit for what should soon be a win, Stahl—via Carrigan—sent Charlie Strickler to the mound to mop up.

The next three innings went by without incident.

The score was 14–0, with two outs in the top of the ninth, when Hal Chase lifted a high fly deep to left field. I turned around and ran onto the outfield grass in case I'd have to take a cutoff throw. I saw that Clyde Fletcher had already taken off and was lumbering back toward the fence. As he approached the hill, I muttered inaudible encouragement, "C'mon, Fletch. You can do it. C'mon . . . That's it . . ."

Fletcher kept his head down, eyes on the tricky ground, and successfully made his way to the top of the slope. Not until then did he look up for the ball, only to find that he'd misjudged it—the ball wasn't carrying all the way to the fence. I saw him freeze momentarily, a look of panic on his face. Then he put his legs in gear to run back in.

About his fourth stride down the hill, Fletcher stumbled and belly-flopped onto the ground. He just lay there, face down, arms and legs splayed.

I raced out to field the ball while Tris Speaker ran over from center field. The ball struck the slope about ten feet from Fletcher's outstretched body. It took one bounce to the wall and then caromed back in my direction. I reached it before Speaker could, and wheeled around to throw to Larry Gardner. He relayed it to Billy Neal in time to nail Chase at the plate. That ended the game with the shutout intact.

I waited a moment until I saw Fletcher getting up under his own power, then I ran off the field to join my teammates in the clubhouse.

The players were raucous with good humor. There's nothing like slaughtering the opposition to put ball players in a good mood.

More than one of my teammates slapped me on the back with congratulations on saving the shutout. This, and the fact that they had twice come out fighting in my defense, made me awfully proud.

Clyde Fletcher finally shuffled into the locker room looking red-faced and flustered. Before we could rib him about his nosedive into the outfield turf, he took the offensive, yelling to the room in general, "Goddam sons of bitches! Every goddam one of you puts in his two bits telling me how to get up that goddam hill, and not one of you got sense enough to tell me how to get back down!"

That out of his system, Fletcher exposed his stained brown teeth and joined in the clubhouse revelry. For the first time, I felt that we were both really part of this team.

The next morning, I bought copies of most of the Boston newspapers, and eagerly turned to the sports sections. Just as I hoped: both Clyde Fletcher and I were prominently mentioned in the stories of the Fenway doubleheader. Usually when I got into a ball game, my performance garnered me no more than a plain line in the box score. It was a rare thrill to see my name in the text of the articles, and it felt a special treat to appear there with my roomie.

Before clipping out the articles, I noticed that in Detroit's game against the Browns Ty Cobb celebrated the holiday by stealing his way around the bases. Second, third, and then home. That Ty Cobb sure knew how to demoralize the opposition. Jeez, why did all that talent have to end up in the world's meanest human?

• • •

Two days after Clyde Fletcher drilled his Fourth of July grand slam, Bob Tyler released him. Fletch wasn't even traded for another player—just dropped from the team. Discarded like a broken bat.

The news came after the closing game of the series with New York. Most of the team was still showering or changing in the locker room.

Fletcher seemed to take his dismissal in stride, but I was shaken by it. I was upset enough, in fact, to surprise myself by blurting out an uncharacteristic proposition. "Hey, Fletch, what do you say to a beer? My treat."

Fletcher looked startled by the offer but he accepted. "Sure, kid, sounds good."

We left the ballpark, and I deferred to Fletcher to recommend a saloon. He picked one out readily enough, and we went in. A haze of cigar smoke and the stench of stale beer filled the room. I gagged on the first mouthful of air, and had to consciously give extra power to my lungs to continue inhaling the dense bitter vapor. It wasn't an inviting atmosphere, but it seemed exactly the right atmosphere for mourning Fletcher's dismissal.

Walking up to the bar, I laid a ten-cent piece on it, and the saloon keeper set us up with two big drafts. The thick yellow head of foam in front of me looked delicious. I scooped up a clump of it with my finger and stuck it in my mouth.

Fletcher didn't approve of my drinking technique. "That ain't an ice cream soda, kid."

"Yeah, I know. I like the foam."

"Suit yourself." Fletcher downed half his glass in one big swallow.

I gave up on eating the foam and followed his example, gulping most of what was in my glass. I was surprised at how nicely it went down. It seemed the best thing in the world to pour down one's throat after a hot dusty ball game. About a minute after guzzling the brew, a soothing warmth slowly rippled up through my stomach. I *like* this stuff.

"I tell yuh, kid, you oughta do this more often. Might improve your hitting."

"Beer will improve my hitting?"

"I said 'might.' Then again, might not. But look at it this way: you don't really drink, you don't smoke, don't chew, don't chase broads, and don't gamble—and you still can't hit over .250! I tell yuh, kid, you're the kind of guy gives clean living a bad name. Take it from me, do some more drinking now and then, run around a little—it'll loosen you up. Put another twenty points on your batting average. Maybe."

I was pretty skeptical, but then after my third draft it didn't seem out of the question that a few beers now and again could enhance my hitting skills.

Into my fourth beer, I started to get maudlin. "Jeez, Fletch, I'm really gonna miss you. How the hell can Stahl let you go after that home run?"

"Don't worry 'bout it, kid. It ain't the first time. At least I got a chance to get that hit. Sure got Warhop's goat didn't it? Jake said they were gonna release me anyway, but he wanted me to get in a game first. Hell, I got no hard feelings against Jake."

"Still, it don't seem right. What do you think you're gonna do?"

"I'll get picked up by somebody. If not, what the hell, I'll play semipro or something. Don't worry 'bout me."

"I'll be right back."

"Again? What are you? A goddam sieve?" His amazement at my frequent trips to the toilet was exceeded only by my own astonishment at his not going at all. Where the hell was he storing it?

After I arrived back at the bar stool, Fletcher asked, "Hey, kid, you know why beer goes through you so fast?"

I shook my head no, and lifted a fifth glass to my lips.

"Because it don't have to stop to change color! Hah!"

Tingly beer shot out through my nose as I burst into laughter. It seemed the most hilarious thing I'd ever heard.

"That one has whiskers on it, Fletch." Billy Neal's voice came from over my shoulder. I looked behind me to see Neal along with Charlie Strickler and Bucky O'Brien. Except for Bucky, this was turning into a bench-warmers convention.

Neal suggested we all get a table together. He gave us the news that Strickler had just joined Fletcher among the ranks of former Red Sox. This would be a goodbye party for both of them.

But before I'd toast Charlie Strickler, I had something to get straight with him. Fletcher and I got off our bar stools, but instead of walking to a table I tapped Strickler's arm and said, "Lemme ask you something."

He stayed back from the others with me, asking, "Yeah? What?"

"You're a liar."

"You're drunk. And watch who you're calling a liar."

"You told me you didn't know Red Corriden."

Strickler smiled. "Oh, that."

"Then I found out you and him were roomies. You lied."

"Yeah, I guess I did at that. Look, kid, when you asked me about him I figured you were a friend of his. So I figured you were one of *them.*"

"What *them?*"

"Bible-thumpers. That kid was always preaching at me 'bout what a sinner I was. Just 'cause I take a drink now and then, or maybe play a little cards. Goddam kid drove me nuts. Judging from your breath, I guess I was wrong about you being a pal of his. Let me buy you a beer."

We joined the others at a table, and I let Strickler buy me the beer. I made it my last. Bidding Fletcher an affectionate goodbye, I left him with the other Sox and staggered home alone.

I snuck back into my room, careful not to make any noise. I hoped that I wouldn't encounter Mrs. O'Brien. She didn't seem the type of landlady who would tolerate drunken boarders.

I felt euphoric after my outing with Fletcher, not least of

all because of the newly discovered fact that I could down half a dozen beers and keep them down.

After wrestling off my clothes, I fell heavily into bed. Maybe the beer had me energized somehow, because I couldn't seem to lie still. Then I realized I *was* still, but everything else was moving. The bed swayed and bobbed as if it were on springs, the walls of the room rotated like a panorama, and my pillow quivered as if it were made of jelly. Feeling that I might be tossed out of the bed, I spread my arms to brace myself against the motion.

Eventually the various movements of the room subsided. I started to drift in and out of a fitful doze punctuated by disjointed thoughts and bizarre fragments of dreams.

Suddenly, amid the strange and convoluted images passing through my pickled mind, an inspired thought jumped to the forefront. It told me who killed Red Corriden.

I still retained enough rational thought to realize that I wouldn't remember the murderer's name in the morning. I needed to write it down. With intense effort, I pulled myself out of bed. As I stood, the bobbing sensation returned. With my equilibrium all but gone, I groped my way around the room until I felt a pencil stub on top of the writing table. I felt around and grabbed one of the articles I had clipped out after the holiday doubleheader. Unable to see what I was writing, I carefully formed the name of the killer near the edge of the clipping and stumbled back to bed.

• • •

I awoke late in the morning, convinced that either my eyeballs had grown during the night or their sockets had shrunk. My eyes felt tightly gripped, and throbbed with pain from the pressure around them.

I tried hard to remember what happened last night. I believed that I had a good time, but if I did, why did I feel so wretched now?

I tried to retrace last night's activities and conversations in my mind. As I worked my way through the muddled recollections and vague impressions, I remembered that at some point I lit on the identity of Corriden's killer. Did I really, or did I just think it came to me? And if it did, who was it?

I had a feeling that I wrote down the name. Painfully, I pulled myself out of bed. After my legs started to feel as if they had enough rigidity to keep me erect, I began a labored tour of the room. Sure enough, on my writing desk was one of my clippings with a name scribbled in the margin: *Cobbb.*

The handwriting was shaky—or my eyes were blurry—but that's what it said. *Cobbb.* As in Ty Cobb.

Jeez, I must have been drunk.

So, according to this scrap of paper, Ty Cobb was the killer. This "solution" promptly raised more questions than it answered. *Why* was it Cobb? Or why did I *know* it was Cobb? Or why did I *think* I knew it was Cobb?

Perhaps it was just wishful thinking on my part. A murderer has to be nasty, and who was nastier than Ty Cobb? But this wasn't really a solution. There wasn't any evidence, just the ramblings of a drunken mind.

I put the clipping in a drawer and decided that I might think about it after my head cleared up—optimistically hoping, but not entirely sure, that it would someday again be clear.

Chapter Fifteen

I could really be on to something here. It seemed unlikely that a credible idea could emerge from the random wanderings of an alcohol-abetted imagination, but maybe it was so. Maybe Ty Cobb did murder Red Corriden.

The Red Sox team was journeying West for a short road trip to St. Louis and Chicago. I had tried to shake off my crazy Ty Cobb dream or hunch or whatever it was, but it kept coming back to me, each time stronger and more insistent. Finally I figured, what the hell, it's a long enough train ride. I'd let myself consider this Ty Cobb idea, and just let the notion play itself out. But once I dropped the restraints on Cobb and let him loose in my thoughts, the idea that he was the killer of Red Corriden moved beyond the realm of drunken rambling and turned into a compelling theory.

I looked at the situation analytically, as I knew Peggy would. Means, motive, and opportunity.

First, means and opportunity: Ty Cobb fit both of these requirements. He was in Fenway Park with Corriden, he had access to baseball bats, and he certainly had the strength and temper to put a bat to violent use.

Then motive. Why would anyone want to murder a young baseball player from Indiana? According to Peggy, husbands and wives often killed each other, but she'd found out that Corriden wasn't married, so that possibility was out. Money was a popular motive, but a rookie ball player was unlikely to be rich. Of course, he could have been killed for his pocket money—but then we're back to it being a mugging.

Revenge then? Revenge for what? Did Red Corriden ever do something so terrible that it warranted such severe retaliation? Perhaps . . . to one man's point of view.

As far as I knew, the only suspicious activity that ever involved Red Corriden was the final day of the 1910 baseball season, when he played out of position to let Nap Lajoie lay down cheap bunt singles. It almost cost Ty Cobb the batting title. The league exonerated Corriden, but did Cobb? Ty Cobb seemed to have his own view of right and wrong. He also seemed to find no shortage of people who had wronged him.

It seemed farfetched on the surface, but I had to look at it from Cobb's point of view. Ty Cobb—a man who feels justified jumping into the stands in midgame to attack a cripple. Would he have any qualms about going after a man who, in his view, almost cost him a batting championship and a valuable automobile?

The more I thought about it, the more my Cobb theory seemed to make sense. Maybe just plain meanness should be added to the standard list of possible motives, a contribution from Ty Cobb.

As I became confident that I was correct about Ty Cobb, I became more sure of myself in this whole investigating business. Perhaps I wasn't as methodical as Peggy or Landfors would be, but I did seem to have an instinct for crime-solving.

I began to entertain myself with highly satisfying day-dreams, envisioning Peggy's proud reaction to my success and Landfors' outrage at being shown up by a mere ball player. And the publicity—a famous baseball player nailed for murder, the crime solved by Mickey Rawlings. This will be bigger news than Harry Thaw's murder of Stanford White!

Then my confidence disintegrated as two other characters injected themselves in my thoughts: Jack O'Connor and Harry Howell. Ty Cobb had a revenge motive, but what about O'Connor and Howell? Cobb *almost* lost the batting title and the car. O'Connor and Howell did get booted from baseball. Did one—or both—of them blame the banishment on Red Corriden?

• • •

Not all of Peggy's ideas were useless. Following her example, I went to the *Sporting News* office when we arrived in St. Louis. I talked to an editor of the "Baseball Bible" who was delighted to let a ball player use their research library—he said I was the first. I pored through the last five years of *Reach Baseball Guides,* and found that Bobby Wallace had been with the Browns when O'Connor and Howell were with the club. I hoped he might have an idea of where O'Connor and Howell were now.

Before the second game of the series in Sportsman's Park, I spotted Bobby Wallace playing a fast-paced pepper game behind third base with four other Browns. When we came to St. Louis in May, Wallace was managing the club; he'd looked weary and his talents seemed to have faded. Then, a month into the season, he gave up the managing chores. Now his skills seemed restored, and he was clearly loving the renewal. He fielded more deftly, and laughed more loudly than his teammates. Managing makes a fellow be an adult, it makes baseball a job. Bobby Wallace was back to being a boy again and playing a game.

I drew closer to the pepper players, enjoying the spectacle and waiting for the game to end. When the players broke to take batting practice, I approached Wallace. It was almost like walking toward a mirror; we had the same infielder build, the same lean facial structure. Other than his hair being darker, he could have been my older brother.

"Hey, Bobby," I called. "I'm Mickey Rawlings. I've seen you play for a long time. It's good to be on the same field with you." Flattery always helps.

"How you doing, Mickey."

"I was wondering . . . since you've been here quite a while I thought you might know . . . I've been trying to find Jack O'Connor and Harry Howell. You have any idea where they went after they left the Browns?"

"You a friend of theirs?"

"No, never met either of 'em. We, uh, we have a mutual friend. Promised him I'd try to look them up if they're still around."

Wallace looked like he was seriously searching his memory. "Howell may still be around. He liked St. Louis, I don't think he'd have left. Haven't seen him since he left the team, though. Oh! You might try the Everleigh Club. He spent a lot of time there, I seem to remember."

"Everleigh Club? Where's that?"

"On Market Street. Shouldn't be hard to find."

"How 'bout Jack O'Connor?"

"You got me there."

"That's okay. If I can find Howell, maybe he'll know. Thanks."

• • •

As a visiting player, I had a practical appreciation of the facilities at the new ballparks: they all provided dressing rooms for opposing teams. With the older parks, visiting players had to dress in the hotel and show up at the field already in uniform. Then worse, they'd have to leave after a game, sweaty and filthy, with no chance to shower and change until back at the hotel.

So after the morning game, I was able to take a quick shower and slip out of Sportsman's Park to head directly for the Everleigh Club. The first cabbie I asked said he knew where it was. He drove me to 2200 Market Street where a large two-story white house sat between a pool hall and a closed-up vaudeville theater. The house was farther back from the road than its neighbors, and was partially shielded by four willow trees.

At the front door, I rapped a rose-shaped brass knocker and waited. And waited. I rapped again, louder, with diminishing patience. Then I grabbed firm hold of the rosebud and hammered the wood forcefully.

I finally heard a pit-a-pat of footsteps and the door opened a cautious few inches. A doll-like colored girl in a maid's outfit looked me up and down, then slowly shook her head. "You *is* an eager one, isn't you?" she said, not seeming to expect an answer. And I wouldn't have known what to answer. I stood frozen, trying to remember why I knocked so hard if I didn't know what I wanted. "Well," she said, "you come on in. I'll fetch Miss Evelyn." The girl let me in to the entrance hall and walked off to climb a staircase that curved upstairs.

As I waited, I heard soft piano notes coming from the parlor. A tall, lean man with coal-black skin, dressed in the same black and white colors as the piano, sat erect in the piano seat. He played with a minimum of movement, gently laying his long fingers on the keys to sound the notes. It looked as if his dark fingers were trying to mesh with the black keys of the keyboard. He played a quiet march, with an alternating rhythm that started my head swaying back and forth to the tempo.

"Business hours don't start until four," a husky female voice said. I looked back at the foot of the staircase. "Why don't you come back in a couple of hours. I'll make sure you're taken real good care of then." Miss Evelyn stood on the bottom step of the staircase, wearing a dark blue gown over a colossal body. The material cascaded straight down from her immense bosom, cloaking any possible trace of a figure. She looked a little like Clyde Fletcher in a dress. Her left hand rested on the bannister, poised to pull herself back upstairs.

"I only need a couple of minutes," I said.

She frowned and repeated with distaste, "A couple of *minutes?*"

I suddenly noticed that the carpeting of the stairs and hallway was red. I glanced back at the parlor, and saw that the chairs, couches, and drapes were all the same scarlet. And I suddenly realized what Everleigh meant, and what kind of club this was.

Blushing and burning, I said, "Uh, I'm not here for uh . . . for uh . . . I was just looking for a fellow I heard used to come here. He was a baseball player—with the Browns. Harry Howell? Do you know him?"

"Know him!" Miss Evelyn exploded. "That bastard worked here for almost a year. He was broke when he got booted out of baseball, so I took him in—he was always hanging around anyway, even without money to spend. I figured he was strong enough to take care of any customers who got out of hand, so I gave him a job as a bouncer. But he was like a drunk tending bar. Made demands on the girls—*unnatural* demands. They were going to quit if I didn't get rid of him, so I fired the bastard." She squinted at me. "You a friend of his?" It sounded like an accusation.

"No, never met him. I was just looking for him to uh . . . ." I wasn't exactly sure exactly *why* I was looking for him. "Uh, do you know where he is now?"

"Don't know, don't care. Just as long as he never comes here again. And you—you can show yourself out." She started back upstairs.

"Are you sure you don't know where I can find him?" I called to her. She shook her head no as she kept climbing the steps.

Defeated, I turned toward the door. Three fast loud chords from the piano halted me. I turned my head to see the piano player beckon me with a nod.

I warily walked into the parlor as the pianist went back to a slow rippling march. I stood behind him to his right. He didn't face me, didn't change the tempo of his playing. He said without emotion, "Harry Howell. He a barber now. Roselli's Barbershop. Twelfth Street."

"You sure?"

"Yup."

"Thanks. Uh . . . why? Why tell me where he is?"

"You mean to bring him something bad."

"What makes you think so?"

"You say you ain't a friend of his, and I know he didn't have no kin. So if you trying to track him down, it's to bring him some trouble. And I like that just fine."

"Did he do something to you?"

"That girl that let you in. She don't do no entertaining here, she just do cleaning and such. And she *mine.* Harry Howell, he tried to force hisself on her when the girls wouldn't take him no more. You settle your score with him, but leave some for me. I'll be making Mister Harry Howell a visit sometime."

I promised to leave some of Harry Howell—and expected to leave all of him—for the piano player.

• • •

Roselli's Barbershop was without customers. The two chairs were both occupied, but one was occupied by a stack of newspapers and the other by the barber. I recognized his face. I'd seen it in *Baseball Magazine,* and on tobacco cards, and in Hilltop Park. It was Harry Howell. I had seen him pitch for the New York Highlanders back when he was Handsome Harry and his arm was still strong. Now here he was, sacked from a whorehouse, cutting hair for a living.

"You open?" I asked.

Howell groaned and reluctantly pulled himself out of his chair. "Yep." He gave the seat a token swat with a grimy towel. Flecks of dried shaving cream dislodged from the towel and fluttered in the air.

I climbed into the seat and kept my eyes focused on the mirror ahead of me, looking at Howell's reflection. His white jacket with the collar buttoned around his throat made him look like a dentist. His hands looked like those of an athlete: large, calloused, and bent. The expression on his face was that of a once-handsome man who'd run out of chances in life and had no plans but to live out his time. Howell tied a sheet around my neck and asked, "How you want it?" He couldn't have sounded less interested.

"Just a trim."

Howell went to work with a comb and scissors, nibbling off snips of my hair. I didn't know what to say to him. How could I ask him about Red Corriden—how could I do it casually?

I decided there was no subtle approach. "You remember Red Corriden?" I blurted.

The metallic clipping noises stopped. "Who?"

I sighed. Why does everyone ask "who" right after I clearly say who? "Red Corriden. He was with you on the Browns."

"You know who I am?"

"Of course. You're Harry Howell."

Howell's reflection smiled. It is nice to be recognized. "You seen me play?"

"Lots of times. Not with the Browns though. I saw you pitch for the Highlanders when I was a kid." The smile fell. I should stop telling guys that I saw them play when I was a kid. "You were a helluva pitcher," I added, trying to get on whatever good side he might have.

Howell smiled wryly. "Yeah, and that was a helluva long time ago." He went back to snipping my hair. "So what do you want to know about Red Corriden?"

"The last day of the season. Two years ago. Cobb and Lajoie were—"

"They were fighting for the batting title. And we tried to give it to Nap Lajoie."

"It's true?"

"Sure it's true. And it's nothing I'm ashamed of. We weren't trying to throw the games. Just give Lajoie some hits. That's all. We didn't do nothing wrong."

"How'd it happen?"

"Well, that batting race went neck and neck all year. The winner was going to get a car, you know."

"A Chalmers."

"Yep, that was it. Anyway, it seemed everybody was pulling for Lajoie to win the title and the car. Or pulling for Cobb to lose—mostly that, I guess. Anyway, we decided to give Lajoie some help. Had the third baseman—Corriden—play real deep and let him lay down easy bunts. You want a shave?"

I knew it didn't need one—and probably wouldn't for another week—but I was flattered he asked and said, "Sure."

Howell lifted a razor and I suddenly wasn't so sure. I was here because I thought he had a motive for killing Red Corriden. Letting him put a razor to my face didn't seem like such a good idea. But it was too late. Howell tilted my seat back. With steel tongs, he pulled a steaming hot towel from a can at the base of the chair. "Close your eyes," he said. I hesitated as the towel dangled over my face, then obeyed. I was suddenly covered by moist heat. And I couldn't see what Howell was doing. I tried to clench my throat as if bracing it for a punch.

I heard the raspy scrape of the razor being slapped on a leather strap. As Howell sharpened the blade, he picked up the story. "The last day of the season was a doubleheader. Wouldn't matter in the standings which team won or lost—

both teams were out of the pennant race. And remember, it was last day of the year. Strange things happen—you know, the bat boy gets to pinch hit, some fifty-year-old coach gets to pitch a few innings . . . Keeps the fans interested. Have some fun before going home for winter. Everybody does it."

My face felt suddenly chilled as the towel was lifted from it. I could see again, and breathe again. Howell began to apply lather to my skin with a brush that was too stiff. "Lajoie went eight for nine in the two games," he continued. "But it wasn't enough—the league gave Cobb the batting championship. We *split* the doubleheader, by the way. Like I said, we weren't throwing games. But nobody remembers that."

"You and Jack O'Connor got kicked out of baseball."

"Yeah, no kidding. Shouldn't have though." Howell carefully cut away the lather along with an occasional whisker. "But everybody could see what we were doing. Corriden played third base standing all the way out in left field, for chrissake. There was such a squawk afterward that Ban Johnson decided he should punish somebody. So it was me and O'Connor."

"It wasn't Corriden's idea to play back?"

"Nah. I forget whose idea it was, but O'Connor liked it, and he told Corriden to play deep. The kid was just doing what he was told. But Jack denied it. He said Corriden didn't know how to play third base in the major leagues."

"Why were *you* kicked out?"

"I got kind of caught up in it, I guess. Lajoie was eight for eight, then in his last at bat he hit into a fielder's choice. So I told the scorekeeper I'd buy him a suit of clothes to change the fielder's choice to a hit. He told Ban Johnson and Johnson kicked me out." Howell made it sound as matter-of-fact as if he had been kicked out of a bar instead of banished from baseball.

"Did Jack O'Connor ever admit that he tried to fix the batting race?"

"Yeah. After a while. He didn't take it real well, though, getting booted out of baseball. He blamed Corriden for it—said the kid ratted on him. He was really pissed that Corriden didn't get in any trouble. Ban Johnson said Corriden wasn't guilty of nothing but doing what he was told. That wasn't what got *me* pissed though—what got me was that Chalmers gave cars to both Cobb and Lajoie. Said it was worth all the publicity they got." Howell dabbed the traces of shaving cream from around my jaw and took off the sheet.

I stood and fished in my pocket for change. "You still see Jack O'Connor at all?"

"Nope. He left town after that business with the league office. I heard he went outlaw. California, I think."

"He's an *outlaw?*"

"Outlaw *league*. You know, not part of organized baseball. Ban Johnson don't have no authority with an outlaw league."

"Oh. You know what team?"

"Nah. California State League, I expect, but don't know which team. I haven't heard from him in more than a year."

I shook Howell's hand. "It was really good talking to you, Harry. Thanks." I gave him fifty cents for a quarter haircut and shave. His eyes told me I was insulting him with the big tip, and I felt like a heel for offending him. Then he shrugged and pocketed the money.

• • •

Harry Howell didn't seem to carry any lingering grudge against Red Corriden. But maybe he once had. Maybe he'd done something to settle a score. Howell seemed a little *too* acclimated with what had happened to him. I couldn't believe he could be that happy with his current lot. And what about O'Connor? Where had he been since leaving baseball? Where was he in April?

And of course there was still Ty Cobb, as good a suspect as ever.

With Strickler and Fletcher gone from the Sox, both Billy Neal and I lost our roommates, so we were paired together on this road trip. Since Neal had been teammates with Cobb on the Tigers, I figured he might be able to give me some firsthand insights into the man.

I'd hardly spent any time at our hotel in St. Louis. Not until we arrived in Chicago did I get to size up my new roommate.

Wearing only shorts, Billy Neal sat at a writing desk playing solitaire and humming a tuneless series of notes. Overall, he looked to be in good shape. He was probably in his early thirties, about the same age as Fletch, but whereas Fletcher's carousing had put an extra ten years of paunch and sluggishness on his body, Neal appeared as firm and fit as a guy in his midtwenties. He also lacked Fletcher's apelike appearance—Neal's curly dark hair was close-cropped and pretty much limited to his head.

What stood out with Billy Neal, was a body that said "catcher." No other occupation could have produced the features that had developed on him. From his knees to his ankles, Neal's shins were gnarled with knots and lumps—he'd been catching for years before Roger Bresnahan invented shin guards. And a slight left-hand twist of his nose indicated that he'd caught at least one game without a mask. Most amazing were Neal's fingers. They were curved and bent and twisted, and some of them looked like they had extra joints broken into them.

The atmosphere of the room seemed odd. Then I realized it was the sound. Gone was Fletch's juicy *Hchoowook, Shptoo, Ping!* The slow regular *Snap* . . . *Snap* . . . *Snap* of Neal crisply turning over each card had taken its place.

I suddenly missed Fletcher and wondered what would become of him. "Billy, you think Fletch will get picked up by another club?"

"Could be. Maybe end of the season, somebody could use him. Can't beat experience when it comes down to the wire."

"I was wondering what happens to guys like Fletch and Strickler. What if nobody does pick them up? What do guys like that do after baseball?"

"After baseball? What do you mean after? You can always play ball. Back in the minors or semipro . . . Hell, I'd even play for a factory team. Got to keep playing ball."

"Huh. I saw Harry Howell back in St. Louis."

"You saw Harry Howell?"

"Yeah, remember him?"

"Sure . . . pretty good pitcher for a few years."

I remembered from the *Reach Baseball Guides* that Neal's name appeared on the St. Louis 1910 roster. "Was he still pitching when you were with the Browns?"

"Nah. His arm was dead. He just scouted for us."

"Well, guess what he's doing now."

Neal shrugged. "Beats me."

"He's a barber. Got fired from a whorehouse, so now he's a barber."

"Well, you don't gotta worry about Clyde Fletcher turning out like that."

"No?"

"Uh-uh. Fletch ever got himself a job in a whorehouse, he'd make sure to hang on to it."

"Hah!" I agreed with him there.

Neal went back to his solitaire game. I watched in fascination as his mutilated fingers nimbly maneuvered the cards.

I finally brought up the Tigers, intending to work my way around to Cobb. "How long were you with the Tigers, Billy?"

"Not long. Joined them last June—or July was it? July."

"Get into many games?"

"Nah, not many. More than I am now though. Caught some, played a couple games in the outfield."

"How did you break into *that* outfield? They're almost as good as ours."

"Maybe better, I dunno. They been together longer . . . But sometimes Cobb would be pissed off at Crawford or Jones, and he wouldn't play if they were out there. That's when I got in. Usually I'd take the place of whichever one he was mad at, but sometimes he'd be mad at both of 'em—then I took Cobb's place." Neal smiled wryly. "That usually seemed to be when he was in a batting slump. He didn't like to play when he wasn't hitting."

"I heard Cobb was tough to get along with. You have any trouble with him?"

"Nah, not really. Mostly I stayed out of his way."

"Huh. From what I hear, that's about the only way to stay on his good side."

"You hear right." Neal put down his cards, and with wonderment in his voice said, "The guy carries a helluva big chip on his shoulder. But it don't really seem personal. He just hates everybody—opponents, teammates, fans . . . everybody. It's like he has a devil inside makes him act that way. Gotta give him his due, though: he's some ball player. Ain't nobody like him when he's on the base paths."

Picking up the cards again, Neal smiled and recalled, "Oh yeah, I guess I did have one run-in with Cobb. You probably heard about him filing sharp edges on his spikes?" I nodded. "Well, once we were playing in Chicago. And before the game, as usual, Cobb is sitting on the bench making a big show out of filing his spikes. Then just before the game's gonna start, I see that the web on my mitt is torn, so I go in the clubhouse for another glove. And there's Cobb. He's putting on another pair of spikes—regular ones, not sharpened. He sees that I caught him, and he tells me you can't get good traction with razor-sharp spikes. Says he just does the filing for show . . . scare the opposition . . . they'll think of it every time he slides into base. Then he says, if I tell anyone, he'll kill me."

"*Kill* you?"

"Yeah, calm and cool, said he'd kill me. Have no idea if he meant it. Wouldn't surprise me though. A few years ago, when I was with Cleveland, the Tigers were in town for a series. But Cobb only played in the first game. Turns out he stabbed some guy in a hotel and had to jump town. The rest of the year when Detroit came in, they were without Cobb. He couldn't come into Ohio—the cops were waiting to arrest him."

"Jeez."

"Yeah, that man does have a demon in him."

Oh, that's right . . . Bob Tyler mentioned something about that Cleveland business being hushed up. I wondered if the man lived . . . Could a *murder* be hushed up?

Chapter Sixteen

On our return to Boston, Joe Wood was slated to pitch the homestand opener against Detroit. He was going for ten wins in a row, and the overriding interest in the game was whether Smoky Joe could manage to chalk up another victory. I was probably the only one at Fenway Park who didn't share that concern. The opposition is what had me interested. Ty Cobb was in town.

This was the first time I had seen Cobb all season, the first time I had ever been on the same field with him.

Although I was starting at second base, I ducked pregame practice. Instead, I focused my attention on Ty Cobb as he warmed up. From the Red Sox dugout, I watched every move he made. I'd gotten the idea into my head—perhaps from watching too many movies with manic-eyed desperadoes—that a killer would look different from everyone else. I stared intently at Cobb, unable to really see his eyes, but occasionally picking out his facial expressions. He looked intense, fierce, driven, determined. The face of a murderer? I couldn't tell.

The fourth inning of the game brought my first personal

contact with Ty Cobb. He was on first base after dragging a bunt single. Our shortstop pointed his finger at me, indicating I was to take the throw on a steal—he must have believed my legs were more expendable than his. Cobb yelled to me, "Watch yourself, busher! Ah'm comin' down!" Was that supposed to be news? He was always coming down. At least I felt less anxious about it, knowing he didn't really have razor-sharp spikes.

Keeping his word, Cobb took off on the first pitch. Rough Carrigan's throw to second came in a little high. I snagged it and brought my glove down fast hoping to still nail Cobb. I did—deliciously hard—right in his face. I tensed, expecting him to spring up fighting. But he just rose slowly and brushed himself off calmly. Then his ice-blue eyes locked on to mine and he softly drawled, "Ah'll be seein' you again, busher." Those weren't the wild villainous eyes I expected. They looked far deadlier. Cold, steady, lethal.

In the seventh, Cobb pulled off a play that only he could. He had again singled, and was taking a bold lead off first. My legs were telling me to be careful. Then the next Tiger batter dropped a bunt to move him to second—but Cobb didn't stop at second base. While the batter was thrown out at first, Cobb kept running. With a hook slide, he scraped safely into third. And on the next pitch he stole home.

A shameful doubt began to flicker through my mind: even if I could prove that Ty Cobb killed Red Corriden, would I do anything about it? If Cobb went to prison who could ever replace him on the baseball field? There was no one like him. It would be a devastating loss for the fans and the game if Ty Cobb could no longer plunder the base paths. A criminal should pay for his crime, I knew. But many of them hadn't, and what difference would it make if one more crime went unsolved?

After the game—despite Cobb's heroics, another win for Joe Wood—I waited outside the players' entrance to the park. Ty Cobb came out first, wearing an expensive charcoal gray business suit and a black homburg. He walked to the side of the entrance and stopped, apparently waiting.

Other Detroit players left the stadium in groups of two and three, making plans for dinner or entertainment. They ignored Cobb, who stood alone, his face with an expression of such haughty arrogance that it ensured a loneliness I could almost pity. A chauffeured Cadillac pulled up, and Ty Cobb drove off with only his enormous pride for company.

I went back to Mrs. O'Brien's for supper, planning to go to the Tigers' hotel afterward. I intended to question some of the Detroit players about both Cobb and Corriden. I'd decided that I *would* find out if Ty Cobb was guilty. And then I would try to do what's right.

As I entered the house, I was greeted by the smells of singed pot roast and fresh-baked rolls. I started upstairs to wash, when I was halted by Mrs. O'Brien calling out to me, "Mickey! You had a telephone call!"

Peggy? I ran into the dining room as Mrs. O'Brien brought in the soup. "Who was it?"

"A gentleman. Give his name as Flitcher. Said he wanted to talk to you about a Mr. Corrydin."

I followed her back into the kitchen. *"Red* Corriden?"

"I believe he did say Red Corrydin. I wrote it down." She picked up a scrap of brown butcher's paper from the kitchen table. "Here we are. Yes, Red Corrydin," she read. "And Mr. Flitcher said he wants you to meet him right away at the same *saloon"*—Mrs. O'Brien glanced up at me disapprovingly—"where you used to go."

I reluctantly made a quick decision to pass up dinner. "Thanks, Mrs. O'Brien. I better skip supper and go see what's up. Sorry."

Walking through the hallway to the front door, I heard Mrs. O'Brien cluck and mutter, "A nice boy like that going to saloons." She sounded disillusioned with me.

It would be good to see Fletch again, but a social beer wasn't what I was looking forward to.

As I got within a few blocks of Fenway Park, I realized that I had absolutely no idea which saloon we had visited. I never noticed the name of the place when we went in, and I was too drunk to notice anything else about it shortly thereafter.

I knew it was near the ballpark, so I started to walk the streets around Fenway. I stuck my head into every tavern I passed. They all seemed the same. I didn't recognize any of the surroundings, and scanning the occupants I didn't see Clyde Fletcher.

I expanded the circle of my search to no avail and eventually gave it up. I returned home puzzled. Did Mrs. O'Brien get the message wrong? Was it another night I was supposed to meet him? Did she forget to tell me the name of the bar?

I walked into the house, started to call out, "Mrs. O—," and abruptly stopped with my mouth still open.

Two uniformed police officers were stiffly seated in the parlor. Both of them rose, and the shorter of the two demanded, "Mickey Rawlings?" I nodded, and the men approached me. "Captain O'Malley asked us to bring you in for some questions."

"About what?"

"He'll tell you when you get there."

"Okay." The demeanor of the officers indicated that I had no choice. What's going on now?

As the two cops ushered me out the door, I turned my head and could see Mrs. O'Brien watching us through the kitchen door. First saloons and now the police. My image was really starting to take a beating.

The officers wordlessly walked me the short distance to Walpole Street. Several blocks ahead, I could see the familiar twin spires of the Braves' South End Grounds where I had played last year. I pointlessly wished that that were our destination instead.

With no helpful communication from my escorts, I tried to guess the reason for my summons. I'd had only one encounter with O'Malley before, and that was at Fenway Park. Is he planning to dredge up the notion that I'm a suspect in Corriden's death? If he is, he won't get very far. I know better now, thanks to Jimmy Macullar. Oh—but I can't let him know that Macullar told me about Corriden's body being moved. Well, if O'Malley wants to go on about me being a suspect, I'll just let him. Let him wonder why I won't quake in fear.

The policeman on my left poked me in the ribs to prompt a right turn up the steep steps of a narrow red brick building. Two large round light bulbs above the door had POLICE stenciled on them in official black letters. The same lettering on the door read DIVISION TWELVE.

We entered the station house, where a brawny sergeant behind a high front desk looked down at me with contempt. The expression seemed to be one that he wore as routinely and comfortably as his uniform.

The officers prodded me through a dingy hallway populated by indolent policemen who chatted among themselves, frantic civilians who were trying to register complaints, and an assortment of seedy individuals who seemed to serve no purpose other than to occupy the few available seats.

My escorts pushed me into a small plain room with a bare table near one end. There were three armless wooden chairs in the room. One of these was in the corner and supported the posterior of Bob Tyler; he looked stern, hands clasped tightly over the head of his cane. Captain O'Malley was in the second chair, seated behind the table. The two policemen each grabbed one of my elbows and jerked me down into the third seat. They then moved to stand on either side of the door with their arms folded across their chests.

I was in the center of the room, facing O'Malley. Tyler was behind me to my right; I couldn't see him without twisting my head. The exposed position was clearly arranged to maximize my discomfort.

If the intent was to make me submissive, it didn't work. I did feel uncomfortable and vulnerable, but I also felt angry. I didn't like being in this place, and I especially didn't like the men who were in it with me. A liberating feeling of calm defiance simmered within me.

O'Malley was the first to speak. "You know why you're here?" he demanded.

"Because those two gentlemen brought me here."

Wrong answer. "Don't be a smartaleck," O'Malley snapped. "You're in real trouble here, and you better learn some respect." O'Malley nodded at one of the cops who mechanically walked over to me, and without any expression whatever, backhanded me across the face.

"Where were you between seven and eight tonight?"

"Why?"

Tyler spoke from behind me for the first time. "That's not a cooperative attitude, Mickey. Tell Captain O'Malley what he wants to know."

O'Malley took it from there. We weren't in Fenway Park now. We were on his turf, and he was in charge. He nodded again, and the second cop repeated the first's assault on my face. Like the first, I found it annoying, but not particularly painful.

"Again: Where were you between seven and eight tonight?"

"I went for a walk."

"Where?"

"Around Fenway."

"Anybody with you?"

"No."

"Anybody see you?"

"Yeah. Other people who were out. Nobody I know though."

"So you can't *prove* where you were."

"I don't know . . . I guess not."

O'Malley seemed pleased. "No alibi, huh? That's tough."

I wanted to ask why, but was now wholly determined to show no interest. I wouldn't give O'Malley any satisfaction.

"How well do you know Jimmy Macullar?"

"Macullar?"

"Macullar! Jimmy Macullar! How well do you know him?" O'Malley was barking now.

"I don't know. He works for the team, for Mr. Tyler I guess. I don't really *know* him."

"When's the last time you saw him?"

"I don't know . . ." I wasn't being evasive; I really didn't know. Macullar had a personality that made it seem he was just barely there even when he was in full view.

"Goddam it! I never met nobody who knows less than you do!" O'Malley was losing patience with me.

Tyler lost patience with both of us. His voice came from over my right shoulder again and got right to the point. "Jimmy Macullar was murdered this evening."

Damn!

O'Malley settled down to take command again, and filled in some details. "Somebody shot him. Out behind Hanratty's Pub. Familiar with the place, Mickey?"

I shook my head.

"It's about two blocks from Fenway Park. Isn't that where you said you were walking?"

"Yeah, around there."

"With nobody who can say *exactly* where you went 'around there'."

"Not that I know of."

"You own a gun, Mickey?"

"No."

"Know how to use one?"

"Yeah, you aim and pull the trigger." I couldn't resist that; I figured it was worth another slap to aggravate O'Malley. I got it—harder this time—and immediately developed a preference that it be the last. No more wisecracks. But I still won't be cooperative.

O'Malley tried a new tack. "You know, Joe Flint would have done a good job on you." He paused and stared at me expectantly. I was supposed to ask who Joe Flint was, but I refused to give O'Malley the moral victory of playing along. He continued, his annoyance at my obstinacy giving an added edge to his voice. "Joe was the Commonwealth's executioner for—well, far back as I can remember. Finest hangman in New England. He'd tie the neatest knot, position it just right behind the ear, drop the trap, and *snap,* clean as a whistle." O'Malley's voice fell. "But then Joe took to drinking, and his hands didn't do such elegant work no more. Not nice and *clean.* He'd hang a guy, and the neck wouldn't break—the guy would just hang there, twitching and jerking every which way . . . his face'd be turning purple and his mouth'd be opening and closing like a fish out of water . . . and then he'd finally strangle to death. Ten, maybe fifteen minutes later."

O'Malley made a show of looking me over. "You got a good neck. Scrawny. Real easy to find where the knot should go. Yeah, even in his later days, Joe woulda done a real fine job on you.

"Of course they electrocute murderers now." O'Malley sounded disappointed with this innovation. "Yeah, they set up one of them chairs in the Charlestown Jail a few years ago. Old Joe did the first one. Didn't like it though, so he quit. Said it didn't take real talent like a good old-fashioned hanging did. All he had to do is throw a switch—then after the guy sizzled, scrape the burnt skin off the chair. What do you think it smells like when a guy gets fried?"

By now it was clear that I wasn't being responsive, so the last question was addressed to Tyler. He answered with indifference, "I wouldn't know. Not good I expect."

"Nope, not good at all. I seen three of 'em this year"—O'Malley virtually beamed at me with eager anticipation—"so far. I was there last month when they put Harry Marshall in the chair. They sponged him with water before hooking him up, and when they gave him the juice this big smelly cloud of steam came off him."

This had more of an effect on me than the hanging scenario. I had once seen Edison's movie *Electrocution of an Elephant.* They really killed an elephant to make it. It took him forever to die, while billows of smoke came from his legs where the wires were attached. Watching the film, I could sense the odor of burning flesh. By the time the animal finally toppled over, I was working my way out of the theater, holding my breath until I could gulp some fresh air.

I felt that I needed fresh air now. I was angry with myself that I let O'Malley's ploy get to me.

O'Malley finally came around to the reason I was brought in. "Here's the situation, Mickey: it looks to me like *you* murdered Jimmy Macullar. And I think it's because he knew when you really came into Fenway Park back in April—when you claimed to have 'found' that body in the ballpark. I know you been talking to Macullar about it—maybe he was threatening to turn you in and tell what really happened.

"You have a bad habit of being around when guys get killed. That's a habit we're gonna cure you of. We haven't found the murder weapon yet, but it'll turn up, and I have a feeling when it does, it'll turn up in your possession. Then you'll be arrested. And then you'll be convicted." O'Malley gave me a self-satisfied smile and concluded, "The only question will be how much juice it's gonna take to fry you."

Tyler asked O'Malley, "Can I have a word with Mickey alone?"

"Sure. He's all yours—for now." O'Malley rose and all three cops left the room.

I skidded my chair around and faced Bob Tyler.

He stared at me with a mixture of pity and disgust.

"You've gotten yourself in a no-win situation, Mickey," he said. "If you minded your own business about that incident at Fenway, you wouldn't have brought attention to yourself. I don't know how you're gonna get out of this mess now. I know O'Malley. Once he gets an idea in his head, he doesn't change his mind. He isn't much influenced by whether his idea is right or wrong. I've got a suggestion though: it's still a good idea to keep your mouth shut. Prying into things is only gonna get you more trouble.

"Meanwhile, like O'Malley said, he's not making an arrest until he has the gun. So you're still a free man. Almost free. I had to take responsibility for you so you could still play. And I'll be keeping a close eye on you, so try to stay—make *sure* you stay—out of trouble." Tyler nodded me out the door, and I left the building with no interference from the police.

When I got home, a worried Mrs. O'Brien greeted me. "Is anything the matter, Mickey? You're not in any trouble are you?"

"No," I lied. "The police just wanted to ask me about an accident I saw."

"I've saved you a bit of supper in the icebox."

"Thanks, Mrs. O'Brien, but I couldn't eat anything right now. I'm just going to turn in early." She looked worried as I started up the stairs, and I wondered what she was thinking of her unsavory boarder.

• • •

O'Malley sounded confident that I would be convicted of Jimmy Macullar's murder—so confident that it appeared guilt or innocence were completely irrelevant. I started to suspect that the gun that killed Macullar would inevitably turn up in my possession.

Somehow, O'Malley knew that I had spoken to Jimmy Macullar—but he couldn't have known what Macullar told me. If he was aware that I knew about Corriden's body being moved, he wouldn't have tried to scare me by bringing up the Fenway Park murder. If the body I found was never officially *at* Fenway, then I couldn't have officially found it there.

First there was one murder: the nameless body I found at Fenway Park. Then there was a second: Red Corriden, killed in Dorchester. Then it was down to one: Corriden *was* the Fenway corpse. Now it's back up to two. Any chance it could be reduced to one again? Not likely.

I looked at the clock and noticed that it had only been a couple of hours since my visit to the police station. The doomed feeling that had taken root in me had already anchored itself so deeply that I thought days or weeks must have passed.

It was an agonizing night for me. I lay in bed, reviewing everything I had been through this season, and feeling myself a victim.

Then, after letting myself sink into a mire of self-pity, I jerked myself out of it. And got mad.

I was mad at O'Malley and Tyler, at the cops who brought me in, at Jimmy Macullar for getting killed. I was angry with myself for not knowing how to handle the situation.

I was mad at Peggy, for not being here to support me, for confusing me with crazy talk about slow-acting poisons and Jacques Futrelle and Red Corriden not being dead and—and *Keokuk* . . .

But mostly I was angry at someone unknown: the murderer—or murderers—of Corriden and Macullar.

The intensity of my vicious silent shrieking finally exhausted me. I slipped into sleep as an orange dawn began to stain my room. It was the color of Red Corriden's hair.

Chapter Seventeen

I was being pinched. By Robert F. Tyler, by Captain O'Malley, and by a killer. Gripped from three directions, with no way to slip out of the grasp. The only way to open an escape route was to pound back at one of the pincers until it broke. Which one would be weakest?

Bob Tyler? He'd already had Red Corriden's body moved—that must be some kind of crime in itself. He also had ties to characters like Hal Chase and Arnold Rothstein—and therefore maybe to other thugs. And as my boss, he could easily keep tabs on me. Hell, he could sell me to Keokuk if he wanted to. Bob Tyler didn't seem poundable.

Captain O'Malley? He wasn't above a little corruption either—he'd gone along with moving Corriden's body out of Fenway. He now seemed determined to make me sacrificial convict in the Macullar case, and he had the means to do it. I could see no way to fight back at a man who had a police force at his disposal.

Crazy though it seemed, the killer looked like my best chance. Of course, that was largely because he was an unknown. Or *they* were unknown. I was using "killer" as a catchall: Corriden's murderer, the gunman who shot at me in Fenway Park, Macullar's murderer. They weren't necessarily the same man.

There was a lot to look into, and it was time to start.

The second murder brought with it new information that I thought would help clarify the overall picture. Assuming the killings were connected, the circumstances of the second crime could shed some light on the first, and likewise the first murder could provide clues to the second.

Obviously, the phone call about meeting Fletcher wasn't made by him. It was a setup to put me on the murder scene. Lucky for me, I couldn't remember which saloon I was supposed to go to. Unlucky for me, walking around looking for it left me without an alibi.

The Detroit Tigers were in Boston when Macullar was killed and when Corriden was murdered. Did Ty Cobb kill both men? My instinct said no, there was too much difference in the methods. Corriden was bludgeoned—an act of violent rage that fit Cobb's personality. Macullar was shot—a calculated crime with the added stratagem of setting me up for it. But the crimes still had to be related—maybe the second was caused by the first.

I'd learned by now that instincts aren't proof, so I set out to get hard facts.

Picking up the morning papers, I started with the most basic. Would Macullar's murder be acknowledged publicly, or would he, too, turn out to be an unidentified body found under a railroad bridge? No, it was official and public, though buried in the back pages: *James F. Macullar, an employee of the Boston Red Sox, was shot to death near a popular Back Bay tavern last night.* The longest newspaper report of his death contained only a couple more sentences than that.

None of the articles mentioned any suspects in the case, and, I was sorry to see, not one included the fact that Macullar had been a major-league baseball player. I thought he would have wanted to be remembered as a ball player.

A quick trip to the library helped me eliminate Ty Cobb as a suspect in Macullar's murder. I remembered that Cobb had embarrassed the Browns in Sportsman's Park on the Fourth of July, just two days before Fletch and I went out drinking. If Cobb was in St. Louis, how could he know what saloon Fletcher and I went to in Boston? I found the newspapers for July 6, and saw that the Tigers were still in St. Louis that day. The box score showed Cobb played in the game, so there was no way he could have been in Boston to see us go into the bar. To set me up at Hanratty's, the killer must have followed us that day—if Hanratty's was in fact the saloon we went into. That was the next thing to be pinned down.

From the library, I walked down Boylston Street in the direction of Fenway Park. With directions from passersby, I found Hanratty's Pub.

Before going in, I looked up at the sign above the door. *Hanratty's* was spelled out with faint peeling green paint. Large shamrocks that were once of the same color, but now even more peeled and faded, were barely discernable on each end of the sign. The exterior of the building didn't look familiar to me.

I walked into a standard saloon atmosphere, still with no feeling of recognition. I ordered a beer, and drank deliberately, letting my eyes wander the establishment. I tried to pick out some identifying mark that would confirm this as the bar where I had come with Fletcher.

I wasn't convinced that this was the right place until halfway through my second beer, when I had to visit the men's room. While discharging the first beer, I started to read some of the scribbles on the wall. Between a couple of French postcards was a poem:

A quiet young lady from Worcester
Stood in front of a fellow who gorcester . . .

That confirmed it—I remembered having seen it there before. So Jimmy Macullar was killed outside the same bar where I had been with Fletch. And the phone caller knew where that was.

Captain O'Malley said Macullar was killed *behind* Hanratty's. I prodded myself to go out for a look—to investigate the scene of the crime, I guess Peggy would say.

The bar had a back door near the men's room. I slowly creaked it open, and cautiously poked my head out. I knew he must have been taken away, but I had a frightening sense of Jimmy Macullar still laying there dead.

I stepped into an alley that was strewn with broken bottles, wooden crates, rusty trash bins, and a huge decomposing rat that was covered with a pulsing swarm of green flies. There was no sign of Macullar, of course, and there was no evidence of his murder—no patch of dried blood marked the spot where he had been killed. I paced over the tightly packed cobblestones of the alley, and kicked away debris that might have covered something. There was nothing. But it would have been different had I been here when the phone caller wanted me to show up. I'd have been standing over Macullar's body.

It *was* different with Red Corriden. I had plenty of evidence for *his* death.

Wait a minute, was that a setup, too? Was I *supposed* to find Corriden's body? No, that couldn't have been a setup. My train had been hours late getting to Boston. The killer couldn't have planned on that.

Then I remembered what Red Corriden's face had looked like. And going after the killer was no longer my preferred course of action.

The alley could tell me nothing more, so I walked home reevaluating Tyler and O'Malley for potential weaknesses.

What was that business at the police station really about? What did Tyler and O'Malley hope to win by the games they were playing with me?

Did they seriously believe I killed either Corriden or Macullar? No, they knew I wasn't a killer. Neither of them gave me credit for having brains enough to be a murderer.

Did they believe they could convict me of murder anyway? Probably. But they would need either fabricated evidence or a forced confession.

Was that episode at the police station an attempt to make me confess? If it was, it was a pitiful one. They'd have to be a lot rougher than that to get an innocent man to confess to murder. Perhaps they would get rougher yet—once the baseball schedule was over and Tyler no longer needed me in one piece.

Or they might be intending to fabricate evidence, frame me for Macullar's murder. O'Malley's words, *it'll turn up in your possession,* kept running through my mind. I had the feeling that either they already had the gun or knew where it was. Maybe they'd simply plant it in my room if they couldn't find the real murderer—if they'd even be looking for the real murderer. But if they already had the gun that killed Macullar, why bring me in to the station? Why not just plant it in my room, arrest me, and get it over with?

The only explanation I could see was that the encounter at the station house wasn't an attempt to break me down into a confession—it was to scare me into keeping quiet until they decided to go ahead with framing me. They were giving me some time—probably because Tyler wanted to wait until the season was over. I preferred to think that Tyler's reprieve was due to the value he placed on my abilities, but it might have been to avoid bad publicity and a loss of ticket sales.

Anyway, I couldn't see where Tyler or O'Malley had any weaknesses I could attack. It was back to finding the killer.

• • •

I really didn't know much about Jimmy Macullar—far less than I knew about Red Corriden. I didn't know who his friends were, if he had family, where he lived. I knew almost nothing about the living Macullar, just how his death had put me at risk of electrocution. It was time to learn something about the quiet Mr. Macullar.

Macullar had mentioned that he was born in Boston, so I thought some of his relatives might still be in the city. I checked back in the newspapers that reported his death, and found that his funeral had been held at the Church of the Immaculate Conception in the South End.

I called the church and said I was a friend of his just in from St. Louis. I was sorry I had missed the funeral, but wanted to pay my respects to the family. I was given the name and address of a sister, Mary Macullar, in Jamaica Plain.

The trolley ride to Jamaica Plain took the route I had

traveled with Peggy when we went to the Arnold Arboretum, almost exactly a year ago.

At the Centre Street address was a tall red-brick house that looked as if it had been plucked off of a Beacon Street foundation and transported to this stretch of road. It was far grander than its neighbors—almost a mansion. I couldn't picture Jimmy Macullar living here.

I expected a maid or an English butler to answer my knock, but instead the door was opened by a brawny young man who made Hippo Vaughn look like Wee Willie Keeler. Despite the heat and humidity, he was wearing a woolen sweater that made me itchy just looking at it.

"Aye?" he demanded.

"My name's Mickey Rawlings. I, uh, I knew Jimmy Macullar. I wanted to pay my respects. Is there a Mary Macullar here?"

"Come in." He gave me barely enough room to slide past him into the front hall. He closed the door and poked me inhospitably in the back. "Hat," he grunted. I quickly removed my boater and held it in front of me with both hands.

The young man left me alone in the hallway. He returned minutes later, pushing a wheelchair that held a pixie of an old woman. She was bony thin, and her wrinkled white skin hung loose from her throat and arms. She wore a dark green dress that was several decades out of fashion. Her fingers played idly with the lace loops of a white shawl that was folded over her lap. The only real sign of life came from her eyes—dark, darting, demanding eyes.

"What's your name?" the woman asked.

"Mickey Rawlings, ma'am. I knew your brother." I paused

in case she wanted to correct me about the relationship; I was only assuming she was Mary Macullar.

"Were you a friend of his?" she asked.

"Yes, ma'am. I didn't know him as well as I would have liked to, but I'd like to think I was his friend. He was the first person I met when I joined the Red Sox. I'm sorry I didn't get to his funeral. And I'm sorry about him, being, uh . . ."

"Being killed," she finished. She didn't sound distraught about it. "Thank you for coming to see us, Mr. Rawlings. It's nice to meet a friend of his. I haven't seen my brother in forty years, so I don't know many of his friends."

"Forty years?"

"Yes, Mr. Rawlings. You see, my brother thought he was a disgrace to the family. Going off to be a *baseball* player, the way he did." She almost gagged on the word "baseball." "We're a proud family, Mr. Rawlings. My father—our father—was Thomas Macullar. He came here in '48 without a penny to his name. And he built a fortune. You've heard of Macullar Ice?"

"Uh, no ma'am." Miss Macullar looked offended by my ignorance. "I've only been in Boston a short while," I added as an excuse.

"Hmph. Well, Mr. Rawlings, my father built the Macullar Ice Company. A shrewd businessman, he was. He set us up harvesting ice from Jamaica Pond. Imagine: farming something that you never have to plant, never fertilize, and every year your crop comes in the same. What could be a better business? People will always need ice, and we will supply it. At a very handsome profit."

"Jimmy didn't want to work for the ice company?"

"No, he made his choice: he went for baseball instead of business. And he stuck with his choice—for life. I give him credit for that. We would have taken him back, but he was too proud. I don't happen to think that baseball is the worst thing in the world—the theater is much worse." She added defiantly, "We've never had an *actor* in the family, Mr. Rawlings."

"I'd like to help find out what happened to Jimmy . . . Do you know why anyone might want to, uh—"

"Kill him. Are you a police officer, Mr. Rawlings?" She plucked harder at her shawl.

"No, ma'am."

"Well, don't you think finding my brother's murderer is a job for the police—not a *baseball* player?"

"Yes, I suppose, but—"

"I appreciate your intentions, Mr. Rawlings, but we can find out what happened to Jimmy." Her fingers tore through one of the lace loops, and she looked sorrowfully at the damage. She spoke softly at the shawl, "We have friends in this city, more friends than that boss of Jimmy's has—they'll let us know what happened to him. And we'll take care of it. We take care of our own."

Then she clamped her jaws shut, and sat motionless. She'd talked as if she had a need to say something about her estranged brother, now that she could never say anything *to* him. My visit was probably her first opportunity to say something about Jimmy.

Mary Macullar looked up slowly and said, "Take my advice, Mr. Rawlings. Go back to your baseball games. Stay out of things you don't understand. It would be safer that way." Suddenly she reached up and slapped the massive left hand that rested on the handle of her chair. "My stick," she ordered. The young man handed her a black twisted cudgel. She clutched it with both hands and pulled herself out of the chair. Fending off an attempt at assistance, she hobbled away without saying goodbye.

As I left, I thought that if I were Jimmy Macullar, I don't think I'd have gone into the family business either.

Chapter Eighteen

A fairly peaceful week went by with no more murders or enforced visits to police stations. I was tempted a few times—about a hundred . . . maybe closer to a thousand—to call Peggy, but I resisted. I put her out of mind—almost completely—and divided my attention between baseball and Jimmy Macullar's murder. Mary Macullar's warning didn't deter me. I was tired of people telling me to stay out of things. Especially since it seemed they only wanted me to sit quietly on the side until they decided what to do with me—or *to* me.

Just over a month was left in the baseball season. The ballpark was no sanctuary for me now; it provided no refuge from thoughts of gallows and electric chairs. I became convinced that my performance on the field was linked to the resolution of the Macullar case. As long as I was an asset to the team and could help Bob Tyler reach the World Series, maybe he would keep Captain O'Malley away from me. If I played poorly, however, he might discard me as he had Clyde Fletcher and Charlie Strickler. Only in my case, I'd be tossed to O'Malley—and then to Joe Flint's successor. So it seemed that by playing good baseball I was playing for time, time that I would use to find the real killer.

The closing days of August were laying a thick blanket of hazy heat and stifling humidity over the city. The conditions were worse at Fenway Park, where the nearby fens—the swamps that gave the ballpark its name—produced a sickening odor and an inexhaustible legion of mosquitoes.

The deadening heat wave restricted the movements of everything in Boston: every person, every horse, the very air, and even the Red Sox ball players. The Sox were starting to play listlessly, aching from a long season of charley horses and strawberries, wilted from the city heat, and lazy from the lack of a serious challenge for the pennant. The only thing that kept the team from falling into a bona fide slump was the pitching of Joe Wood, who still had his winning streak going.

During a Saturday doubleheader against Chicago, surviving the weather seemed to be a higher priority and a greater challenge than winning the game. It was already nearing one hundred degrees when the morning game of the doubleheader got underway. Both teams played sluggishly throughout the match. The fielders walked slowly to and from their positions between innings, the pitchers took extra time between each delivery to keep from overheating. Despite the low final score, 2–0 in favor of the White Sox, the game ended up a long one—just over two hours.

Rough Carrigan was soaked and exhausted after catching the first game, so Billy Neal went behind the plate for the second. Our shortstop took the second game off, too, allowing me to fill in for him.

Ordinarily I wouldn't have been optimistic about us winning the second game, what with our regulars out and Big Ed

Walsh pitching for the White Sox. But we had Smoky Joe Wood on the mound for us.

The heat didn't seem to bother Ed Walsh; he blazed his spitball right by us. He worked economically, not wasting a pitch even when he was up no-balls-and-two-strikes in the count. I became two of the strikeouts he rang up in the early innings.

Joe Wood struggled for us, giving up one run to Chicago in the first inning and another in the second.

The heat and humidity were so oppressive, that I almost looked forward to facing Walsh's spitball in the early innings—I imagined the spray might be refreshing. By the seventh inning, though, that image had completely lost its appeal. Liberal dollops of tobacco juice had been applied to the ball throughout the game, making it a brown, soggy, lopsided lump of leather and string.

The score was still 2–0 when I came up to bat with runners on second and third in the bottom of the seventh. To save whatever strength the heat hadn't sapped from me, I decided to follow Walsh's example of economy during this at bat. Instead of picking out a location where *I* wanted the first pitch, I set my sights on the spot where Walsh liked to deliver most of his pitches: high and tight.

Okay, it'll be a hard spitter inside. Try to pull it.

I pulled it. *Clouted* it. *Tagged* it. Clear over the left field fence! My first major-league home run. A *real* one, out of the ballpark, not a triple that somebody misplayed into an inside-the-parker. I wasn't sure how that mushy ball managed to plow through the gooey air and carry over the fence. It might have been due more to some strange atmospheric phenomenon than to sheer strength on my part, but whatever the cause, I'd take it.

I relished every second of my home run trot around the bases. Like every other place-hitter who claims that he prefers to bunt and just poke at the ball—because the strategy is more *interesting,* and requires more *intelligence*—I'd get an especially powerful thrill on those rare occasions when I'd hit a long ball. But the run was too brief. As I crossed the plate, I was out of breath and my squishing flannels felt like they'd sponged up gallons of sweat. I'd run much faster than I needed to. Next home run I'd have to go slower and savor it.

My homer gave us a 3–2 lead in the game, and those players who had the energy slapped me on the back with congratulations when I returned to the dugout. On the bench, I wondered to myself if the ball would be picked up by some lucky kid, or would it just lie there on Lansdowne Street, a disgusting brown lump indistinguishable from the horse droppings that surrounded it.

The score held, and Smoky Joe Wood chalked up another win. He also won another fan immediately after the contest, when he made a point of thanking me for the game-winning home run. It had always struck me as somewhat unfair that pitchers get credit for the wins even though they seldom drive in the runs. Wood's gratitude seemed more than adequate compensation for this inequity in the box score.

Most of the afterglow of the home run washed away along with the dirt and sweat that I showered off me. I still carried in the back of my mind the notion that I wanted to tell Peggy about everything I did, and it gave me a pang of loss each time I remembered that we were no longer seeing each other. This was such a time—there didn't seem to be much glory in hitting a home run with no one I cared for to listen to me brag about it.

I had almost finished dressing when Jake Stahl quietly told me, "Bob Tyler wants to see you in his office." Here we go again. Who's dead this time?

I found Tyler's office by myself. "Come in!" was barked in answer to my knock. I opened the door slowly and involuntarily scanned the floor. No corpses.

"Come on in, Mickey. Have a seat." I did as ordered, then swung my head to look behind me. "No, Captain O'Malley isn't here. Just the two of us." I relaxed only slightly. Tyler's voice dropped to a soothing tone. "That was quite a performance today," he said. "Your first home run, wasn't it?"

"First in the majors. I've hit a couple in the minors."

"I hope you'll have a chance to hit many more." If Tyler's voice was any indication, it wasn't a particularly fervent hope of his.

Having scolded myself for my belligerent behavior in O'Malley's station house, I was determined to be more discreet and mature. But it wouldn't be easy to hide my distaste for Tyler—especially knowing that he took payoffs from gamblers. After my initial hostility toward Karl Landfors faded, I had come to realize that he was telling the truth about Tyler. Landfors knew too little about baseball to lie convincingly. What he said about Hal Chase throwing games was true—I knew that for sure—so I figured he was right about Tyler and Arnold Rothstein. And there were those sporting friends of Chase at the Fourth of July doubleheader; they had to know somebody in the Red Sox front office to get that box—and Bob Tyler was in charge of the team's ticket sales.

Tyler announced benevolently, "I'd like to be able to

intercede on your behalf with Captain O'Malley. I want to see you keep playing ball."

"You've already helped. If you hadn't vouched for me, O'Malley would already have me in jail." Diplomacy—it made my stomach curdle.

With a wave of his ringed fingers, Tyler dismissed my gratitude. "I think I can do a lot more for you. In fact, I might be able to get you off completely."

"How?"

"If you remember, O'Malley thinks you killed Jimmy because of something to do with that body you found here. And of course he still thinks you might have been responsible for that." Tyler paused. I held my tongue. "I was disappointed that you didn't take my earlier advice about not discussing the matter. I know you talked to Jimmy about it. Maybe you argued with him—that's what O'Malley seems to think. Now, if you were to tell me exactly what you and Jimmy said, then maybe I could convince O'Malley that it was just a harmless conversation."

I hesitated. Tyler tried to convince me with an unconvincing fatherly tone. "Mickey, I know we don't know each other very well, but I can assure you, I am the best friend you could possibly have right now." Still dejected from the realization that I would have no one to tell about my home run, I found his claim to being my "best friend" depressingly near to being true.

Okay, here's the story. "I'm sorry. I didn't know I wasn't supposed to talk to Jimmy *at all*—he already knew what happened, so I thought it was all right. He didn't say much about it. I asked him if anything developed—did they catch who did it or were there any suspects, and he said not as far as he knew. Then he went on and on about when he was a player . . . with Syracuse and Baltimore, he said . . . he seemed to like to talk about his playing days, and I liked hearing about them—reminded me of the stories my uncle used to tell me about the old days. Let's see, Jimmy talked about the different rules back when he played, and some of the players he knew . . . That was pretty much it. So, yeah, I asked him if there was any news about the dead guy I found, but we didn't really talk about it. I didn't much want to—I was just worried about still being a suspect." There, now try to look witless and see if Tyler bought it.

He didn't. "Very well, Mickey. I'll pass that on to Captain O'Malley," Tyler said. Then he leaned forward and hissed, "Maybe he's more gullible than I am."

"I don't know—"

"Shut up. Look, I know you've been poking around in things that are none of your business."

"But I—"

"I said shut up!" Tyler slammed his cane on the floor in emphasis and glared at me with narrowed eyes. "What I can't figure," he growled, "is how such a smart ball player can be such a stupid man." I knew he meant me. And I knew I wasn't supposed to give him an answer. Tyler stared at me with a mixture of rage and bewilderment. "We pay you a good salary. We take you to more cities than most people see in a lifetime, and we put you up in hotels and give you meal money for restaurants. And we build a ballpark where thousands of hard-working people come to watch you play a game. There's a million guys in this country who'd give their left nut to be in your shoes!" Tyler shook his head. "And you want to throw it away because you can't learn to mind your own business."

I tried to looked ashamed.

Wagging a threatening finger, Tyler concluded, "From now till the end of the year, all you do is play baseball. When you're not at the ballpark, you stay home. If we're on the road, you stay in the hotel. You don't even go to any of your goddam movie shows. You understand?"

I nodded.

"Now get the hell out of my sight."

I did.

When I got home, I tried to salvage some sense of triumph from the game. With forced gusto, I told Mrs. O'Brien about my home run. She sounded happy for me, but it wasn't the same. She was no Peggy Shaw.

• • •

Bob Tyler did put a scare into me. But he also told me a few things.

He really wanted to find out how much I knew, how much Macullar told me. Maybe to assure himself—or Captain O'Malley—that it was safe for them to leave me free until the end of the season. It could be that there was some difference of opinion between Tyler and O'Malley, with O'Malley not interested in whether or not I played out the year for the Red Sox.

Perhaps O'Malley felt Tyler was being unfair. O'Malley did Tyler a favor, helping him clean up his mess at Fenway Park by moving Corriden's body out. Now O'Malley was left with a problem: an unsolved murder in his division. O'Malley could want a quick resolution, even if it means framing me, and Tyler might be holding him back.

It was also clear from what Tyler said that somebody was giving him reports on me: that I had spoken with Jimmy

Macullar, that I went to the movies, that I was still poking around for information. Somebody had been following me.

Whatever was going on, I had one thing in my favor that should keep Tyler and O'Malley from coming down on me prematurely: they didn't know that Macullar told me about Corriden's body being moved out of Fenway Park. I was sure they wouldn't let me remain free if they realized I was aware of their cover-up. They'd try to silence me immediately, perhaps permanently. Still, this advantage would expire at the end of the season. It was good only for giving me some time. It was enough to postpone their move perhaps, but not to cancel it.

Chapter Nineteen

"Mickey! Telephone!" For a small woman, Mrs. O'Brien could bellow louder than an umpire.

I raced downstairs. Fletcher? Or a Fletcher impersonator?

"Mickey? This is Peggy." The whisper wasn't Fletch's, but it didn't sound like Peggy either.

"Yeah?" I asked cautiously.

"I need to see you," the soft voice breathed. "It's urgent. I'm at the Majestic Theater—next to Jacob Wirth's. Do you know where that is?"

I still wasn't sure of the caller's identity. And I wasn't going to be set up again. "Who's my favorite movie actress?" I asked.

"What?" blurted into my ear. The whisper was gone, blown away in astonishment at my question. Then I heard giggling, and Peggy answered as if giving a secret password, "Mary Pickford."

"I know where the Majestic is. I'll be right there."

Back to an urgent whispering, she said, "I'm in the lobby. Hurry!"

Without a thought to changing my clothes or combing

my hair, I ran straight to the front door. But just before yanking it open, I remembered that somebody had been spying on me for Bob Tyler. I didn't want any more trouble from Tyler, and I sure didn't want to lead anyone to Peggy. I spun around, and flying past a startled Mrs. O'Brien, went out the kitchen door instead.

Staying off the street, I assaulted the backyard barriers of our neighbors, fighting my way around bushes and squeezing through hedgerows. I came out on Columbus Avenue, certain that I had eluded any observers.

It took five minutes of hard sprinting for me to reach the Majestic Theater. My hair was plastered across my forehead and rivulets of sweat trickled down my neck. I was wheezing for air as I entered the lobby.

Peggy was standing just inside, looking out the glass door. She grabbed my elbow and turned me around to face the door. "Over there," she whispered, pointing out the pane. She showed no signs of returning to normal behavior.

"Where?" I whispered back. "And why are we whispering?"

"The restaurant. Mr. Tyler is in there."

"Then he can't hear us, can he?"

"You never know who's around. *Look.*"

There was nothing to see that I could tell, but I looked across the street at Jacob Wirth's restaurant. "What is it I'm supposed to be looking at?"

"Just watch the door. Mr. Tyler's in there with another man. You need to see what he looks like."

We stood side by side staring out the glass, talking earnestly at the door. We must have looked ridiculous.

"*Why* do I need to see this guy?"

"I think he's—shhh! Here they are."

Tyler came out of the restaurant working a toothpick through his teeth with one hand and swinging his cane with the other. Behind him came a man who stood a head taller than Tyler—six foot six, easy. It wasn't his height that struck me, though. It was his outfit: checked lime green suit, vest open, yellow cap slung low over his eyes. He bit the end off a stout black cigar and spat it out. This was the man Hal Chase had been talking to in the box seats at Fenway.

"Do you know him?" Peggy asked.

I hesitated. "Uh, why? Should I?"

"I don't know. It's too bad his hat is covering his eyes. Do you think you could recognize him if you saw him again."

"I think so." I was sure I could, even if he wore different clothes and shaved his mustache. I clearly remembered his face from Fenway Park. And now I'd seen how tall he was.

"Okay." Peggy sighed. "We can let them go." As if we could have prevented them from going.

Tyler and his friend walked out of view. I touched Peggy's arm gently. "Please. Tell me what this is all about."

She bit her lip and nodded. "All right. Let's go back to my house."

I vetoed the suggestion. Not with Tyler and who knows who else around here. I was not going to attract danger in Peggy's direction. "I can't wait," I said. "Let's go inside."

I crossed the lobby to buy tickets for the movie. The ticket clerk eyed me with a quizzical look; she must have been watching Peggy and me at the door. I fished in my pockets and ordered, "Two, please."

"Be our guests," the girl said. "Just go right in."

Peggy had moved up behind me. "Thank you, Emma," she said. She plucked at my sleeve and we moved inside through the open door. "Emma's a friend of mine," she whispered. "She let me use their phone to call you."

We had no intention of watching the pictures, so I pointed to the back row and she said, "Fine."

Our seats were still squeaking from settling in when I demanded, "Okay. So what's going on?" I didn't have the patience to start with the *How've you been? You look wonderful* routine. Although I wondered about the former and noticed the latter.

Peggy tapped her lips with her forefinger and murmured to herself, "Where to start . . ."

"Wherever you like." Just please get started.

"All right," she said. Then the torrent began. "I was following Mr. Tyler. That's why I knew he was in the restaurant. And was with the tall man. And that's why I called you, so that you could see him—oh, maybe I should back up." I thought maybe she should. "Let's see . . . I read about Mr. Macullar being murdered in the paper. I suppose that's what started it. I didn't do anything after you were last over . . . I had the feeling you wanted to be left alone." She was right about that, but I didn't want to say so. And I couldn't contradict her convincingly, so I said nothing.

Peggy sighed and went on, "You said that Mr. Macullar told you about the body being moved—Mr. Corriden's body. So when I read he was killed—Mr. Macullar—I thought it could be because he knew about it. And then I realized that you knew about it, too. And I thought you could be in danger of the same thing." She showed a worried frown, then brightening up she said, "So I decided to do some investigating on my own."

"That was nice," I conceded. "What did you do?"

"Well, the obvious starting point was Robert Tyler." Why

was that obvious? She picked up steam as she rolled on, "Mr. Tyler already committed other crimes. Having the body moved—that's obstruction of justice. And he took bribes when he was the American League secretary—remember what Karl found out?" I nodded. Of course I remembered. I also noticed that she called every man *Mister* somebody except for that infernal Landfors—he was *Karl.*

"So I looked into Mr. Tyler and what he did when he was in Boston. And I found that he lives in hotels. *Two* of them."

"Two?"

"Yes, one is the Copley Plaza. He has a suite there—it must cost a fortune. And here's the odd thing: he also keeps a room at the Charles Inn."

I thought it odd for anyone to need two places to live in the same town. Peggy made it sound so meaningful, though, that I expected I didn't quite grasp the full significance of her finding. "Why is that the odd thing?"

"It's a shabby hotel, almost falling apart. It doesn't fit him at all. And he keeps it under a false name. An alias. Robert Smith."

"Huh. Which one does he live at?"

"The Copley. He uses the Charles only now and then. For entertaining, uh, young ladies. Inexpensive young ladies."

"Oh. How do you know that?"

"From the desk clerk. I followed Mr. Tyler a few times to see where he spent his time and whom he associated with. Two days ago, I followed him to the hotel and waited outside until it was obvious he was staying the night. I went back this afternoon, and described him to the desk clerk. He thought I was looking for Mr. Tyler—he seemed to think I was there to, uh, meet him. The way that clerk leered at me, I wanted to slap him. Anyway, he gave me Mr. Tyler's name as Mr.

Robert Smith, and the room number, and of course he revealed the reason for the room."

Peggy slowed her speech. "I was walking out of the hotel . . . and Mr. Tyler came walking up with that man . . . I wondered why he would be bringing a man to his trysting place. And then I thought: well, maybe he keeps the room for another reason, too—to meet people he wouldn't want seen at the Copley Plaza. People like that Mr. Rothstein or Mr. Chase that Karl told us about.

"So I went back in, past the clerk and upstairs to Mr. Tyler's room. I listened through the door. They weren't in there long . . . I heard them coming to the door and I ran to the next room pretending it was mine and I was having trouble with the lock . . ." I was impressed; Peggy would make a better detective than me. As good a one, anyway. "I gave them time to get downstairs . . . then I went down, too . . . and I followed them outside. I stayed far enough away that I couldn't hear what they were talking about. When they went into Jacob Wirth's, I figured they would be eating dinner, and there would be enough time for you to get here. To see the man with Mr. Tyler."

"But *why* did I need to see him?"

"Oh! Because you're in *danger.* What I heard in the hotel room—let me get this exactly right—yes, I have it. I heard Mr. Tyler say, *'I called Rothstein. He says if the—'* I'm going to say this exactly as I heard it, *'if the bastard keeps stirring up trouble, you're supposed to take care of him.'* Then the other man mumbled something that I couldn't make out. But Mr. Tyler's answer to him was *'No, not a warning. He's had plenty. Take care of him for good.'* "

Chapter Twenty

I was determined to make sure of one thing: that I wouldn't let Peggy get into trouble for my sake.

Only one way to prevent it came to mind.

Peggy would have to decide on her own to stay out of the Corriden and Macullar cases. I would just have to help her reach that decision. I didn't like it, but there seemed no other choice.

I called Peggy from Mrs. O'Brien's. Using the phone was cowardly, but it was also a safeguard. I didn't believe what I was going to say, and didn't want my face to give away what I really felt.

She picked up on the second ring and sang, "Hello-o-o?"

"Peggy, this is Mickey."

"Oh! I'm glad you called. I had an idea—"

"No! No more ideas!" I snapped. There was silence on her end. Then, in close to the same tone that Tyler had used on me, I poured it on slowly and emphatically. "No more investigating, no more following people—nothing. That's man's work. Playing detective is no kind of thing for a girl to be doing." There, I'd said it.

"Is that a fact?" she asked softly. The receiver suddenly felt cold in my grasp.

"That's right it's a fact. I can take care of myself. I'm not going to have you running around trying to protect me."

"Well. I didn't realize you felt that way. I suppose there's nothing left for me to do then but wish you luck. Good luck, Mr. Rawlings. And goodbye." The soft click that followed left a deafening echo in my ear.

• • •

It was as if the World Series had come a month early this year. Or more like the World Series and a heavyweight prize-fight and the Fourth of July all rolled into one grand extravaganza. The event: Walter Johnson and Smoky Joe Wood facing each other in a Friday afternoon baseball game at Fenway Park.

This season of unprecedented winning streaks would reach its pinnacle on September 6 when Walter Johnson came to town. Johnson had put together a win streak that ended at sixteen in August, good enough for a new American League record. But Joe Wood was still rolling along with thirteen straight. The public clamored to see Johnson and Wood go head to head, to see Johnson defend his month-old record. Jake Stahl gave in to the fans' wishes—perhaps as part-owner of the Red Sox he was eager to see the ticket sales for such a match. Wood was originally scheduled to pitch Saturday's game, but Stahl moved him up to Friday to face Johnson with one less day of rest.

The buildup during the days before the big game blew the Olympics, the presidential race, and everything else out of the newspapers. Writers filled their columns with endless profiles of the two pitchers. Statisticians put together lists comparing the men, not only their pitching records, but height, weight, arm length . . . It was Smoky Joe Wood the challenger going up against reigning champion Walter Johnson the Big Train. Was this going to be a baseball game or Jim Jeffries versus Jack Johnson?

As the day of battle drew closer, the city of Boston was absolutely crazed with excitement and anticipation. I caught some of it—a *lot* of it—myself. It was a welcome break from the thoughts and fears of murder that lately occupied too much of my attention.

I became fixated on the upcoming game, and decided that I wouldn't be able to stand the torment of watching it from the bench. I wanted, more than anything else in the world, to get a chance to hit against Walter Johnson.

It wouldn't matter what happened afterward. If O'Malley and Tyler succeeded in framing me for killing Jimmy Macullar, so be it. If this game lived up to expectations, it would be an historic one, and if I played in it, I'd have my niche in history.

I was so desperate to get into the game, that I went to Stahl's office to let him know how I felt. Through Jake's open door, I saw that he was alone at his desk reading a newspaper. I knocked to get his attention.

"Yeah?"

"Uh, Jake . . ."

Stahl looked up. "Yeah, kid?"

"This game with Washington . . . well, I been hitting pretty good lately . . . got that homer off Ed Walsh. I *really* want to get in this game . . . I've never been up against Johnson before . . . and, well, if you play me you'll get everything I got." I felt silly for begging to get into a ball game.

Stahl didn't respond as angrily as he had to Billy Neal's demand for more playing time. Of course, I asked a whole lot nicer than Neal had. Stahl smiled and said, "You *always* give a hundred percent, kid. That's why I want you on my team. Thing is, a hundred percent of you is about a quarter of Tris Speaker."

Though probably accurate, I felt hurt by that evaluation and Stahl must have noticed. In a kinder tone he said, "It just isn't enough, Mickey. I've got to go with the regular lineup in this game. Fans want to see the starters, and they *are* our best chance to win."

"It wasn't *Speaker*'s spot I was asking for. I don't have to start . . . I just want one at bat against Johnson. Just one."

Stahl thought a bit. "If I can, kid. We'll see how the game goes. If something comes up, I'll try to put you in."

"Okay. Thanks, Jake."

I left speculating on the "somethings" that could come up and give me a chance to get in the game. Let's see . . . one of the starters could get knocked unconscious by a Johnson fastball to the head . . . or maybe break a leg sliding into base. Hmm, not very promising.

Friday finally came, and brought with it the largest crowd that the young ballpark and this young ball player had ever seen. Fans overflowed the stands and filled the perimeter of the field. Along the outfield fence, thousands of spectators lined the wall in fair territory. A rope was strung in front of them to mark the limit of the shrunken playing field.

The players even had to relinquish the dugouts to accommodate the deluge of fans. Along the sidelines, just a couple of feet from the base paths, the two teams sat in folding chairs, pressed from behind by the crowd. There was almost no foul territory; the starting pitchers had to throw their warm-ups on the outfield grass.

In this atmosphere, feverishly charged with expectations and hopes and anxieties, Smoky Joe Wood took the mound to face the top of the Senators' batting order. The duel of the century was underway.

With eager spectators crowding the field from every direction, I had a momentary flash of fear, wondering what their reaction would be if Wood and Johnson succumbed to the massive pressure and were knocked from the box. Would we have a riot of angry baseball fans?

Both Smoky Joe and the Big Train quickly made it clear that I needn't have worried. If anything, the intense pressure simply added to the speed of their fastballs and the sharpness of their control.

Joe Wood had a baby face that a few years ago allowed him to pass for female as the star pitcher of the *Bloomer Girls* barnstorming team. He also had a dynamo for a right arm, which he used now to snap lightning-bolt strikes across home plate.

Walter Johnson was a physical curiosity, with stretched out, dangling arms—it looked as if he could scratch his toes without bending. When he threw, his right arm would rapidly unravel like a long uncoiling watch spring as he propelled fastballs past our batters.

I'd never known a game to be so totally absorbing. Every fan and every player hung on each pitch. The entire stadium hushed each time the pitcher went into his windup. Through the silence, one could then hear the *whizzz*—perhaps audible, perhaps imagined—as the ball hurtled to the plate. Even from the bench I felt drained from total involvement.

Through five innings, the contest was locked in a scoreless tie. Neither pitcher looked to be tiring. On the contrary, they made the early innings look as if they had been only warm-ups.

In the bottom of the sixth, the crowd itself was involved in a critical play. Tris Speaker got hold of one of Johnson's fastballs and knocked a drive into the outfield. The ball carried into the overflow of fans, and was declared a ground rule double. Duffy Lewis then followed with a legitimate double to drive Speaker home and give Joe Wood a 1–0 lead.

Johnson got back on track to strike out the rest of the Sox hitters and end the inning. There was no more scoring through the next inning and a half.

Jake Stahl led off the bottom of the eighth, with Rough Carrigan up next. Stahl had only a brief stay in the batter's box while Johnson threw three quick vaporous strikes past him.

Stahl came back to the Red Sox seats fuming. Carrigan went up to the plate and Larry Gardner hopped out of his chair to go on deck. Stahl waved him back down and barked, "Rawlings! You're up for Gardner." As I walked past him to get my bat, Jake growled at me, "Here's your shot, kid. Let's see if *you* can hit the stuff that son of a bitch is throwing."

From the bat rack, I chose Mabel. I hadn't touched her since May. She felt good, her hickory wood hard and sleek in my grip. I squeezed her tight, and felt her strength flow into my arms.

After Carrigan struck out, I walked slowly to the batter's box. I wasn't worried about the final outcome of my turn at bat; since Johnson was mowing everybody down, there would be no humiliation in adding one more to his strikeout total. I walked deliberately because I was bracing myself for the way I planned to bat against him.

I took my stance with no intention of swinging at the first pitch. I wanted a good close-up look at just how fast Walter Johnson really threw a baseball before complicating things by trying to swing at it.

I saw Johnson go into his motion and unleash that infinite right arm. Then I heard the catcher's mitt go *Pop!* and Billy Evans yell, "Strike!" Wait a minute, here. I missed something. I was supposed to *see* the ball go past me . . . Did I blink or something?

I stepped back out of the box and quickly decided that, for lack of any other plan, I would carry through with my original scheme. I moved up as close as possible to the plate, my toes just an inch or two away from it. Then I leaned over and crouched low. In that position, a fastball that would otherwise be a strike, letter-high on the inside corner, would instead blast into my left ear and exit my right.

With this batting stance, the strike zone was effectively reduced to one-quarter its usual size. I still wouldn't necessarily be able to see what I was swinging at, but with the smaller area, there was at least a greater possibility of the ball hitting the bat.

It was pretty common knowledge that Walter Johnson's only fear was that he might someday kill somebody with his fastball. I felt slightly guilty about taking advantage of his compassionate nature, but this was my only chance—the only way I could compensate for the disparity in our abilities.

I steeled myself for Johnson's second pitch, putting my head and life at the mercy of his soft heart and fine control. He wound up, let loose, and I swung at the low and outside part of the strike zone. The ball grazed the bat for a foul tip. Well, that's a piece of it.

Oh-and-two now. He should be wasting this next pitch. Okay, so I'll be taking. Here it comes. Ball one! Way outside. Hah! Guessed right!

Now I've got to be swinging. I was tightening up in this cramped position, so I backed out once more. Okay, here we go. I crouched over again, ready to punch out at the ball. Johnson lets that arm unwind and here it comes. I take a rip, and . . . contact! A solid shot up the first baseline. Double written all over it.

The first baseman plunges in a desperate dive and—damn! He's got it. If the son of a bitch was left-handed I'd be pulling into second base, maybe third. Nope. Just a loud third out.

Well . . . It *was* a helluva shot—and it was off Walter Johnson.

The game ended with the 1—0 score holding up for Joe Wood. He could break Johnson's record now with three more wins.

The locker room celebration after the game was surprisingly mild. We were more relieved and relaxed than boisterous. It was the biggest game most of us had ever played in, but we were all too drained from the intense pressure of it to have much energy for horseplay.

Jake shook me up when he came over with a furious look on his face. In a loud angry voice that could be heard by everyone, he demanded, "Who the hell taught you how to bat? Sticking your head in the strike zone . . . you're goddam lucky Johnson didn't kill you out there!"

Then, with a laugh that made it was clear he was only pulling my leg, he said, "That took balls, Mick. Way to go." I tried not to, but I could distinctly feel myself puffing up a bit—yes, down there, too—at the compliment.

Chapter Twenty-One

The morning after the big game, I realized I was wrong. It still mattered very much what happened to me.

The first thing I did after I rolled out of bed was check the *Boston American*, skipping to the sports page and the box scores. There I was: *Rawlings*—1 at bat, 0 hits, 0 runs scored. It read like the epitaph of an utterly fruitless endeavor.

That summary didn't convey the tense thrill of that one at bat—the mental skirmish with Johnson, the physical hazard of putting myself in the path of his fastball, the gratifying jolt of meeting the ball with the meat of the bat. Next time I faced Johnson, I'd tag another line drive off him—harder. And it would fall in for something that looked more substantial in the box score. Next time . . .

Jimmy Macullar's words echoed through my brain, *I had my time in the big leagues and I was satisfied.* Those words didn't apply to me yet. I hadn't had my time, I wasn't satisfied. I wanted to play ball—for many more years. And to keep playing ball, I would have to solve the Macullar murder. Maybe Corriden's, too.

I didn't think I could do it alone. Not in the twenty-nine days that remained in the season—perhaps all the time that was left me before O'Malley and Tyler would start warming up the electric chair.

With enough time, I could do it by myself. But I didn't want to risk racing the calendar on my own. I knew one person who might be able to help me—if he would be willing. And if I could find him.

I spent the afternoon in the Boston Public Library. I'd left home by the front door; it didn't matter if I was being followed—how could Tyler object to a trip to the library?

In the reading room, I spread out all the New York newspapers they had. Flipping through page after page, I could find no Karl Landfors in any byline.

An elderly man came up to me and asked, "Are you reading *all* of these?"

"No, I'm finished." I handed him the paper I had just leafed through, then pulled it back. "Sorry, I'm *not* finished. Be done in a minute." The man scowled as I flipped to the sports page. It wasn't there. "Here, I'm done with this one." Somewhat placated, he took it and walked away muttering something about a hog.

Next paper, sports page, an article on the Highlanders. There! *by Fred Lieb.* Back to the front page for the name of the paper: *New York Press.*

• • •

The Red Sox were in New York, on the last Eastern road trip. Then a home stand, a final trip to the West, finish the season at home, and then the World Series. Would my arrest follow next? The gun that killed Macullar planted in my room and O'Malley there to "find" it? . . . *it'll turn up in your possession.*

The first game of our series against the Highlanders was scheduled for one in the afternoon. Billy Neal was still asleep when I quietly left our room and ducked out of the hotel by a service door.

I had breakfast at a delicatessen, then took the subway downtown to look for Spruce Street. I found it between City Hall and the Brooklyn Bridge, and soon located the skyscraper I was seeking.

A directory in the lobby listed the floor I wanted, and after the longest elevator ride of my life, I stepped out into the chaotic city room of the *New York Press*. One vast open space was filled with reporters typing at their desks, copy boys scurrying through the aisles, phones ringing, ticker machines clattering, editors bellowing.

I stopped one harried copy boy and asked directions to Karl Landfors. He pointed to the furthest corner of the room, where the activity was at a slower pace.

Landfors didn't see me as I approached. He was tucked away, out of the mainstream of the room, at a small chipped desk that bordered a storage area. Cartons of typing paper were stacked in a low wall behind him. Obviously, Karl Landfors was not a bigshot. That made me feel better about him.

Holding my hand way out in front of me, I spoke to get his attention. "Karl?"

He appeared startled when he looked up and saw me. "Rawlings?"

My hand felt heavy and clumsy sticking out unnoticed. "It's Mickey, please. I want to apologize. About when we met before . . . I behaved like a jerk."

Landfors visibly relaxed, finally saw my hand, and grasped it. "Well, I behaved like an ass, so I guess we're even." He offered me a seat, and then looked around to see if he could find one. Grabbing a chair from an unoccupied desk, he placed it across from his and I sat down. He seemed very aware of the humbleness of his furnishings. I tried to pretend I didn't notice.

"You're probably wondering why I came here," I said.

"I think I can guess. You want to ask me about Peggy."

I reddened and quickly corrected him. "No. That's not it. Actually, I'd appreciate it if you wouldn't tell her anything about me being here."

"Oh— Well, as you wish."

"You dug up some dope on Bob Tyler. There's no way *I* could have found out that stuff. I have no call to ask you for help, especially after the way I acted at—the last time we met—but, I didn't kill anybody. And that doesn't seem to make any difference to the police. They say I killed another guy now—Jimmy Macullar. I think Tyler might be holding the cops off until the season's over, but that's only a few weeks away. If I don't prove what really happened by then, I'm going to be framed for it. I've found out some things on my own, but there's a lot more to do and I don't have much time. You know how to get information. What I want to ask is: Could you get some for me?"

Landfors looked interested. "I could try. After all, we do have a mutual friend"—I felt myself going red again—"uh, sure, I'll try."

"Thanks."

"Landfors! Where the hell's that Debs piece?"

Landfors yelled back to what I assumed was an editor, "Fifteen minutes!" To me he said, "I'm sorry, Mickey, I have to get this article done right now." He sounded dejected. "The *Press* is supporting Teddy Roosevelt. So they run hatchet jobs on the other candidates—mostly Woodrow Wilson, but they like to take shots at Taft and Eugene Debs, too. They think it's funny to make me do the Debs story—I'm the only Socialist here. My editor will have to do the slanting though; I'm writing a straight piece. Anyway, can we get together later?"

"Sure. I have an afternoon game at Hilltop. How about tonight?"

"That'd be fine. Why don't you call me after the game? I'll be here."

"You're on. It might be late, though. I have to get out without anyone seeing me."

"I'll wait."

• • •

After the game, and some evasive maneuvers that may or may not have been necessary, I met Landfors for dinner at a small German restaurant. Our choice of meeting place was a poor one for discussing crime-solving. The grandmotherly waitresses, homey atmosphere, and simple hearty food were suited for friendly good times, not discussions of murder.

Over steaming plates of red cabbage and knockwurst, with steins of dark beer close at hand, Landfors and I worked stiffly on some conventional conversation before embarking on the specifics of the murder cases.

"How was the game?" he asked.

"Good. We won three-two."

"Did you play?"

"No. Did you get your article done?"

"Yeah. Then they butchered it, just as I expected."

"Why do you stay there?"

"The paper was pretty good until a couple of months ago. Then Frank Munsey bought it to give Roosevelt a newspaper forum in New York. I figure maybe Munsey will sell the paper after the election, then we can back to reporting the news again. Besides, the job is pretty much just to pay the rent. It's my book I'm really interested in. I should have it finished by next year."

I was impressed. "You're writing a *book?*"

Landfors nodded. "Yeah, it's like—do you know who Upton Sinclair is?"

"Sure, he wrote *The Jungle,* right?"

It was Landfors turn to be impressed—well, not impressed, actually he looked surprised. "Yes. You've read it?"

"No, I just heard about it." That seemed to better fit his expectations.

"Well, I'm writing something similar to *The Jungle,* except it's about the garment industry."

"Oh." I couldn't make myself sound interested, but Landfors didn't seem to notice.

"You remember the Triangle Factory Fire last year?"

"I heard about it."

"Well, I was *there.* I had to cover it for the *Press.* The worst thing I've ever seen in my life. The factory was up on the tenth floor, and it was a complete blaze. When I got there, burning people were falling down onto the sidewalk.

"The girls who ran the sewing machines were trapped in the shop—no way to get out. Bastard owners had all the doors sealed so none of the girls could sneak out with a scrap of cloth or a button or anything. When they caught fire, the girls had to jump—it was the only way out.

"And they kept coming down. The worst thing was the sound when they hit: sizzle, thud. Again and again. Been over a year, and I still can't get it out of my ears. A hundred and fifty of them died.

"So I'm doing the only thing I know how to do: I'm writing about it. About all those damn sweatshops." Landfors had a ghastly look on his face, and I knew he was again seeing those women fall burning from the sky and hearing them land. I had experienced the recurrence of horrific events so many times in the last few months, that I knew exactly what he was feeling and sympathized with his anguish.

I decided Karl Landfors wasn't such a bad guy after all.

We sat silently for a while, letting the heavy food settle in our stomachs while we each pursued our own thoughts. Our plates were long empty and our steins newly full. We quietly belched up cabbage and sipped our beers.

Since Landfors had already raised a grim topic, I felt no inhibitions about bringing up the murders of Red Corriden and Jimmy Macullar.

I could tell Landfors was an excellent reporter. Though I was willing to reveal to him everything I knew about the cases, he managed to coax even more out of me than I thought I could give. He prompted me for details I omitted, and sometimes reworded what I said to give the events a perspective I hadn't seen before.

I told him the things I'd withheld from Peggy: the bat in my bed, the gunman who shot at me in Fenway Park, that I was being followed. And I reported what Peggy had heard: Tyler's order to kill me if I kept poking around. His eyes widened at these disclosures.

But it was when I told him what I had last said to Peggy that Landfors reacted most strongly. He squawked, "Oh my god!" Then he said, "It's a good thing you didn't tell her that to her face. There would have been another murder." He understood my motivation, though, and I again made him swear to say nothing to Peggy. I wasn't sure if I could trust him to keep his word—after all, he'd known her for years and had no obligation to me. But deep down maybe I wouldn't have minded if Peggy found out why I'd behaved as I had.

After everything was out, Landfors went over various parts of the complex tale. He seemed especially taken with my idea about Ty Cobb killing Red Corriden. "I read about Cobb attacking the fan in Hilltop Park," he said. "At the time, I thought if he weren't a baseball player he would have been arrested on the spot—he certainly *should* have been. I didn't know about that episode in Cleveland. Your theory sounds good, but do you really think he can be convicted? Even if you can get solid evidence, there are very powerful special interests who'll want to see him keep playing baseball."

"I don't know . . . I suppose I haven't really thought about it for a while. I guess it's pretty callous of me, but lately I've only been thinking about Jimmy Macullar's murder—that's the one *my* neck is on the block for."

"That's not callous, it's survival instinct. So: what is it exactly you want me to do?"

"One thing is to look into Bob Tyler some more. He's obviously one of the keys to all this. I'd especially like to know about his City Hall connections. Both Tyler and Jimmy Macullar said several times that Mayor Fitzgerald is a big Red Sox booster—it sounded like he and Tyler could be cronies. That really has me worried. If the whole Boston government is behind Bob Tyler, I have no chance at all in this."

"I'll check it out. Usually, Boston corruption is more on a neighborhood level. In New York, it's centralized: Tammany Hall controls the city and Wall Street controls Tammany Hall. Tyler could have O'Malley's precinct in his pocket but that's probably the extent of it. I'll see. Oh! You said Corriden's body was found in Dorchester. That's outside O'Malley's precinct, right?"

"Yeah, I guess it is."

"Let's check something out right now." Landfors hailed our waitress, "Gretel!"

She bustled over. "Strudel?"

"No. Well, maybe later. Can we use the phone? It's long distance this time, but the *Press* will pay for it."

"Of course. You know where it is."

"Thanks. C'mon, Mickey."

Landfors led me to a wall phone inside the kitchen. After a series of operators, Landfors got through to Boston. He held the receiver away from his ear so we could both listen. "I'd like to be connected to the police station in Dorchester," he asked.

"Which one?" the Boston operator's voice hissed.

"I don't know, how many are there?"

"Savin Hill and Fields Corner."

"Try Savin Hill."

"One moment please."

A male voice came through. "Division Eighteen."

"Hello, this is—Jack Landers. With the—*Times*. I'm calling to check up on a murder case. A fellow named Red Corriden—John Corriden—was found murdered in Dorchester back in April. I wanted to see if the case has been solved, or at least if there's been any progress."

"Mm—okay. You'd want to talk to Lieutenant Downes. He'd have handled it. Hold on, I'll transfer you."

"Thanks." Landfors winked at me.

"Downes."

"Hello, Lieutenant. This is Jack Landers with the *Times*.

I'm doing a follow-up article on the Red Corriden murder."

"Corriden?"

"Yes, he was killed back in April. Found his body under a railroad trestle, I believe?"

"Oh, yes. Corriden. Not much happening on that one."

"Could you tell me what you do have?"

"Not much to tell. He was beaten real bad—face was just about all gone. Didn't hardly look human anymore. Turned out he was a baseball player. Never did get a handle on who might have done it. Pretty much chalked him up as a mugging victim. That's about it."

"Any suspects?"

"Not a one."

"Leads?"

"Zip."

Peggy's wild idea about Corriden popped into my head. I nudged Landfors and whispered, "Ask who identified him."

"Lieutenant, could you tell me who identified the body?"

"Yeah, hold on a second. I'll check."

Landfors and I smiled at each other. So far so good.

"Here it is. He was identified by a Hugh Jennings. Says here Jennings was his manager."

"That's great. Thanks."

"What paper did you say you're with?"

"*Times.*"

"What *Times?*"

"Downes. Is that D-O-W-N-S?"

"No. D-O-W-N-E-S."

"Got it. Thanks for your help, Lieutenant."

Landfors hung up with a satisfied smirk. "That worked out well," he said. "It told us a lot. That cop just thought somebody was killed in his district. No attempt to conceal information, no hint there was anything shady going on. He's not in on whatever Tyler and O'Malley orchestrated. It could mean that Tyler's clout *is* limited to O'Malley's precinct. But I'll check it out. Anything else?"

"Just whatever you can find out about Bob Tyler. I have a *really* bad feeling about him."

Landfors's eyebrows perked up. "Do you think Tyler could be the murderer?"

"Well, I'm sure he *didn't* kill Corriden. When I first met Tyler—just after I found Corriden—he was dressed too clean and neat, no blood on him, no sweat, nothing."

"What if he was changing when you found the body?"

I shook my head. "Doesn't make sense. If there was time to change clothes, there was time to hide the body first. At least drag it out of sight." Landfors seemed satisfied that I was right about that.

Then I summed up my current thinking. "This is what I think happened: Ty Cobb killed Red Corriden for trying to cost him the batting championship. That left Bob Tyler with a murder in his new ballpark—and Tyler didn't want that, so he had the body taken away. But Tyler can't feel secure, because there's two people who knew somebody was killed in Fenway—me and Jimmy Macullar.

"I think Tyler's been having me watched, to see if I'm going to be a risk. That means he has somebody working for him."

"Any idea who his spy is?"

"It could be the man that Peggy and I saw with Tyler. Or it could be somebody on the team. But whoever he is, he's more than a spy. I think he killed Jimmy Macullar, on orders from Tyler."

"Because of what Macullar knew?"

"And because Macullar didn't like taking part in Tyler's cover-up—maybe he was going to expose it. Tyler wouldn't stand for that."

"So you think Tyler has a hired gun?"

"Yeah, I do. Oh—there is something else you can do. Whoever's working for Tyler, I think the first thing he did was put the bat in my bed—try to scare me into keeping quiet. That had to be done by somebody who knew how Corriden was killed. There were two players, Charlie Strickler and Billy Neal, who didn't join the club until the following day. At first, I didn't think it could be either of them. Then I realized they didn't show up at *Hilltop Park* until they next day—they could have checked into the hotel earlier."

"Tyler got these players just after Corriden was killed?"

"A couple days after, yeah."

"Suspicious timing."

"That occurred to me. But there *were* injuries on the club, and Tyler did tell me he was going to get some more players besides me. Anyway, I'd just like to know for sure if I can rule them out, but *I* can't ask around at the hotel—the whole team is staying there, and it's too easy for me to get caught. Could you find out when Strickler and Neal checked in?"

"Sure, I'll give it a shot. What's the name of the hotel?"

"The Union Hotel on 125th Street. Also: how would somebody get a key to my room?"

"I'll see if I can find out."

"Oh. One last thing. It's about Red Corriden. There could be one more person besides Ty Cobb who would have wanted to kill him: Jack O'Connor. Harry Howell told me O'Connor joined an outlaw league in California—it's not part of organized baseball, so it's not covered in the baseball papers or the guides. Can you check somehow where he was in April?"

"I could try. Let me get this down." Landfors took a notebook and pencil from his jacket pocket. "I have a friend who works on a paper in Sacramento. He might be able to check if O'Connor is still in California. Do you know *where* in California O'Connor went?"

"Not the city. But it would have been the California State League. They probably don't have more than a few teams."

"Okay, I'll do my best. It may take a couple of days . . . how about if I give you a call when I got something?"

"That'd be great. Thanks."

"Glad to. I have a feeling this could turn out to be interesting."

Chapter Twenty-Two

On Monday, back in Boston with an off day, I stayed in my room at Mrs. O'Brien's to await Landfors's promised call. The regular season was down to the final three weeks, and soon we would be facing the National League's champion in the World Series. This was a critical time for the Sox, and my play would be under greater scrutiny than ever. With the high stakes on my performance, I wanted to be as prepared as possible, so I used the time to make sure my equipment was in tip-top shape.

I first went over my glove, tugging and tightening the laces and checking them for tears. Then I gave the glove a light coat of oil to keep the leather soft and pliable.

The bats were next, and Mabel was the first one I pulled out of my bat bag. I'd decided she was the one I would use for the rest of the year. I sat on the edge of my bed and slowly rubbed her down with a ham bone from the kitchen.

With time still to kill, I decided to work on the rest of the bats—if Mabel cracked, I would need the backups. I reached into the bag and grabbed hold of another. The handle didn't feel like one of mine. I slid it halfway out of the bag and saw that it wasn't. The barrel was coated with something that had blackened but still contained traces of red.

I'd found the weapon that killed Red Corriden. In *my* bat bag. I let the bat drop back in the bag out of my sight.

Sliding to the middle of my bed, I pulled my knees up to my chin. I wrapped my arms around them and started to rock back and forth, trying to grasp what was happening here.

This was some kind of double reverse setup. It was the gun that killed Macullar that I was supposed to worry about. Now it's Corriden's murder weapon that turns up in my room. How soon would Captain O'Malley be coming to "find" it?

Well, I wasn't going to make it easy for him. The thing to do was hide the bat. But where? My room didn't have a lot of hiding places: a bed, a desk, and a bureau were the only furniture. I could destroy the bat—break it up, sneak the pieces downstairs, and toss them in the kitchen stove.

No, I couldn't destroy it. The bat was my first real evidence. It might help me make the case against Corriden's killer. I needed to keep the bat, but keep it hidden somewhere. Would it fit in back of a dresser drawer?

I rolled to the edge of the bed and picked up the bat bag again. Grabbing firm hold of the alien bat handle, I pulled it all the way out. I found I was able to look at it a bit more easily than I could when I'd first seen it in the Fenway Park tunnel—maybe because at that time I had also just seen the bat's bloodied target.

One of the first things I saw on the bat was the model: *Ty Cobb* was stamped next to the Louisville Slugger logo. Of course, that didn't necessarily mean the bat was owned by Cobb—probably a quarter of all bats in use were Ty Cobb models.

Looking closer, I saw some hairs matted on the dried

blood. Some of them buckled up out of the crusty mess. They were orange in color—an orange I had seen before. It suddenly wasn't easy to look at the bat anymore. I decided to hide it as quickly as possible.

My room was useless as a hiding place. Was there anywhere else in the house I could stash it? None that occurred to me—I was unfamiliar with most of the house and didn't want Mrs. O'Brien to see me wandering around with a bloody baseball bat trying to find a place to stash it. How about outside?

I went to my bedroom window and opened it all the way. Poking my head out, I could see no helpful hiding place near the window—no convenient tree, no vine-covered trellis. The lack of access to my window told me that whoever planted the bat in my bag hadn't used the window to sneak it into my room.

A flurry of beating wings directly above my head caused me to twist around and look up. A crow took off from the rain gutter on the roof. The gutter looked to be a fine container for a bat—as long as it didn't rain. I pulled myself to a sitting position on the windowsill with my feet inside and my body out. With a slight jump and a long stretch, I was able to reach the gutter and feel inside: twigs, dirt, and something disgusting left by the crow—but no water. A bat should be safe there.

I slid back inside and took out the bat again. To use it for evidence, it had to be protected. I pulled a pair of old socks from my dresser and slid one sock over each end of the bat. They didn't quite meet in the middle so I took a third sock, tore a hole in the toe and slid that one over the gap. Then I did the same with a fourth sock—partly for extra protection and partly because I didn't want to be left with an unmatched sock.

The bat wrapped up, I went back to the window and quickly deposited it in the gutter.

I sat back down on the bed. Waiting for O'Malley to show up, I tried to figure how the bat got in my bag. I couldn't see how anyone could have planted it in my room—no one could have come in through the window, and I couldn't picture anyone coming in downstairs and getting past Mrs. O'Brien. It was more likely put into my bag before we left New York. The problem was, I didn't know when. I just couldn't be sure when the last time was that I had seen the bag with only my own bats in it.

Wait a minute . . . Maybe it *wasn't* a problem getting past Mrs. O'Brien. What if Bucky O'Brien was the one in cahoots with Bob Tyler? It was Bucky who suggested I room at his aunt's house—maybe he even has *her* keeping an eye on me.

• • •

After a Tuesday afternoon game at Fenway, in which Bucky O'Brien lost to Cleveland but I prolonged my life by delivering two RBIs, I went home for the traditional stuffed cabbage feast.

No police had come to find the bat, and I couldn't figure it out. If it was planted evidence, why didn't O'Malley show up immediately? Why give me a chance to get rid of it?

Anyway, my own bats were now in the Fenway clubhouse, the one that killed Corriden was still in the gutter, and I was feeling a little safer. I'd even dropped the idea of Bucky and his aunt working for Tyler—other than that it would be convenient for them to spy on me, there was no reason to suspect them. And I was getting tired of suspecting everyone I met in the last few months.

Mrs. O'Brien was late getting supper on the table. Bucky and I sat in the parlor impatiently waiting to eat. Neither of us spoke. Bucky, I knew, was going over every pitch he made today and silently chewing himself out for every one he deemed a mistake. I was punishing myself with reviews of every mistake I made off the field this year. I wondered if I would get a chance to be washed up like Jimmy Macullar or if I'd get the early retirement Red Corriden had. Maybe I wouldn't have to worry about what I'd do when my playing days were over.

My train of thought worked its way out of my mouth, and I broke the silence. "Hey, Bucky, what are you going to do when you're through playing baseball?"

"So I lost the lousy game! Don't go putting me out to pasture, for chrissake."

"No, no . . . I didn't mean you. I meant—well, I was just wondering what guys do when they can't play anymore. Guys like Fletcher and Strickler. You know, it'll happen to all of us."

"Yeah, well, I'm gonna be playing for a long time. I got years left in me yet."

"I saw Harry Howell in St. Louis. Poor guy's a barber now. I'd hate to be a barber . . . How about Fletcher—what do you think he's going to do?"

"Don't know. Unless he can get paid for drinking. I don't know what else he's good at. Of course, that worked okay for Charlie Strickler—he's tending bar at the Beacon Hotel."

"I'd like to be a movie actor, I think . . . But I'll probably end up an ice farmer or something."

"A *what?*"

"Nothing. Just thinking out loud."

"Boys! Supper!"

An hour after dinner, Karl Landfors came through. I was back in my room when the phone rang, and halfway down the stairs by the time Mrs. O'Brien called my name, "Mickey! Telephone! It's long distance—from New York! Ah, here you are."

"Hello?"

"Hi, Mickey. It's Karl."

"I was hoping it'd be you. Come up with anything?"

"A couple things. First, the Union Hotel—that's a real dump, by the way."

"Yeah, I know. But it's better than most places we stay at. The good hotels don't take ball players."

"Huh. Anyway, Billy Neal and Charlie Strickler registered on April 29 at four P.M. That's about the time your first game at Hilltop was ending, right?"

"Yeah, I think so. So they *could* have gotten into my room, then."

"Easily, in fact. *I* got a room key from the chambermaid. Told her I was with the Pirates—they're in town against the Giants and they're staying at the Union."

The picture of scrawny Landfors being taken for a baseball player amused me. "Boy, if she believed *you* were a ball player, anybody could have gotten a key."

"Actually, she seemed skeptical—until I told her I played second base." Landfors paused to enjoy his little victory with that crack. Then he said, "You're right, though. It could have been anybody. Their arrival at the hotel just means that Strickler and Neal had the same opportunity as everyone else. Although I'm still suspicious about the timing of Tyler getting them. What do you know about those two?"

"Well, they were both with Red Corriden on the Tigers. Charlie Strickler was Corriden's roommate. They didn't get along, but it was no big deal, I don't think. And I don't think Strickler could have been working for Tyler, either—if he was, Tyler wouldn't have let him go."

"What about Billy Neal?"

"I don't think he'd be in on anything with Tyler, either. Neal isn't all that happy about being on the team, and he isn't quiet about it—I heard him giving Jake Stahl hell for not playing him enough. So Neal probably doesn't even *like* Tyler."

"You don't have to like someone to work for him—on or off the field. But from what you said, Neal's definitely in the clear."

"How's that?"

"If Tyler got him for purposes other than playing baseball, Neal would keep quiet. He wouldn't bring attention to the fact that he's not playing."

"Oh. That makes sense, I guess."

"Now: as to Bob Tyler. Nothing solid yet, but it might be good news. At least not bad news."

"What is it?"

"As far as I can find out, Tyler doesn't really seem to have any high-level political influence in Boston—"

"Then what's all his talk about Honey Fitz? Tyler makes it sound like they're tight as thieves."

"Apparently Fitzgerald is just a rabid Red Sox fan. Always has been, no matter who was running the club. There *might* have been some expediting of the building permits to put up Fenway Park, but that's about it—and I can't even confirm that. Tyler probably wants people to think he's close to the mayor just to enhance his own stature. That seems to be important to him—having people think he's a big shot.

"I've been trying to find out what motivates Tyler. Since he took those payoffs from Rothstein, I assumed it was money. Doesn't look like that's the case anymore. Mostly he wants respectability—especially to spite Ban Johnson. They didn't part amicably. Johnson didn't *officially* fire him, but that's what I'm told it amounted to. He forced Tyler to resign. So now Tyler is determined to show Johnson up.

"What this all boils down to is: I think you're probably right about Tyler keeping you safe until the season's over—how long is that now?"

"Twenty-one days."

"Ouch. That's not much. Anyway, Tyler seems obsessed with becoming World Champions—respectability comes with the title, and it will be the best way he can thumb his nose at Johnson. So he probably won't let anything happen to anyone who can help him win."

"Well, that's encouraging. At least I have three more weeks then."

"Yes, but don't be too encouraged. Like I said, that's not much time. Also, it's tough to prove a negative."

"What do you mean?"

"I couldn't *find* where Tyler had influence outside O'Malley's precinct, but that doesn't mean it isn't there—could be that I just couldn't find it. I *was* thorough, but I don't want to give you any false sense of security. Besides, if they want to frame you, they don't necessarily need any further influence. If they can get evidence planted on you, that's all they have to do to get you convicted."

"So I better find out what really happened to Macullar."

"*We* better. I'll do whatever I can to help."

"Thanks, Karl."

"No problem. Let me know if there's anything else you want me to do."

As I hung up, I was already conjuring up a new scenario. Ban Johnson *forced* Tyler to resign. Does that mean Johnson knew about Tyler taking bribes from Arnold Rothstein? Makes sense. He can't *fire* Tyler because he would have to give a reason. Johnson can't let the public know that the American League secretary was in league with gamblers, so he quietly gets Tyler to resign, expecting he'd be rid of him for good. Now Tyler is running the team that's sure to win the American League pennant. Johnson must be fuming. And maybe more than that.

Could Bob Tyler be the real target of the killings—with Ban Johnson behind them? Maybe Johnson figured that a murder at the new ballpark would hurt attendance, embarrass Tyler—even put him on the way to bankruptcy. But Tyler foiled the first attempt by moving Corriden's body out of Fenway. So Johnson's next target is even closer to Tyler: Jimmy Macullar. If this doesn't work, will Johnson go after Tyler directly?

Ban Johnson wouldn't commit murder himself, of course. He'd get someone else to do it. If I were Johnson, I know just who I'd get: Harry Howell and Jack O'Connor—promise to let them back in baseball. All they'd have to do is kill Corriden—somebody they already hated. . . .

This is crazy. Now I'm pretending to be league president and I'm planning murders.

• • •

A piercing caw outside my window woke me early in the morning. After a few minutes of grumbling about the unwelcome wake-up call, I remembered the bat laying in the gutter. And that I'd forgotten to tell Landfors about it.

There wasn't much light in the room; I thought it was because of the early hour. Then I rolled out of bed and saw that day had come, but the morning sky out the window was overcast with dark swirling clouds. My only hard evidence in the Red Corriden case was about to be soaked.

Still in my underclothes, I did my acrobatics on the window ledge and retrieved the bat from its hiding place. Since there no longer seemed to be an impending visit from Captain O'Malley, I now had the time to examine the bat more closely.

I carefully rolled back the socks that protected it. Other than the mess on its barrel, the bat was clean and fairly bright. It must have been nearly new when it was used to kill Corriden. I took a closer look at the blood and the hair, trying to ignore the fact that they were human remains and thinking of them only as "evidence." I spotted a thin white hair sticking out of the dark crust. Would Red Corriden have white hair?

Grabbing my razor from the washstand, I went over the patch of dried blood, scraping carefully and surgically extracting each hair. There were nine of them: five orange, two white, one brown, and one black. Laying them out straight, I could see that three of them were long—maybe four or five inches, much longer than a ball player would wear his hair. Something was wrong with my evidence.

The bone fragments! When I saw the bat in the tunnel, there had been bone fragments imbedded in the wood. I gently ran my fingertips along the bat, rotating it as I went back and forth, like eating a cob of corn. I felt nothing sticking in the wood. Bringing the bat to the window where the light was better, I ran my eyes over the bat the same way. There were no indentations from where bone fragments might have fallen out. This wasn't the bat that killed Red Corriden.

So why was it planted in my bat bag? And whose blood and hair had been left on it?

Another calling card, maybe. The bat left on my hotel bed in April, and now this one—one that had been used.

I carefully wrapped the hairs in a clean handkerchief and put them in a dresser drawer. Maybe they would still be evidence.

• • •

The Beacon Hotel wasn't on Beacon Hill or even on Beacon Street. It was next to Freeman & Son Fish Co., between T and Long Wharfs. On the clapboard front of the hotel were two signs: one proclaimed TRANSIENTS WELCOME, the other—twice as large—advertised BEER. I answered the call of the latter sign, and went into the hotel's bar room.

Charlie Strickler's new uniform suited him: green suspenders hoisted his trousers, the sleeves of his collarless shirt were rolled up above his elbows, and he wore a bar rag over his left arm like a symbol of office.

Strickler slowly drew me a draft, tilting the glass until it was almost full, then holding it upright to give it just the right head. He beamed with pride as he slid the beer in front of me. He was washed up as a ball player, but he was just hitting his stride as a bartender. "On the house," he said.

I wanted to be a paying customer, so I guzzled the first one, then ordered another. As Charlie refilled the glass, I thought maybe I'd have time for a third.

I didn't think of Strickler as a suspect anymore; I'd bought the explanation he gave me when I confronted him at Hanratty's. I knew some roommates could be real nuisances, but nobody gets himself murdered just for being annoying.

My only worry about being here was that Tyler might find out that I came to see him. But I was running out of leads, and needed to take the risk. I thought there was more Strickler could tell me about Corriden.

"This hits the spot, Charlie. Have yourself one on me." He immediately reached for the tap to accept the offer.

"Say, Charlie," I said. "When you were rooming with Red Corriden—"

"Come on, don't go asking me about him. That was a hundred years ago. I got another life now. Baseball gave up on me. Now I got other things to do."

"Just one question? That's all I'll ask."

"All right, one. But I don't like it, I won't answer it."

"Fair enough. I just want to know: was there anything particular that was bothering him? Somebody after him? Something like that?"

"Somebody after him? No, he never said nothing like that. But truth is, I didn't stay in the room much when he was around. And when I did, I ignored what he said. Damn kid was always nagging at me. About drinking too much, and playing poker and craps. Especially about the cards and dice. That kid would carry on about gambling like Billy Sunday preaching against liquor. I just had to stop listening when he'd talk at me. So . . . I don't know if anything was bugging him."

I kept my word and didn't ask any more questions. And Charlie Strickler didn't say anything more about Red Corriden. And then we had a few more beers and argued about who was going to be elected president.

Chapter Twenty-Three

For two months, I'd been convinced that Ty Cobb murdered Red Corriden. Suddenly a number of other contenders emerged with possible motives. And one of them knocked Cobb out of first place on my list of suspects.

Ban Johnson wasn't a serious possibility, of course. And Jack O'Connor was still an unknown; perhaps Landfors would find out something more about him.

Robert F. Tyler is the one who moved into the top spot. As Peggy said, he was already involved in a crime by having the body moved. And I'd figured he was behind Jimmy Macullar's murder. Now I found a motive for him to kill Red Corriden.

According to Charlie Strickler, Corriden was riled up about gambling—he was on some kind of crusade. Who at Fenway Park was involved with gambling? Bob Tyler, who took payoffs from Arnold Rothstein. I thought, somehow, Red Corriden found out what Tyler had done. Then he confronted Tyler on the Tigers first trip to Fenway. And Tyler took extreme measures to squelch him. That would give Tyler an even stronger motive for having the body moved, and for having Macullar killed to complete the cover-up. And for having me killed if I kept nosing around.

That's what I thought. But the only thing I could be really sure of was that Red Corriden didn't kill Jimmy Macullar.

• • •

Since the Red Sox already had the pennant sewed up, Stahl decided to let some of the regulars take a rest before the World Series. I was to play second base during the short road trip to Chicago and Detroit.

The three Chicago games were unmemorable. I played mechanically, my thoughts on the Corriden and Macullar murder cases, my mind laboring for ways to get proof. I had uncovered motives, I had developed theories. But I had found no hard evidence.

And by the time the Chicago series was over, my latest theory bit the dust. I was already certain that Bob Tyler hadn't killed Corriden himself. Now I realized that if he had someone else kill Corriden, he wouldn't have allowed it to be done in Fenway Park. So it wasn't Tyler.

Ty Cobb was back atop the suspect list.

Smoky Joe Wood pitched our first game in Detroit, going for seventeen wins in a row and sole possession of the American League record. The game ended up close, but Wood just didn't have his best stuff. The Tigers hit him for six runs while the Sox could come up with only four. The loss left him in a tie with Walter Johnson for the A. L. record.

The rest of the games were pretty routine. Ty Cobb did come down to second base a few times—safely, but never head first. And my legs stayed intact.

I spent most of my time between games trying to make

the most of what seemed likely to be my last chance to investigate the Corriden case. With time running out on me, I paid little heed to whether or not I was followed, and talked openly to Detroit ball players. I asked what they knew of both Red Corriden and Ty Cobb. The exact responses varied, but the essence of their content could be summed up by "good kid" and "son of a bitch," respectively. Nothing useful.

After the second game of the series, I sought out Hughie Jennings's office. Walking through the corridors of Navin Field, I grimly imagined Red Corriden in the runways of Fenway Park.

Jennings looked out of place behind a desk. I couldn't picture him anywhere but in the third base coaches box, his orange hair and freckles ablaze, spurring on his team with the rebel "Ee-yah" yell that gave him his nickname. I asked him straight out what I wanted to know: how could he be sure that the body he identified in Boston was really Corriden. He seemed to think the inquiry a strange one, but he didn't hesitate to answer. He said the corpse was difficult to look at but easy to identify: he knew it was Corriden by a distinctive spike scar on the left leg.

That wasn't a big help to the investigation, but it was worth tying up a possible loose end. To my surprise, I felt no satisfaction in finding that Peggy was wrong about the body not being Corriden.

During our last night in Detroit, I lay disconsolate in my hotel bed, wondering what to do next. Fourteen days left in the season, and I was completely out of ideas. It's bad enough to see time ticking off so quickly, but to let it pass without knowing how to make use of it was exasperating.

Billy Neal was still up, playing his usual game of solitaire. Snapping the cards, placing jack on queen, ten on jack, nine on ten . . . I resented seeing someone so pointlessly killing time. Didn't he know how valuable it could be?

"Playing solitaire the only thing you ever do, Billy?"

"Nope. Sometimes I play poker, sometimes bridge."

"Oh yeah. Didn't you play with Clyde Fletcher once?"

"Mmm—yeah. A couple years ago, I guess."

"Fletch told me Hal Chase was in the game—and he cheated."

"Yeah, he sure did. Didn't cheat by himself, though."

"He didn't?"

"No, it was a *bridge* game—almost impossible to cheat without a partner. Fact, it was your pal Fletcher who was in on it with him."

"Fletcher? Are you *sure?"*

"Hell, yeah. I should know, I lost a bundle."

Fletch. Jeez.

• • •

I listened intently to Billy Neal's breathing, waiting for it to turn into the slow regular rhythm that would indicate sleep. For the first time, I'd have preferred a roommate who snored. I knew who the murderer was, and needed to call Karl Landfors.

After I was convinced that Neal was asleep, I padded out of our room in my stocking feet and went down to a public phone in the lobby.

Landfors's number was answered with a groggy, "Yeah?"

"Karl, this is Mickey."

"What the—do you know what *time* it is?"

"Yeah, real late. Listen, I know who killed Jimmy Macullar—*and* Red Corriden. And if you help me, I think I can prove it."

"Really?"

"Yeah, I got it solved. Look, we're leaving Detroit first thing in the morning. I should be back in Boston by Thursday. Can you be there—in Boston?"

"Mmm, I think so. Yeah, sure, I should be able to get away."

"Great! When we get together I'll lay it all out for you. There's one more thing: do you know any bookies in New York?"

"No . . . I don't think so."

"Can you find one?"

"Find a bookie in New York? Gee, there's a tough assignment."

"I'll take that as a yes. See if you can put a bet on Joe Jackson to win the batting championship."

"What?"

I repeated, slowly, "Find out if you can put a bet on Joe Jackson to win the American League batting championship. Got it?"

"Yeah, yeah, I got it. Oh! Wait a minute. I heard from my friend in Sacramento: Jack O'Connor's been playing for Alameda in the California State League this year. He's sending me some box scores. They show O'Connor was playing in Bakersfield when Corriden was killed. And he was in Sacramento when Macullar got it. It couldn't have been O'Connor."

"Yeah, I know it wasn't him. It wasn't Ty Cobb, either."

Chapter Twenty-Four

I slowly nursed my second beer, jiggling the glass now and then to give it a bit of a head. I had willingly exceeded my self-imposed limit of one brew, but would not be so reckless as to have more than two.

Hanratty's was starting to fill up with an after-work crowd. The bar was elbow to elbow, and most of the tables were occupied. Each time the door swung open, my stomach tensed with expectation, then slumped with disappointment when it turned out to be just another stranger stopping in for a drink. While my insides rose and fell on this roller coaster of nerves, I considered the prospects of the venture ending successfully. My confidence, already lower than it was when I explained the plan to Karl, continued to slip down with each passing minute. Everything would have to click together just right for this to come off—and so far this year, nothing had worked out smoothly.

When we met in the morning, I had given Landfors the handkerchief with the hairs I'd scraped from the bat. I was pretty sure that the hair and blood weren't a ball player's at all, or even human. Tabby, I thought. Somebody had killed a cat to present me with a bloodied baseball bat. Or maybe a dog—I hoped it wasn't a dog. Anyway, Landfors said he could get the hairs identified.

Finally, Billy Neal entered the saloon. This time my stomach didn't respond at all—maybe it was relieved that the waiting was over or exhausted from all the false alarms of the past hour. I waved and yelled, "Billy! Over here!"

He saw me, and came over to the table where I sat. I'd saved him a seat, which he slid into. "What's up, Mick? What did you want to see me about?"

"Uh—how 'bout a beer?"

"Sure, I could do with one."

I flagged a waitress, and ordered a draft for Neal. While we waited for her to bring it, I asked him what he thought about facing the Giants in the World Series.

"We'll beat 'em I think. They'll be tough, but we got a better team. In a short series you never know though."

"Yeah, that's true."

The beer came, and most of it quickly went down Neal's throat.

"I wanted to ask you about something, Billy."

"What's that?"

"Bob Tyler's filled me in on what's been going on."

"Yeah?"

"Yeah. I wanted to talk to you about it though. He said I could do pretty well for myself by going along with him. But I'm not sure about him—I don't know if I can trust him. He told me about your, uh, association with him. So I wanted to see if you thought he was okay."

"He's okay I guess. What did he tell you?"

"Jimmy Macullar. He told me about Macullar."

"Huh. What *exactly* did he tell you?"

"About how that business with Corriden needed to be forgotten. How Macullar should have kept his mouth shut about moving him out of Fenway Park. How it's to everybody's advantage to keep it from being found out. And: how certain things sometimes have to be done even if they are, uh, unpleasant."

"Yeah, okay. That's pretty much what I told Tyler. Some things just gotta be done. He was pretty pissed about Macullar."

"Seemed okay when he told me about it."

"Yeah, maybe he's coming around. I explained it to him, told him I had to—really wasn't no choice."

"And setting me up for it?"

Neal smiled. "Sorry about that . . . I figured you were nosing around too much, 'specially after you talked to Harry Howell. Tyler was pissed at me for that, too."

"He didn't want you to set me up?"

Neal looked around at the crowd. "Look, we can't talk about it with all these ears in here. How 'bout we go outside?"

I gave a glance at the table behind him and agreed.

Neal nodded toward the back door, and I led the way out into the alley. There were still a couple hours of daylight left, but the sun was below the roof of the bar; it left the cluttered alley in cool shadow.

I heard the door swing shut, and turned to face Neal. Before I could complete the turn, I was slammed by a hard jolting blow to the back of my head. Stumbling forward, I doubled the pain by knocking my forehead into a metal trash barrel. I crumpled to the cobblestones and blearily looked up at my attacker.

Neal quickly followed up on his shot to my head with a

sharp vicious kick to my left ribs. I could hear the snapping sounds of bones cracking, and felt my breathing suddenly constricted.

Billy Neal towered over me, red-faced and breathing heavily. I curled up to make a smaller target, and steeling myself for additional blows draped my right arm over my left side to diminish their force.

Long moments passed with no additional kicks or punches. Neal's breathing gradually became more even. I punctuated the silence by croaking in little gasps of breath as best I could.

Shaking his florid head, Neal finally puffed out, "Damn, you're stupid."

I could only groan in response. I was feeling that he was right about me being stupid. I *knew* this wouldn't go smoothly.

"Tyler didn't tell you nothing, did he?"

I lay there in silence, my brilliant plan as crumpled as my body.

Crack! Another hard kick—this time my arm took the brunt of it. "I said *did he?*"

"He told me some."

"My ass, he told you 'some.' If he did, you'd know that he didn't want you set up, *and* he didn't want Macullar killed, and he sure as hell didn't want Corriden killed."

"You killed Corriden?"

"Yeah, me." Neal crouched down on his haunches, and continued in a quieter voice. "That was a nice try, kid. You had me going for a minute there."

"Why? Why kill Red Corriden?" Every syllable I uttered caused excruciating pain, and I already knew why he killed him, but I desperately wanted to keep Neal talking.

Neal smirked. "Okay, what difference does it make . . . I'll tell you what happened." I could guess why it wouldn't make any difference to tell me, and shuddered at the prospect of one more body turning up behind the pub—or wherever Tyler might choose to relocate it.

"Really, it was self-defense, me killing Corriden."

"It was your idea to fix the batting championship," I wheezed. "Wasn't it?"

Neal sounded surprised, "How'd *you* know? Harry Howell tell you?"

I groaned a noncommittal noise.

Neal shrugged and said, "Yeah, that was my idea. I figured hell, people bet on who wins a game, so how about a bet on who wins a batting title? I ask Hal Chase about it, and he says sure, you can get a bet down on anything. Then he wants to know how I can fix it. I tell him Jack O'Connor's an old pal and it's no problem. Chase says great. He sets up the bet and finds the odds I get are real good. So then Chase wants in. He wants to get down a big bet. *Big.* And he tells me the fix better come off. And he's holding *me* responsible if it don't. Now this ain't something I want to hear, 'cause Chase got some *really* rough pals." I remembered Chase's friend in the green suit, the one who was walking with Bob Tyler.

"O'Connor and Howell—they in on the bet?" I squeaked.

"Nah. That's the great part: I don't tell 'em about the bet, just that it's to get back at Cobb for being such a bastard. So I don't even gotta give 'em a cut. Smart, huh?"

"Mm."

"Well, O'Connor tries to fix it, telling Corriden to play way back. But then the league finds out what Jack was up to, and Cobb gets the title anyway. So it's pretty bad: I'm out a bundle of dough, Jack and Harry get booted out of baseball, and Chase is royally pissed.

"But it don't turn out to be as bad as it could have. Chase knows he wasn't double-crossed by me, so he don't try to get me hurt. I figured it didn't work like I wanted, but no real harm done.

"Then this year, Corriden that stupid son of a bitch comes up to the Tigers. And he decides he's gonna make my life miserable. Seems he found out about the fix. Don't know how, but he did. And he knows I set it up. From opening day the kid's getting on me about it. He blames me and Chase for everybody thinking he's a cheat. So he threatens to squeal on us. Says we hurt his career, his reputation, all that crap.

"So we're on the first road trip in Boston, and he wants to meet me right after the last game at Fenway. He'll tell me what we got to do to make it right. I figure, okay, the kid wants a payoff. So we meet in the runway. Nobody around. I offer him a hundred and he gets mad. Not enough? How 'bout five hundred? No, no good. He gets hopping mad. You know what the dumb bastard wants? He wants us to *confess*. Clear his name, he says. If we don't, he's telling Ban Johnson. Hell, even if I'm willing, which I ain't, Chase would never go along with it. He'd set one of his pals to shut me up.

"So, it's self-defense, see? If this kid squeals, Chase is coming after me. And if I confess, he's coming after me, too Corriden didn't give me no choice. I pick up a bat . . . and that's it. Problem solved. It's his own damn fault."

"And Macullar? That wasn't Tyler's idea?" By now, I had caught on that it wasn't, but I wanted to prod Neal along Keep talking, Billy.

"*Tyler*'s idea! All he wants is everything peaceful. No

troubles in his nice new ballpark. And nothing that would get people interested in how he got where he is.

"Fact, him wanting to avoid trouble almost guaranteed I could get away with Corriden. Gutless son of a bitch was so worried about bad publicity, he had Corriden's body moved clear across town. So it looked pretty good for me, 'cause I could prove I was nowhere near where they moved Corriden to.

"Then Macullar kept making noises that he didn't like a 'cover-up.' The stupid bastard—you'd think a guy his age would have learned how to go along. I gave him a while, tried to talk some sense into him. But I couldn't trust him. If he decided to talk about Corriden being moved, then I could be on the spot again. So I figured I had to take care of him."

"Like you tried to take care of me in Fenway Park—you're the one who shot at me."

"If I shot *at* you, you wouldn't be here. Nah, I was just giving you a little scare." It *was* a little one, compared to how I was feeling now.

"You know," Neal said, "killing Macullar really got Tyler riled. 'When's it gonna stop?' he kept saying. Then he decides he's gonna get tough. Says one more guy gets killed, and he'll kill *me*. So that means you should be safe, kid."

I'm going to get out of this alive?

"Except, like I said, Tyler's gutless. And I figure two, three, what's the difference?"

Damn!

Neal cocked his leg back to unload another kick on me. I kept the arm he'd already smashed over my side, and turned my head to cover it with my other arm. *Crack!* I heard the sound, and braced myself for the pain I knew would follow in about half a second. Two seconds, three seconds . . . no pain. Am I dead?

"Mickey? You okay?"

I uncovered my head and, in agony, turned to answer the stupidest question I had ever been asked. "Never better, Karl. Long as I don't talk, breathe, or move, you dumb . . ." Oh, it hurt to talk—but my spirit felt considerably better.

Landfors had a massive grin on his face and a broken two-by-four in his hand. He stood triumphant over a collapsed Billy Neal.

"Don't look so damn pleased with yourself, Landfors. If Neal's dead you're gonna have some explaining to do. Where the *hell* have you been?" A numbing wave of weakness passed through me. I shouldn't have tried to speak. It took forever to get my breath back with the tiny nibbles of air I could take in.

"Sorry. I tried to follow you out the back door, but it started to squeak. Had to go out the front and work my way around. Thought for sure he was going to hear me creeping up."

"How much did you hear?"

"Enough. Heard him admit to killing Macullar."

"Good."

Landfors knelt down and put his ear near Neal's mouth. "He's breathing, he's okay." Pinching together a lock of Neal's hair, he used it to jerk his head up for examination. "Wow, helluva bump. I really clobbered this guy." Karl sounded as proud as if he had hit a home run. He released his hold and Neal's head banged onto the pavement—it made a similar sound to one I had heard in Fenway Park back in April, but this *thunk* had a sweeter ring to it.

"Is he out?"

"Cold."

"Go make the call."

"What about you?"

"I'll be fine. Hurry though."

"Yeah. Be right back."

Landfors hustled off. I felt queasy in my gut and dizzy in my head. Roaring bursts of speckled light began to erupt in my brain. I wasn't sure if I'd still be conscious when he got back.

Billy Neal let out a groan. Oh, damn. No, it's okay, he's still out. But I may soon be joining him. One more thing to do. I painfully dragged myself over to Neal.

• • •

I came to with Karl Landfors gently shaking my good arm and repeating my name. I looked at him but my eyes didn't focus close-up. They instead took in the two uniformed cops standing behind him. One was writing in a notebook.

"Mickey, you awake?"

With an effort that aggravated my headache, I was able to bring my eyes to focus on Karl. "Yeah, I'm awake."

The officer who was writing told Landfors, "Better take your friend here to a hospital. He don't look so good. We got everything we need for now. We'll be in touch to get your statements."

"Okay, good idea," Karl agreed. "Can you stand?"

"I think so. Legs weren't hurt, they should be okay." Karl helped pull me to my feet, then had to support me because I was too woozy to keep my balance. I felt better after looking down and seeing that Neal was still out.

"C'mon, Mickey. I explained everything to them. Let's get you to a doctor and get you looked at."

"Yeah, okay."

• • •

A broken right arm and three, maybe four, cracked ribs. That's what the doctor who patched me up said when we got to the hospital. He was worried that one of the broken ribs might have punctured a lung, so I had to stay overnight for observation.

Landfors came by the next morning. "How you feeling?"

"Better. Lung seems to be okay."

"Good. You look better. Of course you couldn't look any worse than you did last night."

"Mmm. Funny."

"Just trying to cheer you up."

"If you want to cheer me up, tell me what happened with the cops."

"Well, not much to tell. I called Division Eighteen from the bar and asked for Lieutenant Downes. He wasn't in, but they sent a couple of men out. They showed up pretty quick, and I told them that Neal confessed to murder—"

"*Two* murders. He admitted killing Red Corriden, too."

"Oh. I only heard him admit to Macullar. Anyway, one was enough for the cops to take him in. I gave them our names, and they took my address. I didn't know yours to give them, but I told them they could find out from the Red Sox."

"Did they say when they'd want to talk to us?"

"No, I guess they'll call or come by. Listen, Mickey, I talked to my editor this morning. He wants me back in New

York right away. I had a couple of questions for you, though. Does it hurt for you to talk?"

"It's not too bad."

"Well, I'm still not sure I understand how you knew it was Neal. Why wasn't it Fletcher?"

"Let's see . . ." I tried to put my explanation in a more coherent form than the way I'd first thought it through. "Well," I said, "when Neal told me Clyde Fletcher cheated at cards with Hal Chase, I thought maybe Fletcher *could* be the killer. When Macullar was murdered, I assumed the call I got wasn't from Fletch—it was somebody using his name to set me up. But then I realized it could have been both. It could have really been Fletcher *and* he was setting me up."

"Right! So what made you think it was Neal?"

"Two reasons. For one thing, Fletch and I had only been to Hanratty's once—so he's not going call it 'the saloon *where we used to go.*' That's if you go someplace regularly. But somebody who saw us there, like Billy Neal did, might think we went there a lot. That wasn't enough to eliminate him completely, though. Mrs. O'Brien might not have used his exact words, so I couldn't rely on that.

"Then I realized that Billy Neal had to be the one in cahoots with Chase, because Fletcher wouldn't have said anything to me about the card game if he had cheated."

"*Neal* said something about it."

"Yeah, but that was to cast suspicion on Fletcher. When Fletch told me about it, he didn't accuse anyone but Chase."

"Oh. But what's the big deal about a card game, anyway?" Landfors asked. "What does that have to do with anything?"

"I was looking for connections. See, I thought Tyler was desperate to keep his cover-up intact and had somebody kill

Jimmy Macullar. So I needed a connection with Bob Tyler. And that's where the card game comes in. Tyler was paid off by gamblers to keep Hal Chase playing baseball; Neal was in on a card scam with Chase. *There's* a connection with Tyler. Both Neal and Tyler knew Chase, both were involved in crooked dealings with him, so maybe Neal and Tyler knew each other through Chase.

"Once I started to think that way, other things seemed to fit. When I first came to Boston, Tyler told me there were other injuries on the club and he needed to pick up a couple more players—a pitcher and a first baseman. So why did he get Neal—a catcher? You don't use up a roster spot on a player you don't need. So I figured he wanted Neal for other services: to help him keep a lid on things, and to keep an eye on me."

"But it doesn't make sense! You said Neal made a fuss about not playing—why would he do that if he was hired for another reason? Why draw attention to it?"

"It wouldn't make sense to you, maybe. But it's real simple: when you're a ball player, you gotta play baseball." *I'd even play for a factory team,* Neal had said. *Got to keep playing ball.*

"Ah. So in other words, because he's a baseball player, he doesn't have to be sensible." I didn't expect Landfors to understand.

"Anyway," I said, "I think Tyler either knew or suspected that Neal killed Corriden. So he brought him to the Red Sox where he could control him: he had something on Neal, so he could force Neal to do his dirty work for him—I thought that included killing Jimmy Macullar, but I guess Neal did that on his own. Maybe now Neal will tell us exactly what the deal was with Tyler."

"That's another thing: how could Tyler find out it was Billy Neal, work out a trade to get him, and bring him from Detroit to New York in just a couple of days?"

"With Tyler's connections to Chase and Rothstein, he could have found out about Neal pretty quickly. And there was no trade: Tyler got Neal and Strickler for cash—that's an easy deal to make. Also, Neal didn't come from Detroit—the Tigers were in Philadelphia during our New York series."

"Huh. Well, what about Neal killing Red Corriden in the first place? How'd you figure that one out?"

"I already thought that Corriden was killed because of something to do with the batting race scandal. After I figured out that Neal was the one with connections to Hal Chase, I put some things together: Harry Howell said somebody suggested throwing the title to Nap Lajoie, Neal was with the Browns that year, and Neal had been involved in a gambling scam with Chase. So maybe Neal tried to fix the batting race to put a bet on it. Thing is, I never heard of betting on a batting title."

"That's why you had me put a bet on Joe Jackson to win it this year."

"Right. I wanted to make sure it could be done. By the way, I *didn't* ask you to put a bet on him—I said 'see if you could.' "

"That was ten bucks!"

"Yeah, well, you shouldn't bet on baseball. Anyway, I put together a couple more things: Corriden and Neal were teammates on the Browns in 1910, they were teammates on the Tigers at the start of this year, and Corriden was up in arms about gambling. So I figured he found out about the batting race being fixed; somehow, Billy Neal realized Corriden knew about it and he decided to shut him up.

"But, anyway, with all my figuring, and everything pointing to Neal, there still wasn't any hard proof—that's why I needed to get him to confess."

Landfors was incredulous. "I can't believe you figured it out."

"Well, I didn't figure everything out. I thought Tyler ordered Neal to kill Jimmy Macullar." That seemed to make Landfors feel better.

Chapter Twenty-Five

I was released after two days in the hospital. I was stiff and bandaged and some parts of my body had turned spectacular shades of green and purple, but I was going to be all right. The injuries wouldn't leave any long-term damage to my ball-playing career, and with Billy Neal arrested for killing Jimmy Macullar, my career wouldn't be ended by electrocution either.

I returned to Mrs. O'Brien's rooming house expecting to hear that the police had tried to contact me for my statement about Neal. The only message awaiting me was an official letter from Robert F. Tyler, Treasurer, Boston American League Baseball Club. I was dropped from the team. The letter called it an "unconditional release." My injuries meant that I couldn't contribute to the team, so my best friend Bob Tyler decided I wasn't worth keeping. A week earlier, that would have put me in a panic—I'd have worried that Tyler would let Captain O'Malley at me. But with the case solved, I should be safe.

I called Lieutenant Downes at the Dorchester station house to see what was up with Billy Neal. He said he didn't know what I was talking about. I suddenly didn't feel so safe.

Downes put me through to the front desk. The dispatcher checked his phone log for me: Yes, a call came in Thursday night; no, they didn't send anyone out—they called the Walpole Street station house to have them check it out.

"No! Why did you do that?"

"Standard procedure. It was in their district." Damn!

Next I called the Walpole Street station. Yes, they received a request from Division Eighteen to investigate a disturbance Thursday night. No, there were no arrests. There was no disturbance—it must have been called in by a hoaxer.

Jeez. This wasn't over.

And I was off the team—no reason for Tyler to keep O'Malley away from me. I could still take the fall for Jimmy Macullar's murder.

No! It was worse! Billy Neal was out there somewhere. Never mind O'Malley, *Neal* would be after me. I was going to be dead.

I was still too weak and in too much pain to have the energy to face more of this. As I fought down a tempting impulse to surrender and succumb to the panic that besieged me, I tried to review everything that had happened outside Hanratty's. The episode came back to me in flickering, broken scenes—partial images, fragments of words and sentences.

To help bring the memory into clearer view, I went back to the pub. Standing, teetering, in the alley, I reconstructed what had happened. There's the barrel where I hit my head . . . that's where I was laying when Neal kicked me . . . there's the spot where Landfors dropped Neal's head. The rest started to come back: the words of Neal's story, Karl shaking me to my senses, the two cops standing behind him. The cop—the one who was writing things down—that was the desk sergeant I had seen in O'Malley's station house!

It all came back to me, more vividly than I was comfortable with. There was something else to take care of . . .

My excursion to Hanratty's exhausted me; it took more effort than I should have expended in this early stage of my recovery. I went back home for needed sleep.

No rest came. Laying in bed, trying to sleep, I suffered through garbled daydreams and frightening nightmares, all of them bizarre fantasies populated by grotesque laughing images of Billy Neal, Bob Tyler, Tom O'Malley, Hal Chase, Harry Howell, and Ty Cobb.

More drained than when I went to bed, I got up and called Karl Landfors at the *Press* to tell him what had happened. He was thinking clearly enough to give me some sound advice: "Get your ass out of Boston. Come down to New York, and I'll put you up at my place."

• • •

A trolley took me and my luggage from Grand Central Station to the *Press* building.

Karl was working in his little corner of the city room. He greeted me with a big smile. "One of your worries is over."

"Really? What's up?"

"Read this. Came in this afternoon." He handed me a yellow sheet of paper. *Baseball player Billy Neal was killed yesterday in a hunting accident near Tannersville, New York . . .*

"You're kidding! A *hunting accident?*"

"If I were writing the story on this—don't worry, I'm

not—I would put 'hunting accident' in quotes. I made a couple of calls. Guess who owns a hunting lodge outside Tannersville?"

"Bob Tyler?"

"Close. His old patron. Arnold Rothstein."

"Wow. So Tyler had Rothstein—"

"Do him a favor. That's what I'd guess. Tyler had enough of Billy Neal."

"So he wasn't quite as gutless as Neal thought."

"Guess not. Maybe he was worried with the series coming up—wanted to make sure Neal wouldn't cause him any more problems. Must be a relief for you."

"The man in green!"

"What?"

"That's what Tyler meant! *'No, not a warning. He's had plenty. Take care of him for good.'* That's what he said to Chase's friend. He didn't mean kill *me,* he meant kill Neal!"

"Now the only thing for you to worry about is O'Malley trying to pin Macullar's murder on you."

"No, I don't think he can do that."

"Why not? He still has an open murder case—as far as the cops are concerned, Neal didn't do it."

"They don't have the gun. They can't plant it on me."

"They could have got it from Neal."

"Uh-uh. I have it." I opened my satchel enough for Landfors to look in and see the skinny, ugly revolver.

No one was near us, but he whispered, "What are *you* doing with that?"

"When you went to call the cops, after you knocked Neal out, I felt like I was going to pass out. I got worried that Neal might come to while I was out, and I remembered that

Macullar was shot and I was shot at. So Neal would probably have a gun on him."

"Why didn't you think of that before we went to the bar? We could have been killed!"

"Why didn't *we* think of it. Anyway, when Neal was down, I went over to him to see, and he had the gun in his jacket. I took it out and slid it under a trash bin. Then I passed out."

"Why didn't you *tell* me about the gun?"

"I forgot about it. It was just before I passed out, and, I dunno, I guess it didn't stick in my memory. I didn't remember until I went to the alley this morning. It was still there."

Karl grinned and shook his head. "You *forgot* about it. Well, get rid of the damn thing already! Then there's nothing they can use to convict you for Macullar."

"Yeah, that's a good idea."

"Come on. I know just the place."

It was getting dark when we left the *Press* building and headed down the block toward the Brooklyn Bridge.

"Ah! The hair," Karl blurted.

I turned to him. "The hair?"

"The hair you gave me. I had it checked out at the Museum of Natural History. You were right—it was cat hair. That reminds me: did Neal admit he planted the bat on you?"

"No, I didn't ask about that. It must have been him, though. Doesn't really matter anymore, I guess. As soon as we get rid of the gun, it's all over."

When we reached a pier, Karl said, "I hear the East River is the customary repository for such items." He reached for my satchel and asked, "Would you care to do the honors, or shall I?"

"Me." He opened the bag and I reached in and took out

the gun. I held it out over the water almost reverently. This was going to close out the Red Corriden—Jimmy Macullar—Billy Neal affair, and it seemed appropriate to reflect a little on the case.

"The idea is to let the gun go into the water—not show it off. It's considered suspicious behavior to be seen holding a firearm."

I instantly released my hold on the gun. The hell with it—I'd already given the case a lifetime's worth of reflection. The gulp of the river swallowing the gun wrote *The End* to the saga, and the splash that followed added an exclamation point.

• • •

There was no need now to stay at Karl's apartment. I was going back to Boston. He walked me to Grand Central Station, and I thanked him for everything he had done for me.

"No problem." Landfors smiled and furtively flexed his arm. "Some of it was really quite stimulating."

"You're not going to write about it?"

"No, no. I'm going to get back to my book."

"You know, I couldn't have gotten through this mess without your help. And with Peggy's. Uh, you and Peggy . . . are you two, uh . . ."

"Peggy and me?" Landfors said. "No. Not that I'd mind, but no, there's nothing romantic between us."

"I want to explain it all to her, but I don't know if she'll want to listen to me . . ."

"I already explained most of it to her—at least why you told her to stay out of things the way you did. Hope you don't mind."

"No, it's okay." It was a relief actually.

"But when you get back, I do recommend that you grovel a bit. And bring flowers—she likes roses, by the way."

As it turned out, she liked them very much indeed.

Chapter Twenty-Six

Two days after the close of the regular season, I found myself frustrated and itchy when the Red Sox opened the World Series against John McGraw's New York Giants at the Polo Grounds. This might have been the closest I would ever come to playing in a World Series, and it was mental torture to end up merely a spectator.

The frustration subsided a bit—just a bit—as the Fall Classic progressed. It quickly developed into the most exciting series ever played, and everyone who followed it became so wrapped up in the games that each fan felt more like a participant than an observer.

As everyone knows by now, the 1912 World Series wasn't decided until the final pitch of the final game, with Boston taking the championship four games to three in eight contests. That's right, *eight* contests; the second game of the series was a 6–6 tie when it was called on account of darkness after eleven innings.

The seventh game was an 11–4 rout won by New York to tie the series. The biggest excitement of that contest came just minutes before the game was to start—and it triggered the demise of Robert F. Tyler.

Bob Tyler was in charge of the team's ticket sales. Somehow, he sold the pavilion seats traditionally allocated to the Boston Royal Rooters. Finding their sacred seats occupied, and no other seating available, the Rooters took over the field itself. Led by Mayor John Fitzgerald, the most ardent Royal Rooter of all, five hundred members of the booster club stormed the playing field just as the game was to begin. With their band blaring, Honey Fitz and the rest of the Rooters paraded across the grounds. They easily repelled foot police who tried to usher them off the field, and grew rowdier with their success. Mounted police were called in, and proved more forceful and eventually victorious. Fans were treated to the bizarre sight of seeing the mayor of Boston rammed and prodded off the playing field by his own police force.

Boston citizens were incensed with the Red Sox management for its treatment of the Royal Rooters, and many of them boycotted the series finale at Fenway. The stands were only half filled when Larry Gardner lifted a sacrifice fly in the bottom of the tenth inning to win the game and the World Series for Boston.

Ty Cobb ended the 1912 season with a .410 batting average—fifteen points higher than Shoeless Joe Jackson. It was his second straight year topping the .400 mark and his sixth consecutive batting championship. I took some consolation in the fact that he finished only third in the league in stolen bases.

A couple of weeks after the series ended, Bucky O'Brien told me that one of the players suggested the Red Sox wear black arm bands during the World Series in memory of Billy Neal. Bob Tyler nixed the idea.

As the month of October drew to a close, my arm and ribs began to heal, and I started to see about playing winter ball to stay sharp for next season—wherever that would find me.

The anger of Boston's citizenry toward the Red Sox office management didn't subside with the victorious end of the series. The outraged population accorded Bob Tyler the distinction of being the most despised man in Boston, and demanded that he be fired. By the next season, the fans had their way. Tyler's interest in the club was bought out and he was purged from the Boston Red Sox organization. Then he quietly vanished.

Most people thought that Tyler skulked out of Boston too ashamed to ever show his face again. I believed differently. I believed that if refrigerators hadn't come along and made ice farming obsolete, Bob Tyler would have eventually been harvested from Jamaica Pond.

In the spring of 1919, Hal Chase was dropped from the New York Giants and never played another major-league game. After a career of cheating and throwing games, and being quietly dropped by team after team that couldn't *prove* he was dishonest, the National League finally obtained hard evidence against him. Though not officially banned, he was out for good. But even without playing, he still managed to taint the game. When the White Sox were found to have thrown the '19 World Series in exchange for payoffs from Arnold Rothstein, Hal Chase was named as one of the masterminds behind the fix.

To my regret, I don't know what became of Clyde Fletcher. He just became an early addition to that list that each of us accumulates over the years: the guilt-inducing ledger of people-I-wish-I-had-kept-in-touch-with.

Chapter Twenty-Seven

I stood in front of the colorful array of old tobacco cards, staring at the one artifact that proved I had been a major-league baseball player. After indulging in a lengthy review of *Michael Rawlings,* I took a closer look at the card of *John Corriden, Detroit, 3B,* and then glanced back again at my own. It struck me that, in a way, we looked almost the same. And suddenly everything seemed all right.

For decades, I carried a nagging burden of guilt and frustration about the Red Corriden case. He never did get legal justice—his killer hadn't even been publicly accused.

Now I realized that it just didn't matter anymore whether or not Billy Neal had been tried in a court of law for his crime. It wasn't legal justice that punished Neal for killing Red Corriden and Jimmy Macullar, but it was justice enough. Nothing more could be gained by now accusing a man who was himself long dead.

There isn't even any lingering public interest to satisfy. No one cares that the murderer of a long-forgotten baseball player was never identified—no one remembers the crime.

But people will see the cards: those scuffed pieces of cardboard that portray a couple of eager young ball players named Red Corriden and Mickey Rawlings. What happened since those cards were first issued can't change the way we appear on them. In the baseball shrine at Cooperstown, we will be frozen in time, looking quaintly old-fashioned with outdated haircuts and collars on our uniform jerseys. No one will remember that one of us has been dead since the Taft administration, nor care that the other is still walking the earth. Images on baseball cards—that's all that will last.

I decided it was best to leave the tragedies of the past buried in the thickening dust of failing memories, and I resolved never to tell what I knew about Billy Neal.

I lingered for quite a while in front of the exhibit of old baseball cards, insatiably drinking in my own former likeness, and relishing the warm memories stirred up by the pastel portraits of almost-forgotten heroes and friends. Eventually, I pried myself away from the display. With some time remaining before the exhibition game was to begin, I began to explore more of the museum.

In the Baseball Through the Ages room, I saw marvelous relics of the game bursting with the power to spark magical images and glorious memories. There was Walter Johnson's purple-trimmed Washington Senators uniform . . . Ty Cobb's sheepskin sliding pads . . . the bat Nap Lajoie used to crack out his three thousandth hit.

A tiny old baseball glove caught my eye. It was a dark mummified piece of leather, with a tear at the crotch where the thumb joined the palm. There was no webbing at all on the primitive five-finger glove. The wording on the card next to the mitt read: *Worn by Waddell on July 4, 1905 when he defeated Cy Young, 4–2, in 20 innings at Boston.* Rube Waddell! There was a sepia photo of Waddell in the case, too, showing him at the peak of his strength and glory. For a joyous minute or two, I was a hero-worshipping boy again.

I progressed further through the baseball generations, quickly reviewing Babe Ruth's locker from Yankee Stadium—his uniform still hanging in it, the number 3 carefully displayed; a photo of the 1934 St. Louis Cardinals—Dizzy, Pepper, Frankie, and the rest of the Gas House Gang; the ball Ted Williams hit for a home run in the 1946 All-Star game when Rip Sewell served up his Eephus blooper pitch; the glove used by Willie Mays to catch Vic Wertz's drive in the '54 World Series; the neat line-up of four baseballs from Sandy Koufax's no-hitters—and the even longer row produced by Nolan Ryan.

I saw, too, the awed reverent faces of the visitors who stood entranced by the displays. And I listened to the harmony of personal reminiscences being shared with eager youngsters.

"You see that glove? I was at the game when Willie made that catch. The first World Series game I ever went to. It was at the Polo Grounds, and I was up in the left field bleachers. I was just about your age then . . ."

"You were probably too young to remember it now, but *you* saw Nolan Ryan pitch once. It was back when he was with the Mets at Shea Stadium. Steve Carlton was pitching against him for the St. Louis Cardinals . . ."

"You know, I think we have an old program at home from a game Babe Ruth played in. Grandpa saw him play all the time when he was a boy. He has some great stories about the Babe. First thing when we get home, we'll give Grandpa a call . . ."

There was a reassuring continuity here, in the memories and lore of a woven succession of generations.

I thought that I had completely lost touch with the game, left behind by the new players, the revised rules, and the modern ballparks. But these changes now seemed trivial, at worst no more than minor annoyances. The important things about the game were essentially still the same, and probably always would be.

Somehow I felt myself connected with baseball again. Maybe I had left the game for a while, but having once held a horsehide in my hands its special magic of summer and youth and vitality had seeped into my bloodstream, so the game never really left me.

It was almost time for the exhibition game to begin at Doubleday Field, so I reluctantly left the Hall of Fame building. I hadn't had a chance to look for him, but I knew that Jimmy Macullar was somewhere in the museum, too, if only on the brittle browning roster of a forgotten National League baseball team called the Syracuse Stars. The sun seemed warmer now, and the sky bluer, as I sauntered over to Doubleday Field.

I heard once that if you grow old with someone, nature has a charitable way of making you both always look the same to each other: as one of you gets more wrinkles, the other's eyes get worse, so the aging is never noticed. Baseball and I must have caught up to each other now, because when I arrived at Doubleday Field and looked for the old-timers, I discovered that this happy trick of nature is not restricted to a loving couple. Among the Hall-of-Famers standing along the foul lines, I saw not one paunchy midsection nor one graying head. Each player magically looked like the image on his plaque.

And I myself felt more vertical and vigorous than I had in a long, long time. I threw out the opening pitch with the same effortless zip that I had when playing catch with Uncle Matt